HOW TO SLAY AT CHRISTMAS

SARAH BONNER

B
Boldwood

First published in Great Britain in 2025 by Boldwood Books Ltd.

Copyright © Sarah Bonner, 2025

Cover Design by Head Design Ltd

Cover Images: Bella Howard and Shutterstock

The moral right of Sarah Bonner to be identified as the author of this work has been asserted in accordance with the Copyright, Designs and Patents Act 1988.

All rights reserved. No part of this book may be reproduced in any form or by any electronic or mechanical means, including information storage and retrieval systems, without written permission from the author, except for the use of brief quotations in a book review. This book is a work of fiction and, except in the case of historical fact, any resemblance to actual persons, living or dead, is purely coincidental.

Every effort has been made to obtain the necessary permissions with reference to copyright material, both illustrative and quoted. We apologise for any omissions in this respect and will be pleased to make the appropriate acknowledgements in any future edition.

A CIP catalogue record for this book is available from the British Library.

Paperback ISBN 978-1-83633-552-8

Large Print ISBN 978-1-83633-553-5

Hardback ISBN 978-1-83633-551-1

Ebook ISBN 978-1-83633-554-2

Kindle ISBN 978-1-83633-555-9

Audio CD ISBN 978-1-83633-546-7

MP3 CD ISBN 978-1-83633-547-4

Digital audio download ISBN 978-1-83633-550-4

This book is printed on certified sustainable paper. Boldwood Books is dedicated to putting sustainability at the heart of our business. For more information please visit https://www.boldwoodbooks.com/about-us/sustainability/

Boldwood Books Ltd, 23 Bowerdean Street, London, SW6 3TN

www.boldwoodbooks.com

To my husband.
This book really wouldn't exist without your unwavering support.

1

JESSICA

For me, Christmas begins in the summer with the hunt for a new seasonal job. I can feel the flutter of anticipation in my chest as I think about the winter ahead, even though I'm sitting outside with a Pimm's in my hand and a light August breeze on my face as I begin the search.

Woking in Surrey is looking for a Mrs Claus for the local shopping centre. That could work. I pull up Google Streetview and take a virtual stroll around the main retail area of the town. It looks a bit... well... rubbish... if I'm being honest. I mean, it could work at a push, but it's not really speaking to me. I hop onto Facebook and find a community page called Woking at Christmas. It all seems a bit half-hearted; the lights are a bit naff and there's a tree right in the centre of the town square but it's kind of patchy looking. Hmm... one for the maybe – but hopefully not – pile.

What about Cambridge? It's a lovely city and I bet they really know how to pull off something special for Christmas. Hmm... maybe not. Especially given the proximity to Peterborough; it's probably a good idea to stay quite far from there. There's still an active investigation to find the person who stabbed those men staggering home from parties after harassing every woman they saw and although I know I left zero evidence – because I am meticulous and careful as one must be in these kind of situations – it's probably best not to push my luck too far.

Ooh. Now this looks more like it; I quite fancy a few months in leafy Sussex. Ellsbury Christmas Market is wanting a Mrs Claus for their 'new and improved grotto' and are looking to find someone to help 'create a truly magical experience'. There's an Instagram page for the market – @EllsburyChristmas – and it looks utterly delightful. The market is held in the grounds of the cathedral and the pictures show clusters of wooden chalets decorated with pine garlands and fairy lights, the spire rising behind them.

OK. So far, so wonderful. There's a focus on local vendors; including the promised return of The Truckle Bunnies who make an award-winning cranberry cheddar and Doggy Do-Dahs who sell luxury pet accessories. Plus they have a ton of classic festive hot food options; there's even a Sausage Swing, and everyone loves a bratwurst.

But there's a slight issue when I look at the job advert in more detail. They want an older Mrs Claus, the advert very specifically says women aged fifty plus. That's a bummer. I'm only thirty-five, which is plenty old enough for the kids who tend to think anyone over thirty is old anyway, but the people doing the hiring might need a little more convincing.

I read on regardless, Ellsbury Christmas Market looks so perfect and I'm not going to give up without a fight. Ooh! They're not doing email applications, or even the dreaded video some other places have started asking for. No, Ellsbury are old school and so they're doing in-person auditions next month. No need to book, just turn up on the day. That means I can go there and prove I'm the best Mrs Claus they could possibly imagine; I can charm their pants off with my Christmas spirit, so to speak.

You might be wondering why a thirty-five-year-old is so desperate to get a job as a Mrs Claus. And I'll admit, on the face of it, it is a kind of bizarre career choice.

Except that I love Christmas. Truly adore it. The food: everything is better with cranberry and festive spices and don't even get me started on all the amazing cakes and biscuits. The drink: mulled wine? Yes, please and thank you. The fairy lights twinkling on every surface and giving everywhere a magical glow. The scent of pine intermingled with gingerbread and cinnamon. The cosiness of a warm fire and a jumper featuring cute penguins getting up to mischief. The hustle and bustle and laughter and general excuse to get together and have fun. The way that everyone is smiling and happy and very un-British in their desire to make the people around them cheerful.

Christmas is most definitely my favourite time of year. But there are a few people who ruin it. The fun busters. The people who use Christmas as an excuse to rip off others. Or to take advantage. To exploit. To lie and cheat and steal. The opportunists.

Luckily, I have just the remedy for those people.

Sometimes they still get lauded by the press. 'Local hero cut down in his prime', that kind of thing. You might remember a couple of years ago there was a big story about the pair of entrepreneurs who were found dead in their office? They were held up as bastions of industry, good men with big hearts who would be sorely missed. It was a big deal, made the front page of the nationals. Well, what was never mentioned was that those two men ran a human trafficking ring, supplying 'workers' – the air quotes are necessary because if you're going to call a spade a spade you should call them slaves – to local businesses. So yeah, 'bastions of industry' if you want, but scum who deserved everything I did to them, in my humble opinion.

And do you know who is never suspected of murder? Kindly grandmothers with white hair and a penchant for giving you little gifts. Mrs Claus is the epitome of this kindly grandmother and that is why she is the perfect cover for my mission to punish all the people who have been naughty this year.

When someone is writing a list of people they think could be guilty of garrotting a man with a strand of Christmas lights they are not going to think of Santa's wife, are they? And trust me. No one ever figured out it was me in Peterborough. Or the year before that in Redhill. Or in Eveleigh.

2

FEARNE

It's only September and already I am sick to the fucking back teeth of Christmas. The festive season begins in February in the Dixon house and I am so over the whole thing.

Sebastian is at it again. Pacing up and down in the study, the floorboard by his desk creaking every tenth step as he turns. He's muttering under his breath. I can't hear him down here – thank God – but I can tell by the cadence of his walk that he's chuntering to himself with every step. Is this what a dozen years of marriage boils down to? Knowing the intricacies of your spouse's habits and putting about eighty percent of your available energy into not going up there with a carving knife and finally getting some peace?

'Can you please do something about Dad?' our daughter, Immy, demands from the doorway between the living room and the dining room where she's apparently trying to do her homework. 'I need to study.'

'Can't you put your headphones on?' I ask, trying to keep my tone neutral and not mention the fact I paid well over a hundred pounds for those things.

'They've run out of charge.' Immy pouts a little, as if I'm the one to blame for not charging them at the appropriate time.

'So plug them in,' I reply gently. Everything is said gently at the moment. Like walking on eggshells. My sister-in-law has informed me that Immy will grow out of it 'as long as I maintain the appropriate level of discipline in the household'. Ha! Like I'm the one doing any disciplining. Sebastian is so strict with Immy that I've always played the 'nice' parent. The 'friend'. The one she can twist around her little finger to get the things she wants. Perhaps I've spoilt her. Perhaps this teenage phase is all my fault. But in truth I suspect she's just rebelling against having such an officious prick for a father. And I can hardly blame her, can I?

Step, step, step, step, step, step, step, step, step, creak.
Step, step, step, step, step, step, step, step, step, creak.
Step, step, step, step, step, step, step, step, step, creak.
Step, step, step, step, step, step, step, step, step, creak.

'Seriously, Mum. He's driving me crazy.'

I take a deep breath. 'Fine, I'll take him some tea, see if that helps calm him down.'

Immy gives me a look that says she seriously doubts it will work. But I have to try something. Otherwise I really will be looking for that carving knife.

'I made you some tea,' I say as I poke my head around the door of his home office, which he uses when he can't be bothered to drive to the trading estate. Well, I say home office, but in reality it's the spare room with a crappy desk from Ikea and a chair Sebastian recovered from a skip after last year's market. I offered to help him decorate, to make the space somewhere that feels less like an actual hovel, maybe put up some shelves for the paperwork and paint the wall behind the desk to give it a more calming ambiance. But Sebastian told me to quit badgering him and that if he wanted to 'fanny about' he would do it himself.

He doesn't say anything now, just points to the corner of the rickety desk – the only surface not stacked with papers – as he continues to pace.

'You know, perhaps it would help to bounce some ideas around,' I say lightly.

'It's not that kind of problem,' he tells me.

'OK... well—'

'David Bennett wants four stands,' he interrupts.

'Four? That's a lot.'

'Exactly. He wants the Sausage Swing and also the fish and chips like he had last year. Which is fine. But then he's also applied for some kind of waffle thing and a crumble bar.'

'A crumble bar?'

He hands me the proposal from David Bennett. Apparently it serves what is literally just a deconstructed fruit crumble, so the filling in a bowl plus a scoop of toasted topping plus custard. Huh. Who knew that was a thing?

'It would probably do pretty well,' I say, handing the proposal back to Sebastian. 'And I'm guessing the mark-up would be good.'

'Of course. Why else would David Bennett be interested?' He rolls his eyes in the same way Immy does and I smile a little. He grins back. 'What do you think I should do?' he asks.

'Well, you're the expert at this,' I tell him. He's always liked having his ego stroked. I guess like most men really. But my husband is particularly receptive to a compliment and I often find myself twisted into knots trying to find something positive to buoy him up with.

I don't know when I realised it was easier to just be the woman he wanted instead of the person I really was. I don't think it was a conscious decision, more something that happened over time until one day I woke up and looked around and wondered how in hell I'd got here.

He isn't all bad. Lord knows I could have married someone truly evil, instead of merely shackling myself to his tedium and pedantry. And his *rules*. There are rules for everything, but not in a way that suggests there is a punishment for infringement. The only punishment is a look of utter disappointment and perhaps a cold shoulder for an hour. But when the person who is meant to love and cherish you instead looks at you with pity and sometimes even disdain, it grates on your soul until eventually you find yourself subconsciously making subtle concessions. And consciously making less subtle ones.

Women should have long hair. So I keep it almost to my waist, a curtain of yellow the colour of the summer sun. I want to experiment. Dye it purple. Crop it into a pixie cut. But this is one of those rules that I wouldn't be breaking once and then it would be forgotten in time. It would be every time he looked at me. I think perhaps a part of me is worried that he might not look at me at all and that could be worse.

Yorkshire pudding is only for beef. I hate this one. I would devour an entire plate of Yorkshire puddings with my roast chicken.

The heating should never be above eighteen degrees. In the depths of the winter, when there's frost on the ground outside, I basically live in the kitchen where the Aga pumps out a tiny bit of warmth. I've tried to explain to Sebastian that women feel the cold more than men – honestly, it's a marked difference – but he just cocked his head and gave me the look that said he thought I was some kind of fool.

* * *

'You'll help with the newbies this year, won't you love,' he says over dinner that night. It isn't phrased as a question.

Every year I tell myself that I'm not going to get involved with the market. That I'm just going to insist Sebastian hires someone to help him out with the new vendors. It's a bullshit job, like being a babysitter for a bunch of overgrown idiots, helping the rookies to set up and making sure they follow the rules and being on call for every tiny problem so they don't ever have to think for themselves.

'I was think—' I start to say but he interrupts me.

'I really don't know what I'd do without you.' He grins and digs into his pie as if that is all there is to say.

'But—'

'I knew I could count on you.' He takes a forkful of mash and shovels it into his open mouth.

I sigh. I don't know why I even bother dreaming I could argue. He wouldn't listen anyway. I watch as he chases a few peas around his plate.

Perhaps he'll choke on them.

3

JESSICA

One thing that really works in my favour as a Mrs Claus is the fact I went grey in my early twenties. And not in a 'I found a few rogue hairs' way; I went fully grey over the course of about a year just as I was finally getting my life together. It was another lesson in how people who barely know you like to think they have an opinion on things that don't impact them.

'You should dye it.'

'You can't be grey at your age.'

'Why did you dye it that colour?'

For a while I felt like a pariah, like people were talking about me on the street, hands covering mouths so I wouldn't see what they were whispering. But then along came Covid and the silver movement saw thousands of other young women embracing the grey.

I tend to spend the spring with a pink rinse through it, which looks completely stunning even if I do say so myself. But I don't do that as preparations for the next Christmas season begin. First, Mrs Claus can be many things, but she does *not* rock pink hair. And, second, imagine if I left a strand of pink hair at a scene? Talk about making yourself easy to identify.

The train to Ellsbury takes two hours and I use the time to prep my best Mrs Claus look. I braid my silver hair into two long plaits on either side of my face. Very 'North Pole' chic. I keep my makeup fairly minimal, just lots of mascara and a bright-red lip, which will match the outfit.

I don't wear an actual Santa costume or anything, I'm far more subtle than that, plus it's the third week of September so you have to be a little less weird; you might get away with a that kind of thing in December, but not when there are still leaves on the trees and the scent of coconut suntan lotion in the air. My dress is a dark, almost cherry, red; with a fitted bodice, cap sleeves and a full skirt to just below the knee. A simple black belt cinches it at the waist. I wear a pair of very white plimsole-esque trainers and have a small crossbody bag that brings it all together.

In short, yes, I look too young. But I look like I *could* be Mrs Claus having a day off and that hint of possibility will be enough. I have a few years of experience on my CV and I speak three languages. Plus, I know the names of all the reindeer – without having to sing the song in my head – and that will set me apart from ninety percent of the other applicants. The bar is normally pretty low to be Mrs Claus if I'm honest. Oh, and of course I already have an enhanced DBS certificate to say that I'm cleared to work with children. All in all, I'm perfect.

The auditions are being held in the offices of the market's management company on a trading estate just outside the city centre. It is the least Christmassy building I've ever set eyes on. It's probably a fine example of brutalist architecture, but it looks like a grey box with narrow windows and zero soul.

But inside they've laid out tea and mince pies and Michael

Bublé is singing about a holly jolly Christmas. I feel myself relax the moment I step foot in the space, like I'm coming home. A tiny bubble of excitement pops in my chest and my fingers start to tingle.

Christmas is coming.

My fellow auditionees are significantly older than I am, a sea of grandmotherly types who are no doubt utterly charming. Except the one on the end who has brought her latest knitting project and looks like she'd stab you in the eye with a needle if you looked at her wrong. I find a seat and take a few deep breaths to ground myself. After about five minutes, I'm called into the audition room.

'I'm Sebastian Dixon,' a rather plain-looking middle-aged man says, not bothering to stand. I don't know why it irritates me so much, but it does. Perhaps it's just that it makes it awkward to shake his hand, the angle forcing me to bend over a little and then I have to worry he might be getting an inadvertent eyeful.

'And this is Hanna from Grottos R Us. They manage the grotto.'

Wow, Grottos R Us is a bold choice as a name.

Hanna smiles at me. 'I'd technically be your boss, but most of the time you'd deal directly with Sebastian as he's on site for the duration.'

'It's lovely to meet you both,' I say in my best Mrs Claus voice.

They both smile.

'We're looking for someone who can make sure the grotto runs smoothly,' the man in front of me says, looking me up and down.

'Of course. I have five years' experience in similar operations so I'm very used to the job. I love to focus on making sure that every visit is as special as it can be for the child *and* as easy as possible for the parents.'

'You're a bit young.'

'Well, yes. But in my five years of experience I have learnt so much.'

'But will the children believe?' He drags out the word 'believe'.

'I have a portfolio,' I tell him and hand over the folder stuffed full of photos of me and smiling kiddies, the rapture in their eyes suggesting they very much do believe.

'Hmm. This only seems to cover four years?'

Of course he'd have to notice. The issue being that one year, my third as Mrs Claus, I'd worked for an out-of-town retail park who wanted something a little more 'edgy', and had – in a very misguided moment – decided that Santa had upgraded to a younger wife. That year I wore the skimpiest costume known to man. Think white fishnets, push-up bra and a skirt so short you could see what I had for breakfast. I spent six very unhappy weeks being drooled over by dads, and a fair few granddads for extra grossness. It was a hit for the retail park though and they made a killing out of their Santa. I also made a killing – or ten to be precise, the most I've ever dispatched in a single year – but it was just too easy to find terrible men to get rid of. I had to pace myself in the end before a link was found between them all and the police ended up at my door.

I smile sweetly at Mr Dixon. 'I don't know if either of you are familiar with Eveleigh Park?' I raise an eyebrow.

Hanna snort laughs. 'I am,' she says and then looks up at me. 'I thought I recognised you. It's kind of infamous around Grottos R Us as an example of how *not* to do things.'

'With good reason,' I assure her.

'I promise there's no white fishnets here.'

'What are you talking about?' Sebastian asks, sounding irritated that he's being left out of the joke.

'You wouldn't understand,' Hanna tells him. She grins at me, like we've shared a secret.

I'm asked to stay behind and I make myself comfortable in one corner of the room, taking the best spot to observe the competition. Plus, it's next to the mince pies and I get an occasional waft of delicious cinnamon.

A handful of others are also asked to stay behind, so I can only assume we're going into a second round of the audition process. So far, so standard. I'm at least twenty years younger than my competition but I'm not worried. I have held back my pièce de résistance. Hanna from Grottos R Us was wearing a tiny pin badge on the lapel of her suit jacket; it's for a deaf awareness charity. And guess who knows sign language? This will absolutely tip the balance in my favour.

There are five of us on the final shortlist and we all trot back into the audition room.

'Right then, ladies,' Sebastian says. I do not like the way he says 'ladies'. It sounds patronising. Almost like a slur. 'It's time for us to pick our Mrs Claus. So we're going to go down the line and ask you a few questions. OK?'

We all murmur back in agreement. I'm the fourth one who will be asked. The questions are vanilla, kind of dull. 'What do you think is the true spirit of Christmas?' That kind of thing.

A few of the others stumble over their words. 'Err... I think Christmas is about family. And err... well... I...'

Amateurs.

The question comes to me. 'Christmas is about joy and love and hope for a better world. The purpose of Santa, and Mrs Claus of course, is to bring magic to the children who still believe in something better, something greater.'

Hanna hangs onto my every word. I think Sebastian will try to pick one of the more grandmotherly types. But he can posture and peacock as much as he wants, Hanna will cast the deciding vote. I'm sure of it.

We get to the final question. 'Why do you think you will be the best Mrs Claus?'

There are some more stuttered replies. 'Because I look like her,' one of the women comes up with. She doesn't actually, she has very unkind eyes.

'And you? Jessica Williams?'

I open my mouth to speak, but then I close it again. A cloud crosses Sebastian's face. I begin to sign. 'Because I can speak to all children.'

Hanna looks surprised. 'You can sign?'

'Of course. Inclusivity is so important, don't you think? All children deserve to feel part of the holiday.'

'Oh I couldn't agree more,' she says with a smile. She nudges Sebastian. Her choice has been made.

And, just like that, I become the brand-new Mrs Claus for Ellsbury Christmas Market.

I have a feeling this is going to be a very, *very* good year.

* * *

I overhear him on my way out, talking on the phone to someone.

'I don't think she's right,' Sebastian says. 'Far too young. Too perky to be Santa's wife.'

There's a pause. I'm assuming someone on the other end of the call is talking.

'No. I've been overridden by that bloody woman from Grottos R Us.'

Another pause.

'Hanna is too pushy, too stuck up her own backside. Like she has any idea how to run things.' He sounds so dismissive of any professional skill my new boss has. 'I'm overrun by women who think they know it all. This year is going to be a fucking nightmare and I can't wait until it's over.'

Hmm. For someone who runs a Christmas market he really doesn't sound like he actually likes the holiday. And he certainly doesn't like strong and powerful women.

In my head I bring up my virtual Naughty List and write his name at the top. Just in pencil, mind. It's too early to jump to conclusions, but if he carries on like this I might take out a permanent marker.

4

FEARNE

It's October, only three weeks before the market is due to open, and once again I've been dragged in to help train the newbies on exactly what is expected of them at Ellsbury Christmas Market.

'We run a tight ship here,' I tell the sea of expectant faces with a singsong voice. I want to stab my own eyes out with the whiteboard marker I'm holding in my hand. 'It's hard work, but I promise it'll pay off in the end and we'll give Ellsbury a true taste of the Christmas spirit.' I hate myself as I spit out a whole load of platitudes and general bullshit. The bottom line of this session is to make sure that all the new vendors understand the list of rules laid down by my darling husband. The ones he has promised me are absolutely necessary to the smooth running of the market and not at all to do with his need to control every detail.

One of the vendors raises her hand. She's dressed head-to-toe in tie-dye and I can smell the incense from here. I'm assuming this is Bella. Her stall, Crystals and Gifts, sells – no surprises here – crystals and other such woo woo. Crystals and Shit, I'll be calling it in my head. 'Yes?' I say to her. 'Bella, isn't it?'

'Bella Donna,' she tells me with a smile. Like that is her real name. FFS.

'Right. Did you have a question, Bella?'

'I'm just looking at the location of my chalet.' She squints at the map in the pack I've left on the desks in front of each seat.

'Yes?'

'Well...' she elongates the word and then makes this little grimace face. 'I don't think this is the best place for Crystals and Gifts.'

I swear to myself and pray for God – even though I'm not religious – to give me strength. 'Is there a problem?' I say it with positivity, as if there couldn't possibly be an issue.

'Well... the feng shui is all off.'

I try to recall the exact location of her chalet. It's not in a prime spot I will be the first to admit. But she probably wouldn't want me to repeat what my husband said about the products she's selling. 'Bloody pile of absolute twaddly crap' were his exact words. 'Well, unfortunately the chalet locations are already determined and everyone's spots have been allocated.' I smile sweetly and take the cap off my marker. 'Now then, let's do—'

'But Crystals and Gifts can't be here,' she interrupts me. 'The whole energy of the market will be ruined.'

'The allocations have been made.' Perhaps if I just keep repeating the same line over and over she'll eventually listen. Or at least she might pick up the subtext that I don't actually care about her opinions of the energy of the market.

'But—'

I cut her off. 'Right then. Let's do introductions.' I talk quickly so as not to give Bella a chance to butt in again. 'We'll go round the room and if everyone could tell the group their name and the name of their chalet, and give a little overview of what they sell. I'll pop it all up on this whiteboard so we can refer back to it later.'

I look expectantly at them and they all shift a little under my gaze.

Eventually one of the men raises a tentative hand. He's tall and built like a rugby player with dirty blond floppy hair and a slight air of destitution about him. I can't tell if his jeans are ripped because they're old or because they're a fashion statement.

'Umm... I'll start,' he says in a deep baritone. Bella Donna sits up a little straighter in her chair. He gives a wave, which should have been dorky but somehow he makes look adorable. 'I'm Alvi Jakkinen.' He pauses for a moment. 'I'm Finnish, hence the name,' he says with an almost apologetic shrug. 'And I run an animal rescue centre. This year I'll be taking a stall at the market to try to raise some much-needed funds.'

Having a charity stall was my idea, even though Sebastian is now convinced it was his. I told him it would be a good thing, that he would be giving back to the community. But when the local papers jumped on the story, Sebastian made sure that all the quotes put him in a very philanthropic light. Anyway, I'm over it.

'I just wanted to check something,' Alvi says. 'Can I bring some of the animals with me? Dogs mainly. Although I have just rescued an alpaca, so if she's still with us by the time the market starts, possibly her too. I thought perhaps people might like to meet some of the animals we help at Last Chance Rescue.' He runs his hand through his hair.

'Umm...' To be honest I hadn't even thought about it. I think it's a genius idea though, imagine how much more he'll raise as people will dig much deeper into their pockets if they're staring into the sad eyes of a poor abandoned labrador. But what will

Sebastian think? We've never had pets in the house, despite Immy begging for almost three straight years for a puppy and then another two for a kitten. Fuck it. I'll tell Sebastian it'll be a draw for visitors. 'Sure,' I tell Alvi. 'Why not.'

He smiles at me and his whole face lights up. He suddenly looks familiar.

'Oh. You're Hanna's brother, right?'

'Guilty as charged.'

Hanna works for the company who run the grotto and we're sporadic drinking buddies, especially as Christmas approaches once again. 'She speaks very highly of you.'

He laughs. 'I'm sure she doesn't.' But it's obviously a joke.

'Well, welcome to Ellsbury Christmas Market.' I turn to face the two women sitting next to him. 'Ladies?'

'Hi. We're Amy and Heather Jacobs. We run a small business making decoupage gifts.' The other holds up an example of their stuff. Decoupage is basically cutting out paper shapes and sticking them on top of other things. Or at least that was what I always assumed. I'm forced to admit their stuff is really nice. Quirky and fun and I think it's going to be a huge hit this Christmas.

'And what's your stall called?' asks a slightly serious-looking man in a knitted waistcoat that rather belies the fact he's only in his early thirties.

'The Scissor Sisters.'

There's a smirk from a few of the others.

'Seriously?' the waistcoated man asks.

'It's decoupage. We use scissors,' she tells him, her tone absolutely deadpan.

'Oh.' He looks suitably chastised. I think I love these women.

'And what will you be selling?' one of them asks him.

'Gonks,' he says and motions to a creepy-looking troll-like

thing next to him. He sounds less than thrilled about his product range and my senses prick up. The vendors are deliberately chosen because they genuinely love the products they're selling, or at least that is one of the key criteria. Out of a list of about thirty billion things.

'Gonks!' I exclaim with faux excitement, a poor effort to gee him up a little. 'Why don't you introduce yourself and then elaborate a little for us?'

'I'm James. And, well, they're just gonks.' He shrugs.

'How about you give me your very best sales pitch?' I can't understand how he made it through the interviews with this kind of attitude.

James sighs loudly and stands up. 'Fine.' He sounds like I've asked him to kick a toddler. He clears his throat. And then his whole demeanour shifts and out comes an entirely different person. 'So, I want to introduce you to this year's most desirable decoration. The gonk is inspired by the gnomes of Scandinavian mythology and, according to folklore, these cheeky little guys just love to get cosy by the fire and bring good luck into the home. They are totally adorable and would look amazing in your home this Christmas. Personally, I have one of the enormous ones, but if you're a virgin "gonker",' he adds a cheeky grin, which should feel a bit gross and smarmy but instead is utterly charming, 'I'd recommend a medium-size one. Ease yourself in.'

I think I want a gonk. It could go in the hallway on the shelf above the shoe rack. Perhaps a red one— *woah, what the actual fuck just happened?*

The rest of the group are staring open mouthed at James. 'Holy shit, man,' says Alvi.

'Yeah.' James blushes and looks down at the table, but I can see through the modesty act. He's an epic salesman and he knows it. 'They have a great mark-up too.' He grins.

I no longer care if he genuinely thinks his product is good. He's going to make a fucking killing this year.

After the course, I go to find Sebastian in his office. He looks like a pug who just ate a wasp, his face bathed in the eerie blue light from his computer screen.

'You OK?' I ask, poking my head round the door.

'Hummpf,' he grunts from behind the computer.

'Anything I can help with?'

'Only if you've suddenly learnt how to use a computer,' he grumbles under his breath.

I can actually use a computer. I'm very IT literate. Not that my husband cares about my skills. I only work for him around the time of the market. The rest of the year I write novels. Fairly successful ones too: it isn't amazing money but it's enough to make it worthwhile. And I obviously have to use the computer to write and edit.

Oh, and strictly between us, I self-publish some stuff too, although I tend not to talk too much about the Cherry Dubois books; they're gloriously smutty and my husband would not approve. I dread to think what he'd do if he found out I was writing them.

5

JESSICA

One thing I must say about being a Mrs Claus is the pay is pretty diabolical. I can only assume most of my peers are relying on their husbands to pay the mortgage and the bills and this is more of a hobby for them than a job.

Now, I do not have a husband – I might have mentioned him already if I did – but, luckily, I do have some other talents. I normally make my living in the summer months playing poker. I'm good. Not world-class-televised-games good, but good enough to win some of the smaller online tournaments and top up my earnings with a few weeks in Vegas each spring. But this last year hasn't been quite as lucrative as I'd hoped from a poker perspective and so I'm going to have to economise over the winter. And that is unfortunately going to have to start with my accommodation; Ellsbury is expensive and so I find myself trawling the internet to find somewhere I can afford. *What does a girl have to do to find a bijou cottage with a real log fire, a clawfoot bath and a four-poster bed?*

In the end I find one potential flat in my price range and take the train down to Ellsbury for a viewing on 23 October. It's only a five-minute walk from the offices I went to for my Mrs Claus audition and the building looks like it was designed by the same architect. Another grey box, although this time there's a car park complete with an ancient Corsa on blocks and a group of tween boys in hoodies who think they are bad men but are actually children who should still believe in Santa.

The letting agency told me the landlord would meet me there to show me around.

'I'm very strict about who I rent to,' he says, before he even introduces himself. He's tall, maybe six four, and gawky, with some kind of food stain down the football shirt he's wearing. There's a faint aroma of stale sweat emanating from him.

'Well, I'm a very good tenant,' I tell him with a smile, trying not to look directly at the food stain. It looks like gravy.

'There will be weekly inspections. No messing around, no notice. I have a key and I'll come to check you're not leaving things in a state.'

You know, sometimes you can miss the odd red flag, but this one is being waved in my face so hard it's impossible not to fall over it.

'There's a meter for the electric, so you'll need to load it up at the shop down the road. And only there, mind. The guy who runs the shop will call me if you don't top up regularly, so I can check you aren't letting the place get too cold and damp by leaving the heating off all the time.'

It's a bold claim that me being stingy with the heating would cause damp, given I can see the outline of black blooms through the thin coat of paint he's applied to cover what is an obvious structural problem.

'Oh. And you can't use the freezer section.' He motions to the bottom half of the fridge. 'I store stuff in there.'

Wow. Just wow. I wonder what other delightful treats he has up his sleeve.

'Rent is due every four weeks. Not monthly. We clear on that?'

I nod, even though I have no intention of renting this place.

'And the advert said seven fifty a month, but it's gone up to eight fifty. Cost of living and all that.'

By this point we're back in the musty-smelling hallway and I am desperate to leave.

'So. We have a deal?' He takes a step toward me and I mentally calculate if I could still make it out of the door behind me if he lunged. I think I could. And I could always give him a good sharp kick if need be.

'I'll have to think about it,' I tell him with a saccharine smile.

He narrows his eyes and I plant my feet a little more firmly. 'So this has just been a time waste, eh?'

'Well...' I debate being honest and telling him that this place is a hovel and he is a literal walking nightmare of a landlord who shouldn't be allowed to operate. But there's something in his eyes that tells me to sugarcoat it for my own safety. 'I just need to make sure I can afford the extra hundred a month. I'll get back to you.'

And then I turn and open the door as quickly as I can, half expecting him to slam it shut and trap me inside this hellhole.

My heart is still beating a cacophony in my chest as I walk down the road, sneaking quick glances behind me as I put more and more distance between myself and that awful place. Eventually, I find a coffee shop and order a latte before sinking into one of the overstuffed armchairs.

'You look like you need something stronger than coffee,' says a voice behind me and I jump before turning to face them. It's Hanna, from Grottos R Us.

'Oh, hi Hanna.'

'Everything OK?' she asks and she seems genuinely concerned.

'Oh fine. I just...' but I trail off. She doesn't need to listen to me bitching and moaning. 'It's nothing.' I offer her up a beaming smile. It really is nothing, I'll find something. Things always have a habit of working out in the end.

'I'm a good listener,' she says. 'Unless you'd rather be alone. In which case, just tell me to bugger off.' She says it with a laugh, like she wouldn't be offended. 'I know that sometimes you just need "me time".'

'It's just... Please join me.' I motion to the seat next to me and wait as she settles herself down. 'I went to look at a flat and it was...' I grope for the right word.

'Grotty as hell?'

'Exactly. And the landlord was...' I make a face.

'Grotty as hell?'

'Ha. Yes. Sleazy would be another word.'

'Gross.'

'Yeah. There aren't many good places to rent round here,' I lament.

'Is it just you on your own?' she asks. 'I mean, no kids or anything?'

I shake my head. 'Just little old me.'

'Well in that case you might be in luck.' She smiles, but it's touched by sadness. 'Mum passed away a few months ago and I've just finished renovating her cottage. It's about to go on the market but it'll take a good few months to find a buyer and for everything to go through. If you don't mind the occasional viewing, you'd be more than welcome to move in there for a while. Rent free of course, just pay the bills.' She says it like it's a simple exchange. Like we're friends. Like she hasn't just offered me a golden opportunity without any fanfare at all.

'Oh, I couldn't possibly... that's far too generous.' Of course I want to bite her hand off, there are just ways of doing things, you know.

'Honestly? It would be a favour to me really so the cottage isn't sitting empty. And it's what Mum would have wanted.' She smiles but there's a sadness beneath her upturned lips.

'I'm sorry about your mum,' I say softly.

'Thanks. It's been an odd few months. But Mum adored Christmas and she would love to see Mrs Claus herself living there for the winter.'

'Only if you're absolutely sure?' I cross my fingers underneath the table that she is, in fact, sure.

'Absolutely. When do you need to move in?'

'Ideally next week if possible.'

She pulls out an old-fashioned leather Filofax and opens the diary section. 'Monday?'

'Perfect.'

'Excellent. Now then,' she stares at my almost finished latte. 'How about we go and have a proper drink to celebrate?'

'Hanna,' I say with an air of seriousness. 'I think you may just be a woman after my own heart.'

She laughs. 'Come on. There's a bar down the road that does a cracking Prosecco.'

Hanna shows me some pictures of the cottage and I almost wet myself with how adorable it is. With a double bedroom and a cosy little kitchen and windows with that crisscross lead pattern and a thatched roof. Oh, and get this: a proper hearth. Not just a log fire but one entire wall is dedicated to this huge stone fireplace, complete with an integrated seat. It looks snug. I can sit and read and roast marshmallows and it'll be like a little slice of heaven.

Hanna and I chat about a million and one things. How she hates her job, and thinks her company name is ridiculous – something we can all agree on – and hasn't had a boyfriend in years since her husband left her right after Kelsie's birth. Kelsie is her daughter and the reason for her interest in sign language. She doesn't say that Kelsie's deafness is why the bastard husband left, but she doesn't *not* say it if you catch my drift.

* * *

Later that evening I get a text from Mr Grotty – as I will now call him – the landlord I met this morning.

> MR GROTTY
> Any thoughts on the flat love? Got a lot of interest.

I ignore him. But he messages again.

> MR GROTTY
> If the rent is the problem, I could do a special deal for ya.

> JESSICA
> Sorry, I found somewhere else

I write back. I don't want to give him an 'in' to keep pestering me.

> MR GROTTY
> Your loss. Your not even that pretty.

Interesting message to send a woman who doesn't want to

rent your grotty hellhole of a flat. And great punctuation too. Idiot.

Hmm. Well that's that then. I guess Mr Grotty just got his name added to the provisional Naughty List. We'll just have to wait and see if anyone else leapfrogs to the top spot first.

* * *

On Monday I meet Hanna at the house and it is even better than in the photos. It looks like it belongs in the movie *The Holiday*, it's so adorable.

'Honestly, I can't thank you enough for doing this,' I tell Hanna as she leads me inside.

'To be fair, you're kind of the one doing *me* a favour. It means I don't have to keep coming in to check that nothing's gone wrong, like a pipe bursting or something.' She shows me the living room where a girl of about seven is sitting on the sofa, absolutely engrossed in a book. 'This is Kelsie.'

I take a few steps toward her and she looks up as she senses my presence. 'Hi,' I sign to her. 'I'm Jessica.'

'I'm Kelsie,' she signs back.

'Lovely to meet you.'

She smiles and then returns to the book.

'Oh, and I have a surprise for you,' Hanna says. 'Let me show you upstairs.' Upstairs is the bathroom and the cosy bedroom. There's a small double bed, already made up with a cute winter duvet featuring some adorable polar bears throwing snowballs at each other. And there, laid out like a prize, is my costume for the grotto.

'You know, my dad was from Finland. Over there, Santa is taken *very* seriously and Mrs Claus wears a long apron and a felt cap.' She smiles nostalgically. 'But Grottos R Us have gone for the more traditional British version with your costume.'

There's a hip-length red velvet jacket trimmed with white fur and a thick black leather belt to give it a more fitted look. Plus a red velvet skirt to match and a pair of black leather boots.

'The jacket has a hood,' Hanna tells me. 'Oh, and the skirt has pockets.' She waggles her eyebrows.

The whole ensemble is literally perfect.

I have a feeling this Christmas is going to be the best one yet.

6

IN WHICH SUSPICIONS ARE AROUSED...

The first step in researching someone is simple. Google them. However, 'Jessica Williams' is far from rare and the search results are dominated by an actress with the same name. Apparently Williams is the third most common surname in the UK, after Smith and Jones. I'm envious of the Smiths and Joneses of the world, people get my surname wrong all the time and it's... well this isn't about me. It's about her. And finding out just who this Jessica Williams is.

I quickly exhaust her social media presence, or at least what she has in her own name. Just a Facebook account with very few posts that tell me absolutely nothing at all about her. I can't even tell where she used to live before she came to Ellsbury. Now, I'm not one to jump to conclusions, but that feels odd. Like she's trying to hide something.

But what?

Luckily, despite her apparent efforts at anonymity, I do know that Jessica spent last Christmas as the Mrs Claus at a shopping centre in Peterborough. I've been to Peterborough a few times over the last couple of years and, in fact, I was in the area last December.

Two things happened in Peterborough last Christmas.

First, and apparently very important to the people of the area, was a visceral dislike for the Serpentine Green Shopping Centre's new Christmas tree. It was the latest in a long line of disputes concerning trees and I find myself dragged down an internet black hole about it, reading reams of comments from irate residents, some of whom have an interesting vocabulary and a particular way with words.

But, second, there was a series of unsolved murders in the city that month, including a home invasion in which a husband and wife were killed. I do a Google search and a whole load of results come up. My eye is caught by a headline from a local paper: *A Christmas Slay Ride*. These particular murders were all stabbings, each of the victims just walking home from whatever party they had been too. The police were warning everyone to be careful, not to get too drunk, not to walk home alone. Nothing connected the men, the killings were random, some madman on a rampage.

A Christmas Slay Ride

Christmas is meant to be a time of comfort and joy. But not for the innocent victims of a crazy individual stalking the streets of Peterborough this festive season.

Two days ago, the body of a fourth man was discovered. He had been enjoying some drinks with friends in The Draper's Arms on Cowgate and left around eleven p.m. But he never made it home. Instead his body was discovered by a local business owner as he opened up the following morning.

'It was such a shock,' the business owner, Graham Fewly,

told *Peterborough Matters*. 'I thought it was a mannequin at first. But then I noticed the blood.'

The man, whose name has not yet been released by police, but who is believed to be a resident of Fletton, is the latest victim of who some are calling The Christmas Killer.

The Draper's Arms is a Wetherspoons and literally next door to the shopping centre where Jessica Williams was Mrs Claus. Someone once told me that there's no such thing as coincidence.

7

FEARNE

'Fearne!' he bellows down the stairs. I'm sitting at the kitchen table with a little timer ticking down the minutes of a pomodoro sprint. My next book is due to my editor in three days and I'm up against it, trying to squeeze the words onto the page. 'Fearne!' he bellows again, this time even louder. I try to block him out and close my eyes for a moment to transport myself back to the Ton and preparations for the ball of the season.

I squeal as the screen of my laptop slams down and I'm forced to yank my fingers out of harm's way. 'What the—'

'Fearne, I need—'

'Did you just close my laptop?' I don't even bother to hold in my rage. Who the fuck does that?

'You were ignoring me.' He says it like therefore it was OK.

'I'm on a deadline. You can't just...' but I trail off as I gingerly reopen the laptop. *Please please please don't have my file messed up.*

'I need to get to the market.'

I ignore him as I read through the last few sentences on the screen in front of me. Thank God I bought myself a fancy

MacBook – even if I did tell Sebastian it was a gift from my publisher because I knew he'd throw a fit about the expense of it – and so all my work is still there. I hastily save it, just to be sure.

'Fearne!' This time he shouts. Like a petulant child not getting his mother's attention. Sometimes being married feels like having another kid. An ungrateful, bratty one with zero survival instincts or ability to do its own laundry.

The pomodoro timer beeps to say my sprint is over. 'Great job. Now take a break for five minutes,' it says in its slightly patronising tone, which irritates me no end but has been surprisingly effective in improving my productivity.

'See,' Sebastian says pointing at it. 'You're on a break.'

'I wasn't when you interrupted me,' I point out.

'I need to get to the market. Where's my fleece? The one with the logo on it?'

I sigh. I know I should tell him to fuck off and find his own fleece; deep down I know that a lot of his behaviour is my fault for coddling him all these years and allowing him to push me around until he gets what he wants. Not in a victim blaming way, I still understand that he's a grown man who should realise the impact his behaviour has on the people around him and sort out his own shit. But more in the way that recognises he's learnt that if he shouts loudly enough I will jump to it, that I value peace and quiet over pushing back against him.

'All of your branded stuff is in the wardrobe in the spare room,' I tell him. I washed, dried and hung it all up neatly for him last week so everything would be fresh and clean and easy for him to find. The site set-up is in full swing and sometimes he heads to the market at stupid times in the morning; everything is in the spare room so he doesn't disturb me too much if I'm asleep. Not that I can sleep when I have a deadline looming and

I still need to write almost ten thousand words in the next four days.

'It isn't there,' he says.

'Have you worn it yet?' It's been stupidly mild this year, so he's mainly been wearing a sweatshirt and a gilet instead of the thick fleece coat.

'I wore it yesterday.'

'And where did you put it when you came home?' I ask, trying not to grit my teeth.

'I don't know.' He stares at me as if I must remember, as if I should have been paying more attention to him when he came home last night and demanded his dinner.

My timer beeps. 'Breaktime is over. Back to work,' it commands in the stilted electronic voice I both love – because of the productivity gains – and loathe for being a rather hard taskmaster and condescending shit rolled into one.

Sebastian looks at it. 'But I need my fleece.'

'Did you leave it in the car?' I ask. He has a tendency to take off his outer layer when he's driving, especially now we've bought a car with heated seats and he's developed a penchant for putting his on full blast.

'Oh, yeah.' He doesn't say thanks, not that I was expecting him to. 'I'll just make myself a flask.' There's an edge there, like I should have already made him a hot drink to take with him. I would have done, but sometimes he has tea and sometimes coffee and whichever I make will always be wrong. I have, however, washed and laid out the flask ready for him. He doesn't offer me a cup of tea.

I run my finger over the trackpad to bring my laptop back to life and stare at the words on the page. The timer is already ticking down but I can't concentrate as Sebastian makes a racket.

'You're coming to the market later, right?' he asks.

'Today?' I wasn't planning on it. I was hoping for a peaceful few hours this afternoon in a coffee shop to get another couple of thousand words written.

'The grotto's going in.'

The first year Sebastian ran the market I got roped in to managing Santa's grotto, but then I suggested we outsource to a company who would run it and pay for the privilege and thankfully he agreed. But we used to take Immy every year to see the grotto getting decorated, it was a bit of a tradition. She's fifteen now though and doesn't give a shit.

Immy finds this exact moment to tornado into the kitchen, a whirlwind of blonde hair and hormones. 'Is there toast?' she demands.

'The bread you like is in the breadbin,' I tell her.

'You're coming to the grotto this afternoon, aren't you, sweetheart?' Sebastian asks her.

Immy looks at me with pleading eyes. *Get me out of this hell?* she silently begs.

'Immy has dance practice,' I say, even though I have no idea what is on her schedule, we've agreed she can manage herself this year as long as she doesn't fall behind.

She flashes me a grateful smile. 'Sorry Daddy,' she says as she kisses his cheek.

'No worries. Your mother will still come.'

Of course she fucking will.

* * *

The grotto this year has had a major facelift. It's huge, clad in thick beams of wood to look like a classic log cabin, complete with synthetic snow on the roof and windows. A thousand lights twinkle in shades of red and green and gold, and around the door is a huge twisted garland of foliage and ribbon.

Even my cold dead heart can appreciate how amazing it looks.

'Good, huh?' Sebastian says, coming up behind me. He reaches his arms around and laces his fingers together to rest on my waist. I allow myself to lean back against him for a moment and relish the contact. He is so rarely tactile like this, especially in public. The market installation is obviously going well.

'It's magical,' I tell him. I'm not even lying.

'It's certainly a lot better than it was when we started the market,' he says and then takes a step backwards. Cold air rushes to fill the space at my back. Oh well, that was a nice moment while it lasted. Shame he had to ruin it with a snarky comment about the grotto when I first designed it, like a random housewife from Ellsbury would be able to pull off what a professional company with a budget greater than the two hundred quid he let me spend that first year could.

'When do we get to meet the big man himself?' I ask.

'I've been told to stay out of all things to do with the Clauses,' he says, slightly huffily.

'You're not still upset about Hanna overriding you with the choice for Mrs Claus?'

'She acted like hers was the only opinion on the matter.'

'Well...' I trail off. It's probably not the best thing to tell him hers *is* the only opinion on the matter, given that all staff hiring for the grotto is at her discretion.

'She's too ambitious. You know she only joined Grottos R Us because she thought it'd be a springboard to bigger things. I can't stand women like that.'

Men are strategic, women are calculated. It's like Taylor Swift says.

Although he is right. Hanna does want her current job to lead to something bigger, something better. And kudos to her for it. Ambition should be admired, even if my husband doesn't think so.

8
JESSICA

I meet Hanna at the security gate. She's promised to show me around before the market opens for business tomorrow. Then I'll meet my 'work husband' and we'll run through the whole process for when the kids start arriving.

We walk around the market and it is... Well, I want to say it's wondrous, but the truth is there is still an absolute ton of work to do and everyone is running around like headless chickens. It's complete mayhem.

'Is it always this...?' I trail off and motion around me.

'Yeah. There's never enough time and something always goes wrong and the vendors are here until like four in the morning trying to get everything ready.'

'Why?'

'Why?' she repeats back to me.

'As in, why is it such chaos?'

'Sebastian Dixon.' She looks at me pointedly.

'Oh.' I remember him from the audition.

'Yeah. He likes to be in charge of every little detail.' She rolls her eyes.

'Really?' I feign surprise. 'I hadn't noticed.'

'Honestly. He needs to micromanage every little thing with all his rules and lists and won't ever let anyone help him and so, when something goes wrong, only he can fix it.'

'He must drive you up the wall with the grotto.'

'Yes. But thankfully his wife – she's a darling, you'll love her – convinced him to bring us in a few years ago and I can tell him to fuck off because of how much money we pay the market in rent.' She smiles sweetly, as if she didn't just say that she tells him to fuck off. I don't really swear myself. It's one of those things you absolutely cannot do in front of the children and so I've been trying over the years to wean myself off it. There are times – obviously – when the situation requires an f-bomb, but I try to keep it to the minimum.

The grotto is a lot bigger than I was expecting; normally they are kind of pokey but this one has been designed with a real sense of grandeur. It looks like a log cabin nestled in an alpine village, covered in a layer of fake snow and with smoke puffing gently from the chimney.

'Wow,' I say.

'It looks good, huh?' Hanna replies.

'The kids are going to love it.'

She leads me inside and it keeps on getting better. There's a tree in the corner, covered in a million tiny twinkling coloured lights, a pile of presents wrapped beneath it. Santa's chair is almost a throne, with ornate wooden detailing and a velvet trim, which will match perfectly with my costume. Cinnamon and pine scent the air.

And then in he walks. The big man himself. Or I'm assuming this is Santa, with his shock of white hair and bushy beard.

'Yes, all real,' hisses Hanna in my ear.

'Carl Becker,' he says as he reaches out to shake my hand, his grip warm and strong.

'Jessica,' I reply.

He cocks his head. 'You look a little young to be my wife.' He narrows his eyes as he scrutinises my face.

'Sorry,' I reply.

He laughs. 'No need to apologise. Lucky Mr Claus, eh?' It should be creepy and gross. But there's something so warm and homely and charming about him that I only blush slightly. I can definitely see why they picked him to play Santa. I can only imagine there'll be a few mums developing slightly inappropriate crushes this Christmas.

He's tall and broad and his eyes crinkle when he smiles. His hair is white and slightly curling, almost like a mane, and the beard is utterly perfect. Oh, and he smells like toasted marshmallows. He's by far the best Santa I've ever seen; the kids are going to go crazy when they meet him.

'So, the grotto will run like basically every other,' Hanna tells us, switching into professional mode. I'd kind of forgotten she was my boss if we're honest, but this snap into efficient-Hanna leaves me with no doubt that this woman is a powerhouse. I feel a bloom of pride in my chest – living vicariously through my friends and seeing them smashing it at their lives has always been a great love of mine. She is totally slaying it at work.

'The kids will enter, greet you both, sit on Santa's knee, tell him what they want for Christmas. Jessica, you make a few notes to slip to the parents when they pick up their photo. Honestly, it makes it so much easier as a parent if you just know exactly what they've asked for. Makes all the difference. Then hand over a present and take a photo of them looking kind of goofy holding it.'

'Sounds pretty standard,' I reply.

'We try to make things as easy as possible,' Hanna tells me with practised efficiency. 'The fewer the deviations, the smoother things run. And the elves will do all the admin stuff like scanning tickets and dealing with money, so just don't get involved in all that. There's a manual from head office they'll be following.'

Carl waves his hand a little. 'Don't ruin the magic for me with all the corporate stuff,' he pleads with a smile.

'Even Santa has to make a living,' Hanna tells him.

Carl puts his big hands over his ears. 'La la la la la,' he says. 'Not listening.'

But then all hell breaks loose and the inside of the grotto becomes a flurry of fur accompanied by the smell of wet dog and a high-pitched shriek from just outside. 'Not in there... Oh for the love of Christ!'

I kneel down and grab a bright purple collar belonging to a very raggedy-looking – and extremely enthusiastic – terrier mix. Hanna grabs the collar of a black and white collie. A labradoodle dances around us.

A head pokes though the door. 'I'm so so sorry,' he says with a wince.

'No worries,' Hanna replies.

'I...' I start to say, but the words die on my lips as the rest of him follows through the door. Dressed in scruffy jeans, welly boots and a checked shirt in shades of blue and green, with floppy dark blond hair and warm brown eyes, it's like my ideal man has literally just materialised in front of me. I've always had a thing for guys who look like they really work for a living. You know what I mean by that, right? Like a smart suit looks nice and all, but a man who looks like he gets his hands dirty on the regular is what really does it for me. Extra bonus points if he's covered in dog hair. This guy could probably knit himself a jumper from the amount of fur covering his outfit.

'I'm Alvi,' he says. 'And these badly behaved creatures are meant to be on their best behaviour to try to find their forever homes.'

'Carl. Jessica. This is my brother,' Hanna says.

He smiles. 'I run Last Chance Rescue, it's an animal sanctuary out past the junction onto the motorway. I've got a stall here at the market to try to raise awareness. Well, and funds. Obviously. These guys are eating me out of house and home.'

I think I'm in love. He looks like my ideal man *and* he runs an animal rescue? I might just die right here on the spot.

And then in trots the most adorable scrappy-looking mixed breed, with an upturned ear and a cute little beard. His fur is tan and white and he sits perfectly at Alvi's feet observing the scene in front of him.

Oh. Well now I'm really done for.

9

FEARNE

My alarm goes off at 5 a.m., jolting me from a dream about missing my deadline and my editor turning up on my doorstep to stand over me as I finish writing. But her face was all wrong, more like my old headmistress than her own.

I check my emails on my phone and breathe a sigh of relief when I realise I sent the manuscript off last night. I was up until just gone midnight but it's done. I might even allow myself a few mulled wines later to celebrate. Although for now I need to get up and crowbar Sebastian out of bed.

Today is 2 November and the opening day at the Christmas market. But first we have final inspections to do and I promised my husband a bacon sandwich to start the day off right.

'It's beginning to look a lot like Christmas' is playing on the radio as I put the kettle on. I am going to need a vat of coffee this morning and choose the maple fudge flavour I bought the other day. The aroma of it fills the air and for a brief flash I actually feel Christmassy. Weird.

That same festive feeling ramps up as I follow my husband on his inspection of the chalets. For all I bitch and moan, the market does look amazing this year, with all of the stock out and the lights twinkling and everyone looking happy and smiling as they make sure everything is just so on the stalls.

Alvi from Last Chance Rescue has brought three dogs with him, all wearing gilets with the charity logo on them.

'Are those real dogs in my market?' Sebastian hisses in my ear.

'I told him he could bring some of the animals. It'll be a huge draw for the kids.'

Sebastian harumphs under his breath. But he waves at Alvi as we move past so I think he's going to accept it. I just hope none of the animals make a mess and ruin everything.

Bella Donna at Crystals and Gifts looks miserable.

'Why does she have a face like a slapped arse?' Sebastian asks me.

'She thinks the energy is off with her stall being there,' I tell him.

'Will she be a problem?'

'No, of course not. I told her she's just going to have to deal with it.'

'Good girl,' he says with a smile. As compliments go it's pretty thin, but I feel a small glow that he's at least recognising the work I do.

Most of the food stalls are clustered together to form a square in the centre, with the mulled wine tent – The Apres-Ski – taking pride of place. Even though we won't be opening for a couple of hours, the hog roast – Porkies – is already smelling delicious and I allow myself to daydream for a moment about a pork and stuffing roll with lashings of apple sauce.

'That's the weird crumble place,' Sebastian says.

I take a few steps closer to read the menu. 'Apple and cinnamon. Plum. Peach and pineapple. They sound kind of incredible.'

'You know I'm not good with new stuff,' he says, in the understatement of the year. 'But I think I might try that peach and pineapple one later.'

Well, well, well. Perhaps an old husband can learn new tricks after all.

By lunchtime even Sebastian has to agree that everything is ready for the grand opening. He has a checklist – of course he does – and he goes so far as to crack a smile as he ticks the final item off.

'All done?' I ask as I put a mug of tea in front of him.

'Every single thing,' he confirms, brandishing the list.

We sit in silence as we sip our drinks, enjoying the short lull in the quiet of the office before the chaos of the afternoon begins.

'It's going to be a good year,' I promise him.

He lifts his hand so I can see the way he's crossing his fingers. 'Let's just get through today first,' he says. He drains his tea and puts the mug down with a thud. 'Come on then. It's showtime.'

We make our way from the office to the main entrance to the market. The Mayor of Ellsbury is coming to head up the opening ceremony, and I can feel Sebastian bristling at the thought. Robert Hawcroft is two years younger than Sebastian and they grew up in each other's orbits when Robert dated Sebastian's little sister for a while. He was a posh twat – Robert that is – and Sebastian always hated him.

'Prick thought he could break my baby sister's heart,' he told me when Robert was first inaugurated as Mayor two years ago. The whole story had come out then.

'He was at that fancy Ellsbury House school. His mates dared him to find himself some "rough".' He spat the words, the venom still there after all these years. He'd always been protective of Laura. 'Some "rough". That's all she was to him. But she adored him, thought the sun shone out of his red-trouser-wearing arse. Prick.'

I asked Laura about it last year when she'd had a few too many glasses of wine.

'He was so hot,' she said wistfully.

'Didn't he break your heart?' I asked.

'Well yeah, I was young and foolish.' She rolled her eyes. 'But for a few weeks I convinced myself it was true love and we'd get married and live in a fuck-off mansion and have little toffy kids in designer outfits.' She laughed, a hint of nostalgia there. 'What an idiot,' she said gently, shaking her head. 'So of course I gave him my virginity and then he buggered off back to his ex-girlfriend at Ellsbury House. I cried for like a week. Sebastian was livid.'

'He still is.'

'Bless him.'

Robert Hawcroft is still an entitled prick who thinks he's better than everyone though. Although he's graduated from red trousers to a pair of dark yellow-coloured cords. They are truly hideous.

'Look at the trousers,' I whisper to Sebastian as we head toward him to make sure he has the final instructions for the grand opening.

'Perhaps I should call him Colonel,' Sebastian whispers back, covering his mouth with his hand. I'm assuming just in case our illustrious Mayor has learnt to lipread.

'Colonel Mustard,' I exclaim and giggle.

'Prick,' Sebastian says with venom.

'Prick.' I match his tone. He bumps my shoulder with his. At least we're on the same team here.

'Ahh,' Robert says as we approach, 'Mr Nixon, there you are.' As if he's been looking hard for Sebastian rather than just standing around chatting.

'Dixon,' Sebastian corrects him.

'Of course it is.' The way Robert says it is like Sebastian doesn't know his own name and Robert is merely humouring him in the way you might a small child who you give a prize to for simply trying. I feel my husband's shoulders stiffen beside me.

'Thank you for coming this afternoon,' Sebastian says through gritted teeth.

'Of course, old chap. Wouldn't have missed it for the world, even if it does feel that Christmas comes earlier every year. It's barely November.' He gives a braying laugh that sets my teeth on edge. 'But still, what a great turnout.' He motions behind him to the growing crowd of people waiting for the market to open. 'I didn't expect quite so many people to turn up to see little old me, even if I will be rocking the full regalia.' He motions to the suit carrier being toted by an extremely bored-looking late teen. I recognise him as Charlie, the Mayor's youngest son.

I don't have the heart to tell Robert that the only reason people are queueing for the market is because the first one hundred pints and mulled wines are free. A promotion Remi from The Apres-Ski started running a few years ago that has ensured opening day is always a hit and looks packed for the photos that will grace the front page of the *Ellsbury Gazette* tomorrow.

'I need somewhere to get trussed up,' Robert says.

'You can use my office,' Sebastian tells him. 'Let me show you.' He throws me a weary look and I smile back in encouragement that says *just play nicely for a few hours and then it'll be over.*

I'll make sure he has a large whisky this evening to celebrate the first major hurdle overcome.

I spot a gaggle of girls talking to the security team. One of them has long blonde hair and gesticulates wildly with her hands as she talks. Immy. I wave and she points at me, clearly trying to tell the new security guy who she is so he'll let her and her friends in early.

'She's my daughter,' I tell him as I walk over to rescue them.

'And you are?' he asks. But then realises which side of the fence I'm on and takes a small step back. 'Uh...' He looks around as if someone might come and rescue him.

'I'm Mrs Dixon. You'll know my husband, Sebastian?'

He nods dumbly.

'Can you let my daughter and her friends in please?'.

'Of course, Mrs Dixon,' he mumbles.

'Thanks, Mum,' Immy says as she walks past me. She offers me a quick smile and I know better than to expect a hug or any other gesture of affection in front of her friends.

* * *

Mayor Hawcroft bangs on for ages in his speech, making sure everyone in the audience is bored to tears by his effusive insistence that he's a pillar of the community. I tune him out and imagine a glass of mulled wine in one hand and one of those hog roast baps from Porkies in the other.

Finally he wraps it up and cuts the ribbon with a pair of comically large scissors that he brought with him in their own special case. There's a few seconds' pause as a photo is taken of the Mayor's big shiny face, but then it's as if the floodgates have been opened and a few hundred people rush The Apres-Ski, desperate to get their hands on a free drink.

'Hey, do I know you?' Charlie, the Mayor's son, asks Immy, who is standing with her friends close by.

'No,' she says and I watch with pride as she gives him the once-over.

'Are you sure? I think we know each other from school.'

'No.' She turns away from him and I watch as the smile immediately drops from his face.

He reaches out to grab her hand and pull her back to face him.

'Fuck off,' she tells him, shaking him off.

'Oh come on. Don't be mean.' He sticks out his bottom lip in a way I can only assume he thinks might be endearing.

'No.'

'But—'

'No is a complete sentence.' She turns away from him once again as if to say *case closed*. My heart swells with pride. I don't like it when she directs that sass at me, but when she uses it to get rid of older boys hitting on her I'm fucking ecstatic.

'What about you, sweetheart?' he says to one of Immy's friends, Riya.

'I'm fifteen, you perv.'

'So?' he says.

'Eughh. Fucking gross.' Riya almost spits the words in his face. 'Come on girls, let's get away from this loser.' She links arms with Immy and the pack shimmies away.

Should I pull Immy up later on her friend's bad language?

But my attention is snagged back to Charlie. I watch him watching them and a cool hand creeps up the back of my neck. There's definitely something not right about that boy and I hope he stays the hell away from the girls. Otherwise I might not be accountable for my actions.

10

JESSICA

One thing I've noticed in each of the places I've been Mrs Claus is that the festive spirit so rarely extends to communal staff areas and these can be some of the most hideously depressing places you will ever set foot in. They normally have a hint of stale sock in the air and the feeling of a doctor's waiting room.

But, however bad the other staffrooms have been, I think it's going to take all my skills to make this market's one even vaguely passable. It's a shed. One that has been constructed in such a way that there are gaps in the corners and the roof is crooked. The raw wood floor has been covered in a tatty bit of carpet that looks like it's been pulled from someone's loft after fifty years; perfect for transporting a dead body, less perfect for creating a welcoming space to spend the precious breaktime of a ten-hour shift.

Luckily, Ellsbury has not one, not two, but five charity shops lining its cobbled high street and so I've been able to pick up a load of fluffy rugs and cushions to scatter around. I even found two giant beanbags for the princely sum of five quid.

Unluckily, I get busted by Sebastian Dixon as I'm driving my tiny Nissan up to the staffroom the day after the market opens.

'You can't bring your vehicle in here!' he shouts, loudly enough so I can hear him from inside the car and with Sia's *Every Day Is Christmas* album playing.

I roll down the window and poke my head out. 'I'm just dropping off some stuff to spruce up the staffroom,' I tell him in a singsong voice, plastering a smile on my face.

'You can't bring your vehicle in here.'

'I won't be long.'

'You can't bring your vehicle in here.' Jeez, he sounds like a broken record. 'Vendors need to restock. There's a rota.'

Of course there's a rota. I imagine Sebastian has a rota for every minutia of his life. 'I'll be quick.' I broaden my smile.

'You're in the way.'

I look around for all the other people I'm apparently inconveniencing with the presence of my car. The rest of the market is silent.

'If you give me a hand unloading I'll be done in half the time.'

'But... but...' he says. Then he huffs. 'Fine. But if you pull a stunt like this again I'll be forced to... umm...'

The penalty for 'improper loading' is a fine to the stallholder. There's a notice in the staffroom I'm desperately trying to make habitable. But I'm not a stallholder and so there isn't really anything Sebastian can do. Instead he just huffs again and comes round to the rear of the car.

I pop the boot. Maybe it was a stroke of luck to get accosted by Sebastian; it'll make getting everything from the car so much easier.

* * *

The first shift in the grotto goes off without a hitch. The kids adore Carl, whose costume makes him look like the real deal. It's the same shade of red velvet as mine, with a similar white fur trim; large black buttons grace the front of the coat and the trousers are cut wide so they sit perfectly on top of his chunky black leather boots. He looks like he could trek across snowy mountains with a sack of presents slung over his shoulder.

'Are you sure you're not really him?' I ask when we have a quiet few moments before the next wave of children descends on the grotto.

Carl taps the side of his nose and then winks. He refuses to say any more on the subject.

* * *

That evening, there's a staff party in The Apres-Ski.

'I know the grotto only opened today, but shouldn't the party have been on the first night the stalls started trading?' I ask Hanna as we meet up outside the grotto so we can head there together.

'You'd think,' she replies. 'But because most of the stall-holders have to work so hard to get everything ready, they basically just crash and burn on the first night so we've started having the party on the second.'

Makes sense I suppose. We wait patiently in the beer tent to order some mulled wines.

'We call this *glögi* in Finland,' she tells me. '*Kippis*,' she says looking me directly in the eye as she taps her plastic cup against mine.

'*Kippis*,' says a deep voice behind me. I turn to find Hanna's brother. The gorgeous Alvi. A blush creeps up my cheeks. I'm going to look like an absolute fool.

'Ah, my favourite brother. Come join us.' Hanna pats the seat next to her.

We drink some mulled wine and I fall into a pleasant fog of watching and listening to the hubbub around me. I love being part of a crowd, feeling the mood ebb and swell, part of something bigger than myself but not the focus. Until the bench next to me creaks with the weight of someone sitting down. I turn to stare into a pair of chocolate-brown eyes.

'You seemed kind of overwhelmed,' Alvi says, his voice soft and with just a hint of sexy caramel. 'So I thought I'd check in.'

I smile at him, a little stupidly if we're being honest. 'Just taking it all in,' I say quietly.

'It's kind of a rowdy bunch,' he acknowledges, looking around at all the stallholders and other staff members who have packed the tent to celebrate the first full day of trade.

'I guess they have a lot of steam to blow off.'

'Yeah. It's been…' he trails off and pushes his thick hair away from his eyes. It immediately springs back into position and I have to sit on my free hand to stop myself from reaching out to touch it. 'Let's just say that the market management have a certain way of doing things.'

'I assume you're talking about Sebastian Dixon?' I raise both eyebrows as I say it, just so he knows which side I'm on.

'Absolute taskmaster,' Alvi tells me, leaning a little to close the distance between us, just in case anyone is listening. Although I suspect that everyone here would be of the same opinion. 'I'm a charity, just trying to save some animals. But he wanted me to fill in a million forms and provide so many pieces of paperwork, it was insane. He wanted four bits of ID to prove who I was and three referees.'

'Ouch.'

'I almost had to pull out, because I was getting to the point where it was eating all the time I have to spend on actually helping with the animals. I don't get a lot of spare time to be honest.' He looks sad. And if I squint a little I see the lines of tiredness around his eyes. 'Or spare cash as I needed to pay someone to certify my documents and it just gobbled up money like there was no tomorrow.' My eyes travel from his face to his outfit: his jumper is kind of threadbare and his jeans have that trendy ripped look, but I think it's more that they're old and starting to fall apart then being a fashion statement.

'But you made it through all that.' I wince a little inside, I sound like I'm just putting a positive spin on it all. Or, worse, excusing Sebastian's behaviour somehow.

'Yeah.' He smiles and it lights up his entire face. 'If I can even make half of my projection, then I'll be able to keep the rescue centre open for the whole of next year.'

An hour or so later, Alvi offers to walk me home and I gratefully accept. I'm still getting my bearings and Ellsbury is a bit of a warren. We're at the edge of the market when music starts to play.

'This is one of my favourites,' Alvi says with a shy smile.

'"Carol of the bells",' I say. 'I love it too.'

But behind me I hear a huff and then a quiet voice begins to sing along. 'Bitch what the fuck, bitch what the fuck, bitch what the fuck.' I have to admit the words – despite the profanity – do fit the tune perfectly but the look on Alvi's face is of perfect shock. I pull him off the path and we hide behind the waffle stand to watch the person pass.

'Who's that?' I hiss under my breath. She's wearing a midi-skirt with leather boots and a wax jacket. Her long blonde hair is twisted into a chignon. She's beautiful, one of those women who look like they've stepped out of a renaissance painting, all perfect features and radiant skin. But she walks with her hands stuffed in her pockets, leaning forward slightly, boots scuffing the ground as if she doesn't really have the energy to lift her feet properly.

'That's Fearne Dixon.'

'As in…' I raise my eyebrows.

'Yep. That poor woman is married to Sebastian himself.'

'How come she hasn't killed him?' I whisper.

She must have far more self-control than I do.

11

FEARNE

Day three of the market passes without a hitch and I start to feel the embers of hope that this year will be one of those non-event seasons where everything just kind of runs smoothly and no one does anything too heinous.

By day four I've been lulled into a false sense of security. I'm in the little office Sebastian has built, making sure I stay on site for the first few days in case the newbies have questions or just need an extra hand with some of the more technical elements of being a Christmas market vendor. Suddenly the door bursts open, slamming into the desk wedged in the corner where I'm sitting and causing me to jump out of my skin.

'Fuck!' I scream as the coffee I was just about to sip sloshes all over me.

Sebastian – the perpetrator of the door slam – looks at me for a moment, a flash of puzzlement across his face. But then he shakes his head and ignores my coffee-soaked predicament. 'You are never going to believe what someone has graffitied on the side of the waffle stand.'

There is only one possible thing it can be, from the look of abject horror on his face.

'A... a...' He physically gropes the air as he tries to find a nice polite euphemism. He's never been able to say 'cock'. It's rather stifled any attempt at sexy-talk between us. 'A *willy*.' See what I mean, hardly a knicker-wetter as a term.

I make him a cup of tea and add an extra sugar. He needs to watch his diet but I think now is not the time to be overly zealous. One more sugar is probably better than a full-on heart attack.

'Thanks, love,' he says, as he slumps into a seat with the steaming mug. 'It was quite the shock.'

'I bet,' I say in a soothing voice. 'Any idea who did it?'

He shakes his head. 'I think we're going to have to put up some extra cameras.'

I nod in agreement. 'That sounds like an excellent idea.' I don't remind him that I told him last year to buy some more cameras as the coverage was patchy.

A few hours later and there's a knock on the door. 'Got a delivery for you, darling,' the head that pokes around the door says. 'Was told to bring 'em here.'

'What is it?' I ask.

'Looks like cameras, darling.'

'Oh.' That was quick. Normally it takes Sebastian about three years to actually do things. Shame he can't be this efficient at home, I've been asking him to fix the garage door since 2014.

I head outside, grabbing a fleece from the hooks by the door in case it's chilly. It smells like damp dog and fag butts – it must belong to one of the supervisors who share the office space with Sebastian – so I'm lucky it isn't actually that cold and I don't need it.

'These are all for here?' I ask the delivery guy.

He shrugs. 'I guess so.' He scans the clipboard in front of him. 'Yeah, fifty WiFi cameras.'

'Fifty?' I must sound oddly accusatory, because he takes a small step backwards.

'I'm just doing my job, darling.'

'Of course, sorry. It's just that feels like a lot of cameras...' I stare at the huge pile of boxes.

'Safety first and all that,' the guy mumbles as he hands me the clipboard to sign for them.

'I think I should just check with my husband.'

'Whatever, darling. I don't have all day.' He huffs loudly as I slip back inside the office and grab my phone. But of course Sebastian doesn't answer. 'Seriously, love. I've other deliveries to do.' He taps the clipboard loudly.

'Fine.' I sign my name and off he goes, leaving me with all these boxes and no idea what I'm meant to do with them.

'What the hell are all these?' booms a voice from behind me.

I whirl round to face Sebastian. 'I tried to call you. These are the cameras you ordered.'

'Cameras?' He looks completely bamboozled by the idea. 'Oh, CCTV.' His eyes narrow as he looks at the stack. 'I ordered five.'

'You ordered fifty,' I correct him.

'Nope.'

'Well, they delivered fifty.'

'You shouldn't have signed for them.'

I throw the stinky fleece at him and stride off. I'm going to get myself a hot chocolate with a shot of Baileys in it. Fuck all this shit.

In the end the security team sets up most of the cameras.

They run off WiFi and connect to the main computer, triggering when the motion sensors detect something.

Sebastian – who appears to have come round to the idea of a *lot* of cameras – is like an excited schoolboy as Jet, the Head of Security, takes him through the new system. I have no doubt he'll get bored soon and go back to blaming me for accepting fifty cameras when he wanted five, but for now he's happy and so I'm going to relish the peace.

'What the—' Sebastian shoots out of his chair, pointing at the screen. 'Is he? *Is he?*' The horror in his voice is unmistakable.

'Oh dear,' Jet says.

'Dirty bastard!'

I'm intrigued now and so I head round to his desk so I can see what's going on. 'Oh.' I have no more words. On the screen a young man is crouching round the back of Santa's grotto, his trousers round his ankles as he takes a shit on the ground, a huge grin on his face. Dirty bastard indeed. 'Hang on.' I peer more closely at the screen. 'Is that Zachary Hawcroft?'

'The Mayor's son would not be doing a poo in my Christmas market.'

'I really think he is.'

Sebastian squints. 'It fucking is him.' My husband is now apoplectic. 'I'll kill him.'

* * *

So I'd thought that Charlie – as in creepy Charlie who seems to have an inappropriate interest in my teenage daughter and her friends – was the son of our illustrious Mayor we needed to worry about. But, given what just happened, it appears that the crown goes to twenty-three-year-old Zachary, who is apparently going by the moniker Z – pronounced Zee not Zed – now and leads a group of six young men who begin to make a nuisance of themselves.

Over the next few days – and despite my husband's warnings and repeated threats to inform his father – Z and his band of merry dickheads become more and more of a problem. A queue begins to form outside the office as stallholders line up to complain. Unfortunately, Sebastian is dealing with yet another problem – this time with one of the generators – and so I'm on my own to face the rabble.

'They've been stealing from Waffleicious. Literally just leaning over the barrier into the waffle stand and swiping chocolate bars and stuff. And then eating them as they go round like a pack of ravenous dogs,' David Bennett tells me. Well, 'tell' is a mild word for what is basically a major ticking-off. As if it's my fault. He's the kind of man who thinks he should be in charge, who believes the world should bend to his whims.

'They've been bringing their own vodka,' Remi from The Apres-Ski adds. 'And I think they've been selling it to some of the younger kids. What about my licence? I don't want to get blamed for this.' Remi is a sweetheart and I know his concerns are genuine. He has a husband and three small kids to look after; if he loses his licence to operate at the market it would have huge repercussions for him. I give him a smile, one that tells him I'm on his side.

'They've been putting my gonks into compromising positions.' James takes out his phone and swipes through a series of photos depicting the things simulating various interesting acts.

'They were taking the mickey out of my rune bags,' Bella Donna adds. Although, to be fair, I can hardly blame them when I also take the piss out of the shit she sells.

'I'm worried they'll start swiping stuff from The Truckle Bunnies.'

'And what if they target Heaven Scents Candles?'

'Look. Everyone should put their concerns in writing,' I say. There's too much for me to deal with right now. 'And send me the photos of the gonks,' I add to James. Some of the positions are surprisingly adventurous and they might give me some pointers for one of the books I'm writing under my pen name. Cherry Dubois could use some more ideas.

12

JESSICA

I bump into Alvi on my way into work. This time he has three very small, very thin and very timid-looking dogs with him. Each of them is dressed in a little coat to keep them warm.

'This is Ziggy and Twiggy,' he says, pointing at two of them. 'And this little guy was just rescued and doesn't have a name yet.'

I stoop down and appraise the nameless dog a little more carefully. He has the saddest-looking eyes I've ever seen and all I want to do is take him home. 'What happened to him?' I ask.

'He was a stray so we don't really know.'

'He looks so sad.'

'Don't be fooled by the big brown eyes, all Iggies have them.'

'Iggies?' I look up at Alvi, but blush when I realise this angle gives me a rather good view of his muscular thighs encased in their tatty jeans.

'Italian greyhounds.'

'Oh. Well, it is Christmas, so why don't you call him Figgy?'

'As in pudding?' He places his hand gently on the dog's small head. 'I think it's perfect.'

I stand up, trying to look graceful but probably failing miserably. 'You should get him a little jumper with puddings on it.'

'Genius.' He grins at me. 'I'll go and ask Joseph if he has anything I can borrow. I really want to get these three rehomed before Christmas and some nice festive sweaters might just tip the balance. Apparently Doggy Do-Dahs got turned over last night. Some of the stock was stolen but a whole load more was ruined. Joseph can't sell it but these little guys won't mind if they have a jumper that's a little grubby from being thrown on the ground.'

'Oh no. Poor Joseph.'

'Yeah. The rumour is that it's that Z dude and his pals.' Alvi shakes his head. 'Anyway, I'd better get to work.' He smiles. 'Have a fabulous day, Mrs Claus,' he says and then gives me this funny little bow. It's gawky and utterly adorable.

'You too, good sir.' I do a curtsey. *Why did I curtsey?* I scuttle off, trying not to fall over and make even more of a prat of myself. A curtsey? The shame.

* * *

All everyone can talk about is this Z guy and what he and his friends are up to. Now, I will admit that some of their antics are fairly humorous: the thing with the gonks was kind of brilliant, but some are hideous. Defecating behind the grotto is definitely against the spirit of Christmas and then ransacking Doggy Do-Dahs. Poor Joseph has poured his heart and soul into making jumpers and accessories for Ellsbury's fur babies and he doesn't deserve to have his stock ruined.

When I get home, I make myself a peppermint hot chocolate and settle into the nook by the fire with my laptop. It's time to do some digging and find out a little more about these hooligans.

Zachary Ellis Hawcroft is better known to his friends as Z. Which sounds stupid. Like he's pretending to be some kind of gangster with an interesting moniker. In reality, it appears he's just another rich manchild who thinks the world owes him. Although I don't even know what is owed. Nothing he does seems to make any sense in terms of achieving a goal. It's merely destruction for destruction's sake.

People might think I'm a psychopath, but at least I have reasons for what I do. Goals I'm reaching for. Oh, and a moral compass, grey as it may be.

Z is the son of the Mayor of Ellsbury and still lives with Mummy and Daddy in their huge farmhouse on the outskirts of town. He's twenty-three years old and, from what I can tell, has never had a job, or done anything meaningful with his time like education or charity work.

He was a student at Ellsbury House school from 2013 to 2018 and by the looks of things had everything going for him. House prefect, on the cricket team, featured in photos advertising the school, all that kind of thing. The school website is still using one of those pictures – him and three other boys in the woods sitting around a fire – to demonstrate all the wholesome activities on offer to justify the... I click on a link to the school fees.

Thirteen thousand pounds a term.

Thirteen thousand? A term?

That feels like daylight robbery. And I do hope Daddy Hawcroft has asked for a refund given the man his son became.

I manage to find a few articles from the *Ellsbury Gazette* archive that report on various petty crimes and the arrest of a local youth meeting Zachary's description. They didn't name him in the articles, but a few people in the comments section had done the honours. *We all know this is Zachary Hawcroft,* one person said. So much for anonymity.

But nothing was ever done and Zachary has continued to cause a nuisance without repercussion. I can only assume Daddy is able to protect him. What a boon it must be to have a rich and well-respected father. Imagine the risks you could take if you knew someone had your back like that. Think of all the awful people I could get rid of with impunity if I were in his shoes. It irks me that he uses what amounts to a superpower to do nothing more than terrorise and disrupt.

I don't want you to think I'm placing him on the Naughty List – although still in pencil, I don't want to make rash decisions so early in the season – out of jealousy of his position. I'm not petty like that. But I think we can all agree that something needs to be done about his behaviour.

I take a look at some of his friends too.

Jared Abel. This guy *has* been named in the *Ellsbury Gazette*. A fair few times in fact. And it looks like he doesn't have a rich daddy to protect him because he spent six months in HMP Bristol last year.

Noah Welling. Last year he was accused of sexual assault but the case was subsequently dropped when the victim pulled their statement. But here's the thing about the internet, you can threaten your victim to redact, or offer them enough money to stay quiet, but once the internet knows, the internet remembers. And other people pick up the fight. #JusticeForMaria still trends occasionally.

Max Kirby. He has a tattoo of a spiderweb on his neck and apparently goes by Parker. Another former student of Ellsbury House and the son of a local businessman. Daddy Kirby runs a company that ostensibly owns a plethora of gentleman's barber shops and a few takeaways in the wider Ellsbury area. All the kind of businesses where lots of paper money changes hands. I'm not one to cast aspersions, but I would not be surprised if

Daddy Kirby has a reason for running cash businesses that goes beyond a healthy mistrust of credit card companies. I don't want to say money laundering, so I'll just whisper it very quietly.

All in all, they seem a delightful bunch of young men. I wonder how many of them will graduate to the Naughty List before the festive season is finished?

13

FEARNE

I wake up on Thursday morning with an impending sense of doom. Like the world is about to end and of course it will all be my fault. All I want to do is stay in bed with the covers pulled over my head and pretend that nothing else exists.

You could pretend to be sick? a little voice whispers in the back of my brain. I don't normally like to; it feels a bit too much like tempting fate.

There's been a lot of Covid going round this month... But if I feign Covid I know I will then get sick for real.

But you could stay home in the warm and finish writing the story you've been working on and drink hot chocolate and then start that new Cherry Dubois book you've been thinking about...

I poke my head out from under the duvet and try a few tentative coughs.

'You'd better not be getting sick,' Sebastian grumbles next to me and pulls more of the duvet onto his side. Luckily I bought a super-king duvet – even though the bed is only a king – so there's plenty to go round. Honestly, the best hundred quid I ever spent and I'd highly recommend it for anyone who shares a bed. Especially with a cover-hog like I do.

Sebastian's mobile rings. 'Fuck's sake,' he says loudly. I take the opportunity to try a few less tentative coughs. If Sebastian's getting a call at this time in the morning then it can only be one of two things. His mother, which always comes with the risk that she's calling to invite herself to come and stay, like she did for an entire week in the summer when I almost killed both of them. Or work, which means some kind of crisis. In either of these scenarios, I'm going to feign sick and run the risk of karma catching up with me later.

I can hear the tinny voice on the other end of the line. It's the nighttime security guard for the market whose job is to do the final lock-up of the site and then review the CCTV from the warmth of the office. Occasionally he's meant to do what Sebastian calls a 'perimeter sweep', which is just a fancy way of saying that he ambles around the market with a torch and makes sure no one is causing trouble.

'There's been a break-in,' he tells Sebastian. 'The Ellsbury Still.'

'How?'

'Looks like a crowbar.'

'Did you catch it on the CCTV?'

'Yeah, but, by the time I got to the Still, the guy was gone.'

'Did you recognise him?'

'Balaclava, boss.'

'Fuck's sake.' There's a groan from Sebastian as he heaves himself into a sitting position. 'I'll be there in—'

I cut him off with a coughing fit. Hmm, perhaps I should pursue this acting malarky; I'm really very good.

'I'm on my way,' Sebastian says into the phone as he turns to give me a filthy look. Or at least that's what I assume his face is doing, it's too dark to say for sure, but I've lived with him for thirteen years so it isn't a huge leap on my part.

'I think I'm sick,' I say, my tone rather pathetic.

'There's been a break-in at the market. We need to go in early.'

'I really think I'm sick.'

'So come on, you can make coffee while I have a quick shower.'

'I'm sick.' I'm a little more forceful this time.

'There's no time for you to be sick.' He says it like it's the biggest inconvenience in the world. If I was actually sick I would be fucking livid with how little he seems to care.

'It might be Covid...' I deliberately trail off. Covid has always been a bit of a sore point with my husband. When the first lockdowns happened he thought it was all a huge overreaction and kept ranting on about how we couldn't afford to pay all these people not to work. The 'we' in that sentence being the UK government, obviously. But then Christmas 2020 approached and Covid was still rampant, with new surges and threats of another lockdown. He did a total one-eighty, demanding that we be compensated. The 'we' in that sentence being us personally. Since then he's been very cautious and the first indicator of Covid in the house forces a full quarantine protocol until the individual is proven cured, or it becomes clear it wasn't Covid to begin with.

'You need to stay here and isolate.'

'I'll go to the spare room.'

'You should.'

He doesn't ask how I'm feeling. For now all he cares about is stopping the spread. But before you think he's a total prick, later he will stop at Tesco and put together a whole survival kit for me. With crisps and chocolate and magazines and Lemsip. Oh and that delicious chicken soup that is 'fresh', as in it's in the chilled section in a plastic pot and not from a tin. He'll even make sure there's a stock of those baguettes you finish cooking in the oven so it feels like having freshly baked bread.

* * *

From my quarantine room I am kept updated with stories of a series of break-ins over the next few days.

'He wears a black balaclava so we can't see his face,' Sebastian tells me over video call from the living room.

'And there's no distinguishing marks? Logos on his clothes or visible tattoos?' I ask before popping another Guylian chocolate shell into my mouth. One of the best things about the run-up to Christmas is that everything is on offer: all the supermarket boxes of chocolates suddenly become cheap as chips so indulging in seashells, or Bendicks mint selection, or even some Marc de Champagne truffles feels like a moral duty and a genuine saving.

'He's wearing a hoodie. But he does have a tattoo on his neck. You can just see the spider web peeking out.' He sounds suddenly more animated. 'Would that be enough to figure out who he is?'

'Maybe.' I actually have no idea, but it's good to keep Sebastian's hopes up. 'You should ask around tomorrow. See if anyone knows him.'

'Hmm... I could put some posters in the staffroom. See if anyone knows him. Yes, that's a great idea. I'll have this solved in no time.' He sounds a bit smug, like he didn't just literally repeat me verbatim.

I eat another seashell and allow him to wallow in his own perceived brilliance.

'You're looking better,' he says after a few moments.

'Oh, I'm...' *Shit!* I wasn't paying enough attention to the charade.

'Perhaps it isn't Covid.' He cocks his head and looks at me.

'Well, fingers crossed.' I do the gesture. 'Let's see how I feel tomorrow and then I'll do a test. If it isn't Covid then I guess I can leave quarantine.'

A cloud of suspicion crosses his features for a moment. 'Well. It would be useful to have you back at work.'

I sigh under my breath. Oh well, the peace and quiet was nice while it lasted. And at least if there's a thief on the loose then things might be a little more exciting at the market.

14

JESSICA

There's a printed sheet of paper tacked up in the staffroom, complete with a grainy photo.

Do you know this man??????

Yes, there really are six question marks. Now, I understand multiple exclamation points to show something is *really* exciting or *really* shocking, but there aren't different levels of questions. No question is more questioning than another; it's either a question or it isn't.

I peer at the picture. He's wearing a balaclava so all his features are covered, but I can see the tattoo on his neck, the same one that one of Z's friends has. Which one was it? Ah, yes. Max Kirby, son of the potential money launderer.

Interesting.

Apparently, I'm meant to tell Sebastian *IMMEDIATELY!!!!!* – yes all in caps and with five exclamation marks – if I have any information about the '*perpatrater*' – spelt incorrectly – and that it is my duty to do so. But my break is over in ten minutes and I still need to pee, which is a bit of a palaver in the costume.

* * *

I get a call in the morning from a rather distraught Hanna. Apparently, last night someone broke into Alvi's stall and stole donations the kind-hearted people of Ellsbury had made to the animal charity.

'They stole everything,' she tells me. 'Tins of food and boxes of treats and spare blankets and squeaky toys.'

'That's awful,' I say.

'Yeah. He's beside himself. And they took his cash float. The one he keeps to break bills for donations. It wasn't much, maybe a hundred pounds, but even so.'

'Poor Alvi. Does he know who it was?'

'The same guy who stole from all the others by the looks of things. The one in the balaclava.'

We say our goodbyes and hang up the call.

Who the *fuck* – and yes, this is one of those moments when the f-bomb is absolutely necessary – steals donations to an animal shelter?

Well, I guess it is a rather rhetorical question. Because I know exactly who did.

Max Kirby.

Do you know what is guaranteed to get you to the very top of the Naughty List?

Stealing from a charity that is run by a guy I have a minor crush on and who gives everything he has to provide a safe haven for abused animals.

To say that I am livid would be an understatement.

Action is required.

I can't take back what Max did. But I can make sure he never does it again.

I put on some Christmas music – not carols or instrumental, more Kelly Clarkson and Ariana Grande belting out 'Santa, Can't You Hear Me' – and mix myself a festive cocktail. The Winter Spiced Negroni is a twist on the classic and it's strong, absolutely delicious and the ultimate accompaniment for the task I'm about to undertake.

At my last office job – which used to be my preferred hunting ground as it's amazing the kind of awful people who work in medical insurance claims processing – we had a Secret Santa one year and someone bought me a notebook. At the time I remember being disappointed; who buys stationery for their Secret Santa? But then I opened it up and found that each page was titled 'Jessica's Naughty List' in a fancy script. It was so perfect I could have cried. I mean, I didn't, obviously. I'm not prone to blubbering in the middle of the office Christmas party; dripping tears onto lukewarm vol-au-vents is hardly my style.

I use this notebook to plan each of my murders. I don't write them inside, this isn't a manifesto, or a way I'm secretly hoping to get caught when I leave it in the pub. I use a craft knife to carefully remove a fresh sheet of paper and balance it on an old magazine. Both will go in the fire once I'm done. Maybe now you'll understand why I was so pleased to get that huge hearth?

Max Kirby. I write his name at the very top, followed by his crime: *theft from charity*. I shake my head as I write the words. Of all the degenerate things to do.

Now onto the fun bit. I crack my knuckles and then take a large swig of the negroni. We're on to the 'how' part of the equation.

I like to be avant garde, especially with the first kill of the year. There is no point in punishing terrible people if no one knows about it. Max's death should serve as a warning that this kind of behaviour is not tolerated. And as a comfort to others – the good, law-abiding, Christmas-loving people of Ellsbury – so they know they're safe and protected.

But if I'm too obvious, the finger of suspicion will swing toward Alvi. And although I know he is a gentle man with a kind heart who would literally not hurt a fly, the police may not share that opinion. Even a whiff that he may have been involved would cause him trouble. Mr Sebastian 'Jobsworth' Dixon might even hold it against him for the rest of the market and Alvi needs this.

I make another drink while I mull things over, allowing my brain to work as I sip. I want the body to be found at the market. That is the non-negotiable part of the plan. But I think I should make it look like another gang did it, some kind of retaliation against Max by a rival, rather than revenge for all the awful things he's done to the stallholders.

* * *

Max Kirby lives in a soulless newbuild flat not far from the market. His is on the ground floor, with a terrace accessible from the street. The back door is open and I can hear the thump of music from inside and smell the weed. I loiter outside, trying to decipher how many of them there might be. After about five minutes, three young men – including Z – leave and the music is switched off. No further sound comes from the flat.

I put on a beanie hat to cover my hair and pull up my hood so my features will be in shadow, and then I jump over the fence that surrounds his terrace. The door is still open and the miasma of weed is even stronger so he must be having a smoke.

That's good. It'll make him slow, more lumbering. It will give me time to make sure I stay ahead of him.

'Oi,' I hiss from the doorway. 'Max.'

'Fuck off,' he says, but his voice is a teeny bit slurred.

'Oi,' I say again.

'I told you to fuck off.'

I had a plan to lure him to the market under the pretence of being a friend of Z. But now I think I might take an easier approach. And so I take a deep breath and brace myself for the words I'm about to say. 'Oi, you fucking twat. Thieving little cunt.'

He looks up and sees me. Sees how much smaller than him I am. How much weaker he thinks I'll be. A glint of a smile flashes in the half light of his flat. 'What did you just call me?' he asks, standing up.

'I called you a thieving little cunt,' I repeat, even as the word makes me want to wash my own mouth out with soap.

'And you think you can come to my flat and call me names, do you?' He takes a few steps toward me.

'Yes, you massive dickhead.' The slur doesn't sound quite right, it's too old fashioned, it isn't the kind of phrase men like Max Kirby use. But as long as it makes him angry it doesn't really matter.

He takes another step as he appraises me. But whatever he thinks about his chances against little old me, he'll be wrong. I just need him to take the bait.

'Twat,' I say. And then I spot an opportunity. A little bag of pills just sitting there on the side, within easy reach. This is guaranteed to make him mad enough to chase me. I grab them and stuff them into my pocket. 'I'll just help myself like you do.'

'Oh you fucking bitch,' he yells and then launches himself toward me.

I turn and run, vaulting over the fence and down the road.
He follows.
I'm fast and sober – well, sober-ish.
He's slow and stoned.
It isn't a fair fight.

As I approach the far corner of the market, I press the small transmitter in the pocket of my leggings. It's a WiFi jammer and it will basically take out all the cameras in the vicinity. I used it earlier a few times so when someone checks the footage they will see random outages. It will be chalked up as a system malfunction. Such a shame to lose evidence of a murder because someone didn't set up the network properly.

There's a fence around the perimeter of the market, but it's dotted with gates to make it easy for customers to come and go. Each gate is secured with a simple padlock and all the codes are the same. *2410*. It's Sebastian Dixon's wife's birthday. Which would be kind of sweet if it wasn't so predictable, and if people didn't post their personal information all over social media for the world to see. Anyone could figure out the code. I already unlocked this entrance on my way to Max Kirby's flat and so the gate swings open to my touch.

I wait for the stoned snail to catch up, watching him lumbering up the incline to the gate, breathing heavily. I guess cardio isn't part of his lifestyle.

'Over here,' I call from the shadow of the waffle stand.

'You little bitch,' he says, between attempts to suck air into his lungs. It's really not as threatening as he thinks it is. I slip the knife from its hiding place up the sleeve of my coat. It's large and fairly light. Well, it was cheap. I want the police to think this was a rival, and I doubt the kind of guys Max normally locks horns with would be buying expensive Japanese steel.

Once he's in range I step forward. 'This is for all the people and the defenceless animals you stole from,' I say as I plunge the blade into his heart. The look of shock on his face is a picture and I wish I could capture it for posterity.

But I am not the kind of killer who takes a trophy, even a virtual one. That's a very good way to get caught and I'm too good at this to make that kind of stupid mistake.

15

FEARNE

Sebastian is livid. 'There's a dead body in my market. A fucking *body*.' He looks green, like he's about to be sick. Not that I can blame him, I suppose. He's just seen a man who was stabbed through the heart and left to bleed out across the cobbled path that winds between the stalls. It must have been very traumatic and I guess I should cut him some slack this morning.

I decide to take him some tea and he gulps it down gratefully. 'Are you OK?' I ask softly.

'I just saw a dead body in my market,' he tells me, his tone insinuating that my question was the dumbest thing he's ever been asked, that *of course* he isn't OK. He might have a point to be fair.

'Have the police said anything more?'

He shakes his head and I put my hand on his shoulder. For a second, he covers it with his own, fingers squeezing mine. 'It was him.'

'Who?'

'The thief. I recognised the tattoo on his neck.'

'Shit.' I say it on an exhale, lengthening the word.

'You don't think it was some kind of revenge thing?' He raises his eyes to meet mine. 'That would really scupper the market. I mean, imagine if it was one of the stallholders?'

I take a few moments to flick through a mental rolodex of everyone we have on site this year. None of them look like murderers. 'I doubt it. I mean, can you imagine Connor from The Ellsbury Still killing someone? Or Alvi from the animal rescue charity?'

'Definitely not Alvi. Even if he is related to that bloody woman.' Talking of Hanna reminds me she and I haven't met up for a while; I should sort that out, a glass of ice-cold Prosecco sounds fucking fantastic right now.

'No, I can't see it,' Sebastian adds. 'But, in that case, we have a random killer on the loose.' He looks stricken.

'It'll all be fine,' I promise. 'It's probably a rival gang or something.'

'Yeah.'

But neither of us is convinced. This is Ellsbury, a quaint place that is only designated a city by virtue of the cathedral. Ellsbury doesn't have gangs. Even if it does appear to have a murderer.

I offer to do a tour of the market and check in on our stallholders, make sure they are all alright and not freaking out.

'Thanks, love. You're a star,' Sebastian says as I leave the office. I think this whole thing has really unsettled him.

The market is busier than usual and I wonder if word has spread about the murder. You might think that would put people off, but I've worked with the public for so long I know it's exactly the opposite, at least in the immediate aftermath. Humans have a bizarre attraction to the macabre and plenty of them will be trying to snap a photo of the now fenced-off area where the murder happened, smiling faces next to the bright yellow crime scene tape.

I walk past The Ellsbury Still but don't stop. Especially when I hear Connor's booming voice describing the process of how his gin is made to a potential customer.

'I always thought it was a sill,' the customer says, looking slightly puzzled as he stares at the name of the stall.

'It's a *still*,' Connor enunciates every letter of the word. 'You don't dis-*sill* something, do you?'

I think I might need to have a little chat about customer service and not berating the people who are planning to spend fifty of their hard-earned pounds on a bottle of your gin. But not right now. Today is about checking no one is having a mental breakdown.

Alvi waves from the rescue centre stall and I wave back, before blowing kisses for the two adorable Staffordshire terriers he's brought with him today. He doesn't seem the type to get upset about things so I leave him to it and head to find James and his gonks.

'How are you doing?' I ask.

'Busy. Really, really, busy,' he says with an air of puzzlement.

'That's good.' I inject deliberate positivity into my tone.

'I guess...' He trails off. 'Umm... you might want to check in on Bella Donna at Crystals and Gifts.' He grimaces slightly.

'I'm on my way,' I say and grit my teeth as I head over toward her stall. I have a feeling this isn't going to be fun.

'I told you the energy of the market would be off,' she tells me with this funny little half smile half smirk. As though she's secretly thrilled that someone died and now she's been proven right.

'It has nothing to do with the location of Crystals and Gifts.'

'Really? You're going to actually look me in the face and tell me that the energy of this place is fine? With a man stabbed to death mere metres away?'

'I promise that has nothing to—'

'I demand you move me.' She actually stamps her foot and juts out her chin. It's like a cartoon and I feel a bubble of laughter threaten to escape from the back of my throat.

'I can't do that,' I tell her.

'But you have to. For the sake of the market.'

'I literally can't do that.'

'Well. In that case you leave me without a choice.' She makes this odd harumph noise and spins on her heels to leave the hut.

I don't know what kind of protest she's planning on making, but something tells me it's only going to make my life even harder.

Fuck this, I need a gin.

I head to The Apres-Ski. It's only about half full, but I suppose it is only three in the afternoon.

'Gin and tonic please,' I ask Remi. It's his third year running the tent and he's always a lovely ray of sunshine in a sea of never-ending shit.

'Bad day?' he asks as he pops the top off a bottle of Fever-Tree.

'Oh, nothing too terrible,' I reply, pasting a fake smile across my face. I obviously can't tell him the truth; it isn't like I can bitch and moan to the vendors. My husband is their boss after all.

'The murder?'

'Yeah. It's a lot to deal with.'

'Well, you know I'm always here if you need someone to talk to.' He beams at me and I feel a small kernel of warmth in my heart. Although it could just be the gin I suppose.

I drink quickly, desperate for the alcohol to take the edge off my irritation. I'll only have the one. Or perhaps I should have a second. Build up the insulation a little? But, before I can decide, there's a commotion outside the tent. I should probably go and investigate.

'What's going on?' I ask Barry from the security team who's standing guard on The Apres-Ski to make sure no one leaves with any glass.

His walkie-talkie crackles a few times. 'I need Security Three to attend chalet twelve,' says a voice from his hip.

'Is that for you?' I ask.

'I'm Security Two,' he tells me. 'But let me get the goss.' He picks up the handset. 'Security Two to Security Three, what is happening? Over.'

'Security Three to Security Two. Altercation by chalet twelve. Standby. Over.'

'Security Two to Security Three. Standing by. Over.'

'Security Three to Security Two. Apparently the woman from Crystals and Shit is demanding that Doggy Do-Dahs swap chalets with her. Over.'

I stifle my laughter at the fact they also have developed nicknames for the vendors. But then my brain processes what was just said. That fucking woman.

'Security Two to Security Three. What is happening? Over.'

'I think I'm going to need backup. Yep.' The pitch of his voice rises. 'Backup. Mayday, mayday.'

'What the actual fuck,' Barry mutters and then looks at me. 'He's going to have to figure this out for himself. I can't leave my post.' He shrugs.

'Backup,' comes another squawk from his walkie-talkie.

'I think you probably should...' I motion to it.

'Yeah. Probably. Fuck's sake,' he mutters under his breath and lumbers over to chalet twelve. I follow him. This might be entertaining.

16

JESSICA

You know how they say that you wait forever for a bus and then three come along at once? Well, the same thing tends to be true of people to put on the Naughty List. No sooner have I dispatched – that's a nice word, isn't it? – Max Kirby, do I start to hear rumours about someone else who might just be a contender for the List.

David Bennett.

On the outside, Mr David Bennett looks like the model citizen. Another one of those 'pillar of the community' types who creates employment for the people of Ellsbury and donates to a range of charities, regularly being seen at social events to raise funds for good causes. Of course, charity is tax deductible, so we should always be a little suspicious of the wealthy writing a cheque for a hundred quid to the local Scouts. Some people aren't quite as altruistic as they appear at first glance.

David runs a catering company called Hot Eatz. Yes. With a Z on the end. But not even I think that is enough rope to hang him with. Although perhaps when I couple it with the rumours I've started to hear it's enough to start investigating a little. Just a sniff around, nothing major.

Hot Eatz runs four stalls at the market. The Sausage Swing, which sells a traditional range of German bratwurst for an eyewatering sum of money. Waffleicious, which sells... well... waffles. I have to confess that I am rather a fan of Waffleicious, especially the one they do with Biscoff spread and squirty cream. Hot Eatz also runs the fish and chips place and Crumble Top, which sounds ridiculous but I'm kind of intrigued and might have to treat myself at some point.

I asked Hanna yesterday how much a vendor might make on a stall this winter. Just out of curiosity. She probably thinks I might be tempted to make the switch from Mrs Claus to purveyor of fine artisan goods.

'Umm. It depends on what you're selling obviously.' She gave me a flash of a smile in apology for teaching me to suck lemons. 'You'd make more money selling posh gin than decoupage decorations for example.'

'What about the food stalls?' I asked, with casual nonchalance.

'That's where the money is, to be fair. Or at least it can be if you can get the prime spots and the core "Christmas fayre" like the Sausage Swing or the hog roast. I probably shouldn't tell you this,' but she was leaning in to me as she said it. She was one hundred percent about to spill all the beans, 'let's just say that if you run that for the five weeks of the market, and you're good, like the product is spot on and everyone is singing your praises... then... yeah. It's lucrative.'

'So if you had a few of these stalls...'

'Licence to print money. Honestly, it's a bit of a travesty that one man can have a cluster. I heard that David made a claim to

Sebastian that he needed critical mass in terms of size to operate effectively.' She looked almost scandalised.

'Bribery?' I asked.

'Who can say for sure...' she says it so enigmatically that she may as well have just confirmed it as an absolute given.

But making money isn't a crime. Even though maybe it should be. Although, if you're making money hand over fist, then it wouldn't hurt to share it with the people who are busting their guts to make it for you. And I have heard a few rumours of my own that old David Bennett does not in fact share the financial love with his staff. Very much the opposite.

* * *

We close the grotto from three to four in the afternoon to make sure Santa – I'm starting to convince myself that Carl is actually the real deal – and I can have a break before the afterschool rush comes in. An opportunity for a pee and a coffee, maybe even one of those delicious waffles and a chance to gather more intel on the man behind the empire.

The waffle stand is on the corner of one of the market streets, which means it gets less footfall than some of the other stalls and is therefore less busy than the more prime locations. The less time I have to queue, the more of a break I actually get. Especially as my hour off is actually shortened to about forty minutes by the time I've taken off the costume and then put it back on just before the grotto reopens.

It's also super close to the smoking area. I gave up years ago but I still find myself drawn to the smell; apparently, once a smoker, always a smoker. I've thought about getting a nice peppermint vape for the season but I'd only get addicted and it's probably not a good look for Mrs Claus.

It's such a shame though as it's a brilliant breeding ground for gossip. I can see two of the girls from The Sausage Swing are having a bitch and a moan and I creep closer to listen in. Sofia and Valentina are twins, but I have no idea which is which. I know that identical twins aren't really that identical, and that if I got to know them better I'd find them easy to distinguish, but I've only met them once and that was pretty much in passing. They're speaking in Spanish, but thankfully I'm basically fluent; I might miss a little in terms of the nuance, but I can understand the gist and that's what's important.

They're talking about work. Maybe I'll learn something new about David Bennett? It's the usual stuff. Long hours. Poor pay. But paying minimum wage isn't a crime. Nor is making your staff work some seriously antisocial hours. It *should* be a crime, don't get me wrong, but it isn't something even I can kill a man over. Otherwise there'd be no one left to run almost all the businesses in the city.

'I guess you're reformed?' A voice behind me makes me jump. It's Santa.

'Hi San— Carl,' I correct myself. 'I have been reformed a very long time.'

'But yet here you are.' He motions at the smoking area.

'Indeed.' I smile at him but I'm also trying to listen to what the twins are saying.

'We would only need one,' one of them says to the other. 'Then you could go home and post it back to me so I can go back.'

'That's fraud.' She sounds horrified at the suggestion.

'It's necessity,' the other hisses in return.

What are they talking about?

'We should probably head back to the grotto,' Carl says.

'There's already a queue of the little rascals. Going to be a busy afternoon.'

'Absolutely,' I reply, one ear still on the girls. Talking in English and listening to Spanish is a skill I haven't fully mastered. But I swear I hear one of them saying they could go to prison.

'He's the one who should go to prison,' the other twin replies.

* * *

I have a text from Hanna when I check my phone at the end of my shift.

HANNA

> Fancy some drinks tomorrow night? I've invited Fearne too. I think you'll get on great.

JESSICA

> Fearne?

I text back.

JESSICA

> As in Dixon. But we don't hold her taste in men against her! It'll be fun. I promise.

I really should be spending my free time digging into what David Bennett is up to. But I suppose that all work and no play really does make Jessica a very dull girl.

JESSICA

> Count me in

I message back.

And you never know, Fearne Dixon might prove to be a good source of information, she and her husband have been part of the market since the very beginning.

If anyone knows where the bodies are buried – figuratively of course – it's her.

17

IN WHICH NOEL LUMENS MET HIS FESTIVE
FATE...

In the winter of 2023, Jessica was working at the Belfry Shopping Centre in Redhill in Sussex. It takes me hours to find anything about what went down in Redhill, but eventually I stumble across a rather niche podcast that seems to focus on people who meet interesting demises in the run-up to Christmas. It's called *May All Your Christmases Be Red... Blood Red*. And once again it's someone who is far too perky for their own good; is there some kind of course YouTubers and other influencer types go on? The presenter, Justin, describes himself as 'a purveyor of truth with a dash of the macabre and a dollop of fun'.

> Good morning, afternoon, evening. Just a little catch-all there for those of you tuning in from around the world. This is *May All Your Christmases Be Red... Blood Red*. The podcast where we dissect all the terrible things that happen to people, but with a Christmas twist.
>
> Today's episode is called 'What's In A Name'. You know how some people just suit their names? As if they have

moulded their personalities and honed their looks around the moniker they were given as babies? I went to school with a girl called Elfie, which I thought was a nickname but was actually on her birth certificate. Luckily for Elfie she didn't grow up to be a six-foot-tall rugby player and instead was about five foot three and seven stone soaking wet.

Well, sometimes people don't just live by their names.

They die by them.

And so today I'm going to tell you the story of a man called Noel Lumens.

Noel Lumens always wanted to be an electrician. According to his mum, that was all he ever wanted to be. And so, when he was twenty-one, he finished college and started up his own business doing small bits of electrical work for people. He was happy. Life was good.

After a few years, he got offered the job of a lifetime. The contract to put up the Christmas lights for his hometown of Redhill. He thought he'd made it, that this would catapult him into the big time. He told everyone he met about the lights and invited them all to the grand switch on. It was a party. He went to the pub with his friends and the festivities continued.

And then he got in his van and drove home. Only, on the way, a woman stepped off the kerb and he hit her. BAM. She survived. Just. She'll never walk again. But, two days later, Noel Lumens was found hanging from the Christmas lights just outside the pub he'd been drinking in.

Was it an accident? Was he merely replacing a faulty bulb?

Was it suicide? A man unable to deal with the destruction he wrought?

Or was it a murder? Revenge for the lives he ruined?

Whatever the truth, he really did live and die by his name.
Noel Lumens.
Christmas Lights.

18

FEARNE

I spend over an hour debating what to wear this evening. Drinks with Hanna is normally pretty casual. To be fair, *all* of Ellsbury is pretty casual, it's not as if anywhere requires a cocktail dress. But some places in Ellsbury do demand a certain *type* of casual; a nice pair of jeans and a jumper from Boden and either ankle boots or a pair of brand-new trainers that have never seen the inside of the gym. But it's normally just the two of us and the inclusion of Jessica from the grotto has thrown me.

'Do you really think it's appropriate?' Sebastian asks from the doorway.

'The jumper?' I'm holding a pale-blue cashmere-mix crew-neck against myself, trying to decide if it will look OK with my new wide-leg dark jeans – Good American no less, though I did get them in the sale. But there's nothing inappropriate about it.

'I mean fraternising with the market workers.'

'Jessica is Mrs Claus.' My words sound more like a question as I have no idea what he's talking about. It isn't like he's Jessica's boss.

'But she's still an employee working on the market.'

'So?'

'I just...' but he trails off. I think even Sebastian realises his line of argument makes no sense. 'I thought we could watch a film this evening.'

And there it is, the truth of the matter. He doesn't mind who I go out with, he'd just rather I didn't go out at all. 'We can watch it tomorrow,' I tell him. Heaven knows I don't get to go out very often and so there is no way I'm giving up an opportunity for some gossip and Prosecco.

'Promise?' Sebastian's face lights up a little and for a moment I feel bad about disappointing him this evening. But no, I want to go out. He can wait twenty-four hours.

'Promise. I'll even cook that chilli you like.'

'Deal.' He grins and then closes the gap between us, reaching down to pick up the deep purple V-neck jumper I've already discarded. 'Wear this. You look beautiful in this one.'

* * *

I get to the bar before the others and manage to snag a table in the window. My phone beeps with a notification from Facebook. Apparently I've been tagged in a stupid giveaway by some woman I went to school with. *I should probably unfriend her*, I think idly as I look at her profile. The last thing she posted was red text on a green background, the whole thing pulsating as if to give it a sense of urgency:

ONLY FORTY-ONE DAYS TIL CHRISTMAS!

Give me strength.

'Can I get you a drink?' The waitress is at my side despite me only arriving about a minute ago. That's one of the reasons this place is so popular; the staff are very attentive and glasses are never empty for more than a few moments. There's an efficiency to getting a bit pissed here and I appreciate it.

I'd normally order a bottle of Prosecco, but I have no idea what Jessica will be drinking. 'I'll just have a Cassis Manhattan for now,' I say, pointing at the mini-whiteboard on the table, which details their festive cocktail selection. I can drink that while I wait to see what the others are having.

But, before I've taken a sip, my phone dings. It's Hanna.

> So sorry. Kelsie's just been sick and the babysitter is having a meltdown about it. Not going to make tonight. Have fun and catch up soon xx

Ah, shit. Well, I guess that's that then. I look at my full cocktail. If I neck it, can I pay and get out of here before Jessica arrives? I don't want it to be just the two of us. That feels like it would be really weird.

'Hey. You must be Fearne.'

Too late. I look up to see Mrs Claus, although of course tonight she's not in her costume and I suddenly realise just how young she is. 'Uh, hi.' The words come out a bit high pitched, the kind of voice you'd use if you bumped into a celebrity you were in awe of. That's just great, she'll probably think I'm a moron now.

If Jessica notices, she's polite enough to pretend she doesn't. 'Did you get a message from Hanna?'

I nod. 'Yeah.'

'I hope Kelsie's OK.'

I feel bad that my first thought when I got the message was about myself and how this evening would be ruined, rather than concern for a sick child.

The waitress approaches.

'What are you drinking?' Jessica asks me, pointing at my deep red cocktail.

'Cassis Manhattan.'

'Nice. I'll have one of those too please.' The waitress scurries off to get her drink. 'Wow, I just love that sweater,' she says, reaching out to touch my shoulder gently. 'What a fabulous colour on you.'

An hour later – and another cocktail down – we decide to move onto Prosecco. We're getting on like a house on fire, bouncing around topics like we've been friends for years.

'What do you do? For work I mean,' Jessica asks me.

'Oh. I... umm... I'm a writer.'

'What do you write?'

I hate this question because my answer always sounds kind of weird, either bragging or delusional depending on what the other person thinks I mean. 'Umm... Novels.' The response when you say you write novels is normally to ask if they would have heard of your books, or if they can buy them in Waterstones, or to tell you about their own writing. Although, to be fair, that last one is normally reserved for the men, who will then tell you in great lengths about the 'next great American novel' they've been working on for a decade – despite being from Greater London and having never done anything of significance with their lives.

'Cool. Tell me about them.'

Oh. This isn't normally how this works. 'Well, the first one came out in 2015 and I've done one a year since then, so that's what, ten out now. They do well. Not like household name well or anything, but...' I spread my hands out in front of me as if to say that's all.

'That's amazing. Ten books. What kind?'

'Regency romance mainly.'

'Like *Bridgerton*?' She leans forward slightly, a salacious grin forming.

'Kind of. But without all the steamy sex.'

She sits back a little. 'Oh.' She sounds disappointed.

When I first told Sebastian I wanted to write a book he looked at me like I'd grown another head. But eventually he supported me and even gave me his old laptop to write on. His only rule was I couldn't write any of the 'raunchy stuff', in case people thought I was writing about him. Fat chance of that. But, anyway, I agreed. And I love my books. They earn a bit, not enough to live like a princess or anything, but enough to pay for a nice holiday each year and the odd treat for the family. Sebastian calls it 'pin money', like we live in the 1950s.

But do you know where there *is* money? Lots and lots of money, if you're good at it? Erotic fiction. Fearne Dixon writes closed-door romance of the regency era, where the steamiest scene is a pre-marital kiss. Cherry Dubois, on the other hand, writes glorious filth about fae and shapeshifters and horny werewolves. Cherry Dubois makes a fortune and I'm starting to get paranoid that Sebastian will find my bank statement and realise just how many lies I've been telling him.

Jessica refills her Prosecco and then motions the bottle toward me. I down the last few gulps from my glass before handing it to her for a top-up.

Fuck it. I'm going to throw caution to the wind. I've been sitting on this for so long and I need to tell someone.

'Actually,' I say, my voice breaking a little on the word. I take another sip of wine to lubricate my throat. 'I do write something else too. But it's a secret.' I look around me to make sure no one I know has crept up behind me in the tiny bar.

How to Slay at Christmas

'Ooh.' She leans forward again. 'Tell me.' Her eyes gleam. I like Jessica. I think she and I could actually be friends.

'My husband doesn't know.'

She mimes zipping up her lips.

'I... umm...' I can feel the blush already blooming on my cheeks and up my neck. 'I write erotica too.' The words tumble out before I can take them back and now they are sitting there between us like thick fat slugs. *You shouldn't have said anything.* I try to ignore the voice in my head, the one that tells me my confession was a mistake.

'Tell me more,' Jessica demands.

'Mainly paranormal. Fae. Shifters. That kind of thing. A few months ago, I started a new series about werewolves and it's been alarmingly successful.'

'Wow. You really are a dark horse, Fearne.'

'It's... fun.'

'Why doesn't Sebastian know?'

'He wouldn't approve.'

'Have you asked him?'

'He made me promise when I first started out that I wouldn't write that stuff in case people thought it was about him.'

Jessica stares at me for a few moments, cocking her head a little. And then she bursts into laughter. 'I don't want to speak ill of your husband, but he doesn't look like he'd have it in him.'

'Maybe that's the problem,' I reply, my tone deadpan.

'Oh my God. You didn't just say that?' She laughs again and I join in. Perhaps the wine has gone to our heads. But, Jesus, I've missed this, having a friend, having a gossip, feeling like I'm fun and witty and someone you'd choose to spend time with rather than just a mother and a wife who is tolerated.

19

JESSICA

Wow. Well that really does go to prove you can't judge a book by its cover. She looks so prim and proper and then BAM! It's all fairy porn and werewolf harems. Fair play to her, though, she's obviously good at it. Plus, you can never knock something that brings happiness to another person's life, and that wicked glint in her eye is testament to that joy. Is it the writing of the books, or the hiding it from Sebastian, that makes her happiest? I think it's probably both, if we're being honest.

I get us another bottle of wine.

'I'll get shitfaced,' Fearne tells me but she's holding out her glass for a refill so I don't think she's actually complaining. 'So, then, Jessica. Now you know my biggest secret, you have to tell me yours.'

For a split second I imagine what she'd do if she knew the truth. But that would be ludicrous. She's fun, far more so than I'd imagined, but I don't think she'd find my serial killer alter ego a good drinking partner. 'There isn't a lot to tell,' I say with a shrug.

'You're single?' She looks at my left hand as she asks.

'There was a husband once upon a time.'

'But no more?'

'Let's just say we had a difference of opinions.' Like he wanted someone to beat on and I wanted him dead. But I don't add that last bit out loud.

'Boyfriend?' Fearne asks.

'No.' But, to my horror, there's something odd in my voice, a little catch.

Fearne seizes on it. 'But you like someone?' She's looking at me intently over the rim of her wineglass and I can feel myself being drawn closer into her orbit. I want to tell her everything. It's like she's hypnotising me. Or maybe I'm just a bit tipsy.

'Kind of.' The words are out before I can stop them.

'Is it the guy from the rescue centre? What's his name?' She pauses as if she's trying to think of it, but I can see through the act. She just wants me to be the one to say it.

'Alvi.'

'Alvi!' she exclaims. 'Of course. He's Hanna's brother. He's cute...'

'It's complicated.'

'Is it?'

'No.' I'm forced to admit. 'Not really.' I flash a shy smile. 'But I'll only be here for another month and so...'

'First,' she says, her voice turning stern as if I'm about to get a lecture. 'You can have a fling. There is nothing wrong with having a bit of fun, letting your hair down.' She reaches out to touch my braid. 'And your hair is truly fabulous. That colour looks incredible on you.'

'It's natural,' I tell her.

'Is it?' She sits back as if in surprise. 'I just assumed you'd dyed it to play Mrs Claus. Oh, wow. I love it.'

It feels nice for someone to react positively and not immediately give me the number of their own colourist.

'Anyway, back to the whole fling thing.' She waggles her eyebrows. 'You could call it a little "festive joy". And,' she puts up a finger as if I was about to interject and not let her finish, despite the fact I'm silently drinking my Prosecco and debating the veracity of her argument. Because maybe I *could* have a fling. 'Who says you have to leave in a month? You could always just stay here in Ellsbury.'

She says it like a fait accompli. Like I won't be a wanted woman with a trail of bodies behind me by then. Reality comes crashing back down over me. I can't have a fling, I can't risk bringing someone too close to me. And I certainly can't even dream about staying, not unless I turn over a new leaf.

Don't worry, I'm not going to suddenly swear off the murder and settle down with the hot guy with all the adorable dogs. This isn't that kind of story and I know you're only here for the worst types of people getting their comeuppance.

The whole point of the constant moving, of finding a new city each year, is risk management. There are rules to murder, ones that mitigate the chance of getting caught. Leave no physical evidence: no fingerprints or DNA. Have no obvious connection to the victim; nothing more than the same level of proximity as a hundred other people. Don't stay too long: move before the pattern of activities gets established. No one will connect a handful of murders in one city to a handful in another city in another year.

I realise I've been silent for too long.

'You really like him, don't you?' Fearne says, obviously mistaking my lack of reply with deep contemplation of Alvi's assets.

'He's kind of easy on the eye,' I say eventually and then give her a salacious eyebrow wiggle.

'Amen.' She clinks her glass against mine. 'You should totally smash that.'

I give her a WTF look in return.

'Apparently it's what the kids are saying.' She shrugs.

'Well, here's to... smashing.' We clink glasses again.

We move on to gossiping about some of the stuff that happens on the market and I'm glad to lead the conversation away from my love life.

Fearne tells me a few stories about nightmare customers, ending in one about poor Amy and Heather from the decoupage stall and the person who tried to return a greetings card after they had written in it.

'People are so odd,' I tell her. 'So this customer wrote the card and then was like, "Nah, I won't give this to my loved one, I'll just take it back"?'

'Yep. Amy refused, obviously, and then the customer tried to make a formal complaint to Sebastian about her and Heather.'

'Just wild.' I laugh. 'You know, they don't look much alike. For sisters, I mean.'

Fearne looks at me, her face impassive. She stays like that for a full thirty seconds.

'What?' I ask eventually, unable to bear the silence any longer.

'Do you genuinely think they're sisters?' she asks, her tone slightly incredulous, but with a jokey edge, like she's poking fun out of me.

'Are they not...'

'They share a surname. The stall is called the *Scissor* Sisters.'

'I... Ohhhhh.'

'Yeah, they're a married couple.'

I feel the blush burn my cheeks and I clap my hand to my mouth. 'I thought they were literally sisters,' I say. 'Oh, well, fair play. It makes a lot more sense.'

'A lot of the paper in their creations are pages of famous queer books, like *Oranges Are Not the Only Fruit* and *The Price of Salt*. The little old ladies of Ellsbury buying them probably have no idea.'

'Oh wow. I love that. Hopefully a few bigots will also buy them by accident.'

'Here's hoping.' Fearne shows me her crossed fingers and then we both start laughing. I haven't felt this relaxed in ages. I could get used to evenings like this.

'What other gossip do you have from the market?' I ask her.

'Hmm... like what kind of thing?' she asks.

'Like who is the most nightmare stallholder?' I ask.

'Bella Donna.' She answers so quickly, with not even a second of hesitation.

'Crystals and Gif—'

'Crystals and Shit,' she interrupts. 'Sorry. It's terribly unprofessional of me, but I just can't stand the woman. Honestly, every day she has another complaint.'

'Is she the one who flipped out the other day and security had to calm her down?'

'One and the same.'

'Wow. What's her problem?'

'She thinks the location of her stall is causing bad energy in the market.' Fearne's tone is deadpan.

'Jeez.'

'She thinks that's why there was a murder.'

'That feels like a stretch,' I reply. Especially as I know exactly what caused the murder and it had absolutely nothing to do with Bella Donna and her crystals. But obviously I don't say that to Fearne.

Even if part of me thinks she might actually understand, at least on some level, why I do what I do. I sense an anger in her, a thirst for justice, and the embers of a fire burning deep within her.

20

FEARNE

I have a website for the Cherry Dubois books, a way of ensuring that people can contact me but without being able to link the nom de plume back to my staid regency romances. Every day I get a couple of readers writing to tell me how much they love the series and often asking for specific titbits to happen between characters. It's a great tool. But I also get at least half a dozen spammy emails offering me a range of publishing services: everything from cover design to proofreading to marketing support.

> Sell a million copies with our secret method!

> Reach new readers with our mailing list – now only $500 to join!

> Do you want to be a bestseller? Click here for 100 tips and tricks!

Hey Author. You've been selected for our Reviewer Plus scheme. Guaranteed five-star reviews!

You've been nominated for an award at this year's Steamies.

Hang on a sec. The Steamies? That has got to be spam. My cursor hovers over the email. Should I open it? Every fibre of my being screams not to. That's how you get viruses and other malware and whatnot. But the Steamies are only the biggest erotic fiction awards in the business.

I pull up their website instead. Nominations for the 2025 awards have been announced this morning. And there, sitting under a banner for Best Newcomer, is my name. Well, Cherry Dubois's name. It's actually real. I read on to discover there's a huge gala event for the award ceremony. At the Dorchester Hotel in London. All expenses paid, including the hotel stay and first-class train travel from anywhere in the UK. *Oh my God.*

I want to dance and sing and pop champagne even though it's only ten in the morning.

But then reality comes crashing down. I can't go to a fancy gala event in London. Cherry Dubois doesn't exist. Not in this house anyway. Sebastian would lose his shit if he knew what I was writing.

I spend the rest of the morning doing chores. Angrily. Taking all my frustration out on the laundry and the hoovering and scrubbing the burnt remains of yesterday's lasagne from the baking dish. Eventually my rage dissipates and disappointment takes its place. It would have been such a fun evening. Just imagine getting all glammed up and having people actually appreciate the work you do? Have them take it seriously and say that you're really good at it.

The chores grind to a halt as I think about what could have

been. But there's no point in moping about. And there isn't time either. I still need to prep dinner – it's Friday and so Sebastian will be expecting something fancier than a ready meal or a pizza chucked in the oven – and do the ironing and a million other things.

At least I was nominated. That has to count for something, right? People are noticing my work. They think it's good. They think *I'm* good. They think I'm a genuine contender for Best Newcomer. Buoyed by a new injection of positivity I decide to say fuck it and not bother with dinner. We'll have takeaway and I'll have a nice glass of wine – one of the fancy ones I only drink on special occasions – and I'll celebrate the win of just being considered for a Steamie.

Immy's in her room, blasting Blackpink at full volume and singing along at the top of her voice. Even the parts in Korean. And no, she doesn't speak Korean, so it just sounds like a mangled mess. I know I'm meant to go upstairs and tell her to turn it down. I know that she probably wants me to, that it's all a part of the whole 'teenage rebellion' thing. She is fifteen, after all.

But here's a little secret. I actually like K-pop. The cheesiness of it all with the heavily stylised dance routines and strangely addictive beats. Not that I would ever tell Immy that. I wait to see what the next song is; it's not one of my favourites so I'll take this opportunity to head upstairs and do my motherly duties.

I tap on the door three times and then wait for a count of ten. Sebastian thinks we should have an open-door policy in the house, that 'we're family' and so don't need to hide things from each other. My husband was never a teenage girl. Immy deserves her privacy.

I crack open the door. 'Will you turn that racket down?' I call into the room.

'Fuck's sake, Mum. You need to knock.'

'I did.'

'Oh.' She knows I always knock and why we need to have this conversation every day I don't know. 'Is the music too loud?'

'A bit.'

'I'll turn it down.' There's a hint of huffiness to her tone. Like this is all such a huge effort for her and I'm being a pain in the backside.

'Thank you, sweetheart.' We both know she'll turn it up again the second I get back downstairs. 'Would you like a cuppa?'

'Sure.'

'There's cake downstairs too if you fancy a slice?' I don't want to sound too desperate or too needy. I've perfected the appropriate level of nonchalance to imbue into these kinds of invitations.

'Carrot?' she asks, narrowing her eyes.

'Of course.' I also bought cinnamon, chocolate and caramel apple. She's constantly changing her mind as to which is her favourite so I make sure we have one of each that I can whip out at any moment. She thinks I can read her mind.

'Perfect. I'll be down in five minutes.'

But she doesn't come down for fifteen minutes, by which time I've already caved and eaten a slice of carrot cake. I'll have to have a second piece with her. I try not to stare but she looks like she's been crying, her eyes red rimmed and puffy, her mascara smudged at the corners.

'Sorry I was so long,' she says quietly.

'No worries,' I reply, my voice light. I want to ask her what's wrong. I want to find out who has made my baby girl cry. I want to hurt them. My rage begins to rise but I tamp it down. I would do anything to protect my daughter, but getting angry now won't help in getting her to open up to me.

I wrack my brain for something to say. Oh. Yes, that could work. 'How about we go out this evening? The ice rink's open.' We used to go every year and every year Immy would decide that what she wanted to be more than anything when she grew up was an ice dancer and perform with Disney on Ice. But the dream would be forgotten the next day and so it became one of those 'holiday stories' that families tell.

But instead of a look of excited glee, she scrunches up her nose. 'I kind of need to study.'

'Really?' I raise my eyebrows. Not that I don't think she should study, heaven knows things are so much more competitive than they were twenty-five years ago, but I'm sure she said to Riya earlier that she'd done all her homework already. I think Immy is lying to me, although there's nothing I can say, it isn't like I can admit to eavesdropping on her conversations.

'Fine. We'll go ice skating.' She says it likes she's doing me a favour, but I also know that smile she's wearing. It's real and it means she's secretly excited but doesn't want to lose her veneer of being cool.

* * *

The ice rink is just down the road from the Christmas market and so I shelve my idea about takeaway and instead promise Immy we'll go to one of the food stands afterwards for dinner.

'Can I have waffles?' she asks.

'If you want.' Personally I avoid anything that David Bennett touches as much as I can help it – it'll be a Porkies hog roast bap for me – but Immy doesn't need to be burdened by my principles. Besides, have you ever tried to tell a teenage girl she can't have something she's set her heart on?

We have to queue for fifteen minutes for a pair of skates, but as soon as we're out on the ice it's worth it. East 17's 'Stay Another Day' is blaring as I glide serenely – or at least that is what I think I look like; I haven't fallen over yet.

'What is this music?' Immy asks.

'It was the Christmas number one in 1994.'

'Oh.' I can tell it means nothing to her, but for me this song always creates a glowing ball of nostalgia in the pit of my stomach. Of a time when December was full of magic and expectation. A time before markets and stress and getting up at the crack of dawn to see my husband off to work.

With this song playing I can almost believe it's 1994 again and that anything is possible.

21

JESSICA

I bump into Fearne in the staffroom on my break.

'I guess we should take this down,' she says, motioning to the picture of Max Kirby – Do you know this man?????? – on the board. 'I doubt anyone is going to forget him in a hurry.' She sounds almost sad. Like he didn't get what was coming to him. Who steals from defenceless animals and expects to get away with it?

'Yeah.' I keep my tone as neutral as possible. It's never a good idea to have too many opinions about the dead. Especially if you were the one to dispatch them.

She takes the page down and stares at it for a few moments. And then she rips it in half, straight down the middle, bisecting his nose. The action is decisive. 'Well, good riddance, I guess,' she says. It feels at odds with her sadness from before and she must catch my look of confusion. She looks around to check no one will overhear. 'I'm not saying he deserved to die or anything, but he was hardly a model citizen. I just wish it hadn't been here at the market, Sebastian's been a fucking nightmare ever since.'

'Oh.' I feel a flash of guilt. Or perhaps it's shame. Whatever it is, it's new and I'm not sure I like it. But I feel bad for making her life even more difficult. Being married to Sebastian Dixon sounds hideous at the best of times.

'Sorry, I shouldn't have said that.' Her cheeks turn red. 'You really don't need to hear about my husband.'

'It's OK. Honestly, I'm here if you need a chat. Or a rant. Or whatever.' Especially because it sounds like the root of this recent nightmare behaviour is my little murder habit.

'I got nominated for something. It's silly really. Just a little award for one of my Cherry Dubois books. But I can't go.' She looks thoroughly dejected and my heart breaks for her.

'Why not?'

'Can you imagine the look on Sebastian's face when I trot off to the Dorchester Hotel in London?'

'The Dorchester?' Wow, it must be some award.

'Yeah. The nomination is for a Steamie, they're like the Oscars of the erotic fiction world. I mean it's not a big deal in the overall scheme of things but...'

It is a big deal. It's a huge deal. And that husband of hers is taking it away from her.

Ho hum. Well, guess who just added themselves to the Naughty List?

* * *

That evening I meet Hanna for a late dinner. The rest of the market is in full swing as I walk past and I'm thankful there's no plans for the grotto to ever open past seven thirty. We head into the cobbled heart of Ellsbury.

'There's this steakhouse that is just... chef's kiss,' she tells me, looping her arm through mine as if we've been pals forever. 'You're not vegetarian, are you? I didn't even think.' She sounds disappointed in herself. 'Here I am just dragging you off without even asking what you'd actually like.'

'I'm not vegetarian. And steak sounds perfect,' I reassure her.

'You're sure? Only I have this tendency to just take over and be a bit overbearing.'

'You're not.'

'It's what Kelsie's father used to say. That I was bossy and domineering.'

'You know that, if you were a man, he would have called you confident, self-assured and authoritative? See how those words sound so much more positive?'

'That's what Fearne always says. That there's a difference between the words used for women and those used for men. Strategic versus calculated. That kind of thing.'

'She's right,' I say just as we arrive at Sear Genius. It looks divine; warm and inviting and busy enough to have a lovely hum in the air while not being so packed you feel like a nuisance to the staff if you want another drink. The air is filled with the aroma of roasting meat and my stomach growls audibly.

'Was that...?' Hanna asks, pointing at my midriff.

'Yep. I guess my belly just confirmed she's happy with the choice of restaurant.'

'Wonderful.' She does a funny little half skip and drags me the last few metres. 'Let's get settled with a drink and you can tell me all about your evening out with Fearne.'

* * *

'The thing I don't understand is why she stays with him,' I say to Hanna, as my third Mistletoe Manhattan cocktail is delivered to the table.

'She loves him. He's not a terrible man, not in the overall scheme of terrible men.'

'Isn't that just setting the bar on the floor?'

'Maybe. But she fought so hard for him, back in the day. Her family did not approve.' She raises an eyebrow.

'Why not?' I lean forward and drop my voice. It feels like I'm about to get a tasty morsel of gossip.

'She was late twenties, young, free and single. He was older, not like creepily so, but he was a forty-year-old widower with a young daughter. Her family thought she was shackling herself to a life of domesticity, that he was looking for a nanny rather than a partner.'

'So Immy isn't her daughter?'

'Woah. I would never say that to her. She loves that girl more than life itself. Fearne always knew she couldn't have biological kids but she says she wouldn't change a thing about how she became a parent because it gave her Immy.'

'So she stays with Sebastian for Immy...' I trail off. I get it. I do. It's just... it feels like such a waste of a life to be chained to a man so... mediocre... so nothing... but still someone who refuses to let her shine as brightly as she could.

'We all make our compromises,' Hanna says.

Do we? I don't think I do. I give in to my baser instincts, live my life on my terms. Go where I want. When I want.

But you don't have anyone to share it with. There's a small voice in my head who sometimes makes treacherous little digs. I try to ignore her. Hers isn't an opinion I want to give airtime.

After pudding – a cheesecake with gingerbread flavours and a sticky Baileys-infused sauce, which was like heaven on a plate – Hanna gets a text. 'It's Alvi. He's in the pub down the road. We should join him for a drink.'

'I... err... I should probably head home,' I say awkwardly, in a way that couldn't confirm my burgeoning crush on her brother any more if I tried.

'So I see the Alvi-magic is working on you?' She grins. 'Oops, I didn't mean that to sound like it did. He isn't a player or anything. Just that women tend to fall for him; probably that whole starving-charity-worker-with-dogs thing. But most women get bored after a while and realise the fairytale of the rescue centre is very far from the truth.'

'I imagine it must be incredibly hard work,' I tell her.

'More than you would ever believe.'

'You sound like you don't approve.'

'I'm proud of him. Of course I am. He's saved so many of them. But at what cost to himself? He's still single, still living in the draughty old farmhouse our aunt and uncle owned, still has no money, no prospects. I just worry that one day he's going to wake up and realise his charms have dwindled and he's left everything too late.'

'Ouch,' I reply to her evisceration of her brother.

'Sorry. Was that too harsh? It was too harsh. I'm just... what am I doing?' She pauses for a moment, staring off into the middle distance as if trying to order her thoughts. 'I can tell he likes you. And you obviously like him, it's written all over your face.'

'It isn't.'

'Is.' She laughs. 'I just don't want him to get hurt. Or you, for that matter.'

'So you're just making sure my eyes are open?'

'That is it exactly.' She looks at me gratefully. 'Have some fun. Just don't break each other's hearts.'

I wonder if she'd be telling me to have fun with her brother if she had any idea of the kind of things I do in my spare time.

Alvi might not be relationship material, but I sure as anything am not.

We meet Alvi in the King's Head, a pretty standard pub with low ceilings and a faint whiff of stale beer in the ancient carpets.

He's sweet and attentive and he smells curiously like cinnamon buns, as if he's just got off work in a bakery rather than spent his whole day surrounded by dogs. He listens when I talk, and I don't mean in that fake pretend way people do when secretly they are just waiting for a space in the conversation to jump in with their own opinions or anecdote or whatever. He actually listens. Leaning forward to make sure he catches every word, his eyes on mine, his expression soft.

And there's something about the way he is with the dogs. This time he's brought a slightly overweight chocolate labrador and a black and white collie with him. Both are snoozing at his feet, the picture of relaxed contentment, and occasionally his hand will drift down to pat one gently, a slight touch of reassurance that he's still there and they are safe with him.

But I can't like him, not romantically.

I definitely don't have time to get involved with someone right now.

22

FEARNE

Every Sunday we sit down as a family to a proper roast dinner. It's become something of a tradition in the house, a way of making sure we at least spend a little bit of quality time together, especially when work is extra busy around November and December. It's a lot of effort making a full roast with all the trimmings, but in some ways I find it kind of therapeutic, or at least I used to, before I had book deadlines and teenage angst and a burgeoning rage at the entire world. Sebastian thinks the anger is perimenopause. I think it's just the accumulation of years of feeling like I'm being taken advantage of and not knowing how else to deal with the frustration.

Anyway, Sebastian had to work today, so the roast dinner is later than usual. I'm cooking a half leg of lamb with a blackcurrant glaze, rosemary potatoes and an assortment of vegetables, including a cauliflower cheese with a breadcrumb topping. For dessert, I've spent hours making Immy's favourite: apple strudel with a rich vanilla sauce, the same we had the first time we went to Bavaria a few years ago to check out the Christmas shop in Oberammergau.

I probably should have started the mammoth task of writing a million Christmas cards to acquaintances we never see, but it's only the middle of November so I've still got time. Last year I missed the final post and Sebastian got pissy; apparently Christmas cards are one of the 'remaining bastions of a functioning society' or something. Personally, I think they're a waste of time but it isn't like he listens to me anyway.

'Is it nearly ready, Mum?' Immy pads into the kitchen with her headphones around her neck. 'I'm starving.'

'Your father isn't home yet,' I tell her, peeking through the glass front of the oven to make sure the potatoes aren't burning. They've reached the perfect point of crispiness and I'm worried they'll be ruined if he's much longer.

'Fuck's sake,' she hisses under her breath.

'Please don't swear,' I say, the words coming out of my mouth on autopilot.

'You do,' she reminds me.

'So?'

She huffs at the unfairness of it all and I feel she does have a point.

'Maybe you could give Dad a ring?' I ask, turning down the heat on the hob before the gravy boils dry.

She huffs again.

'Is everything OK?' I ask gently. She seems kind of on edge.

'Fine,' she replies, too quickly. 'I'll call Dad.'

But before she can even get her phone out, I hear the car pull onto the drive. 'That'll be him.'

We talk about nothing much as we eat and – even if I do say it myself – the meal is delicious. The only thing that would have improved the lamb is a side of Yorkshire puddings, but it's not worth the fight. Immy chats away but there is definitely something going on with her, like a frantic undercurrent.

The strudel has been particularly successful this time and Sebastian even gives me a little round of applause as I place it on the table.

'This looks fantastic, love,' he says.

It also tastes pretty good and he makes a lot of appreciative noises as he eats a huge portion. Immy gives me a side eye as he moans a little and I have to stop myself from giggling. He sounds like he's *really* enjoying the strudel.

Immy clears the plates as soon as Sebastian puts down the spoon he's been using to scrape up every last vestige of vanilla sauce. And then she comes back to the table, twisting her hands in front of her. 'I want to talk to you both about something,' she says, her voice small.

Sebastian and I share a look. *Do you know what this is about?* he asks without saying a word. *Not a clue,* I reply. He reaches out to touch my hand under the table.

Immy clears her throat. 'There's this man,' she says, the words coming out quickly. 'He's been following me and Riya. Like after school and stuff. He drives this van and he'll creep along the road next to us.'

Fear spikes in my belly. 'Do you know who he is?' I ask gently, trying to keep my reaction neutral so I don't scare her.

She shakes her head. 'It only started a week or so ago. And he'll say things.' She looks up and meets my eye.

'What kind of things?'

'Horrible things. Gross things. And he whistles.' She grimaces. I think every woman knows exactly the kinds of things he's saying and the way in which he's saying them.

'Are you sure you aren't imagining it?'

Immy stares her father straight in the eye for a count of three. And then she storms out of the room, slamming the door behind her.

'You deserved that,' I tell Sebastian.

'Why?'

'You told her you didn't believe her.'

'But she's always overreacting to things, flying off the handle and blowing everything out of all proportion.'

I bite back a retort. I don't want to fight him over this; he won't understand, or even try to, and it'll only end up in a shouting match.

* * *

The next day, I take Immy to school in the car. Sebastian said I was coddling her, that I'll turn her into a neurotic mess who runs to her mummy to fix every problem. Luckily, he left for work at seven this morning so I didn't have to listen to him banging on for too long.

'That's him,' Immy says as we pass a white transit van about a street away from the Priory School.

I slow to a crawl. 'You're sure?'

She nods. 'I remember the number plate ends in TRK and there's a dent in the side.'

I drop her off at the school gates and then double back. There's a space on the opposite side of the road and I pull my Prius into it. I've brought a cinnamon latte with me in a travel mug and so I'm just going to sit here and drink my coffee and hope to get a glimpse of him.

What can I do with his number plate? It's times like these when I wish I wrote crime instead of romance, I'm sure a good crime writer would know how to get a name and address. Isn't there like a database or something? Or can only the police use that? Why don't I know a helpful – but slightly bent – police officer?

In the end, trusty old Google comes up with the disappointing answer. I can request the information from the DVLA with a V888 form but I must have 'reasonable cause'. Would freaking out my teenage daughter and her friends count?

Or do I just go straight to the police?

Just as I'm debating my options, the rear door of the transit opens and out hops a man who must have been inside this whole time. He has long, lank, greasy-looking hair, and the face of a glasses-wearing weasel. He slams the back door and walks round to the driver's side door, giving me an opportunity to get a closer look at him. He's not very tall, maybe five foot eight, and slim, almost wiry. He's dressed in mid-wash jeans and a plain black zip-up hoodie.

But it's the look on his face that really makes me take notice of him, a cold chill blasting up the back of my neck. He's smiling, but the sly secret smile of someone who has just gotten away with something and is extremely proud of themselves. It tickles my lizard brain. He *looks* like the kind of guy who would stalk vulnerable teens. And I know we're not meant to say things like that, but in this case it's true.

Fuck this.

I pick up my phone and call 101. 'I'd like to report a man for inappropriate conduct toward my teenage daughter and her friends.'

Eventually I'm put through to an officer in the local station, who sounds thoroughly sympathetic but not exactly raring to go in terms of taking any action. They promise to look into it, but impress on me just how busy they are at the moment. 'You've heard about the murder down at the market? Well, that's taking up a lot of our resources.'

Am I going to have to take matters into my own hands?

23

JESSICA

Alvi messages me just before I leave for work. A cute picture of the labrador and collie from the other night, with text underneath that reads:

> It was an honour to meet you, Mrs Claus.

Adorable.
But I do not like him.
I don't have time to get entangled with some hot guy with a cute dog. Dogs. Plural. So so so many dogs.
I walk to the grotto, feeling light as air. There's a real sensation of winter, the wind icy but the sun shining, giving everything that really crisp feeling. The perfect weather for the perfect morning.
But no. I do not like Alvi.
There's a girl, probably in her mid to late teens, sitting on the wall not far from the entrance to the market. Long dark-brown hair, delicate almost doll-like features, skinny body over-

whelmed by a huge padded coat. I wouldn't have noticed her, but for the two huge bags of stuff at her feet. One is a giant bag for life from Sports Direct – I can only assume they moved on from giant mugs – and the other at least has a zip on it, but it's so stuffed to bursting I doubt it'll last for long.

There's a sadness to her. A desolation.

'Are you alright?' I ask gently.

She looks up, her eyes red rimmed from crying. She scrubs the back of her hand across her face. 'I'm fine.' She says it in a way that screams 'leave me alone'. But up close I can see that her nails are dirty and her hair greasy. There's a hollowness to her cheeks too, like perhaps she hasn't had a proper meal for a while.

'I'm just going to get myself a coffee,' I say, pointing to a cafe a few doors down. 'Would you let me get you a hot chocolate?'

'I'm fine,' she repeats. But her chin wobbles slightly.

I dig into my pocket and pull out a couple of loyalty cards for the cafe chain. 'I have free ones and I can't drink both by myself.'

Her face lights up a little. 'OK then.'

I remember having nothing.

And I remember the way people would think you owed them for their gestures of kindness, so much so that I would rarely accept anything, especially from a stranger. But a free hot chocolate? That can't come with strings attached.

'I'm Jessica,' I say as we walk side by side toward the cafe.

'Lena,' she says quietly, huffing slightly under the weight of the two huge bags she's carrying.

'I could take one of those for you?' I offer, motioning toward them.

'No,' she says. 'I mean, no, thanks,' she corrects herself. 'Sorry.'

'It's OK.'

We take a seat by the window and I watch as Lena tries to make herself as small as possible. I can only assume people have been moving her on, making sure she isn't cluttering their doorsteps, their establishments.

We sit in silence as we wait for our drinks to be delivered to the table. I ordered extra cream and marshmallows on her hot chocolate and her eyes light up when she sees it. Plus the cheese and tomato toastie I bought her.

'Why are you being nice to me?' she eventually plucks up the courage to ask when the waitress leaves us.

I busy myself putting sugar in my coffee, even though it's already loaded with syrup. 'I think I was in a similar situation to you once upon a time.'

'I got kicked out of home.' She says it with a quiet rage, one that simmers just below the surface.

'You can tell me about it, if you'd like?'

'Ha. There isn't much to tell. I've been living with my uncle. He had a friend over. Yadda yadda yadda. I don't think I need to spell it out for you. My uncle said I was a liar. Told me if I was going to tell tales about his pals then I should find somewhere else to live.' She shrugs.

'You don't have any other family? Any friends?'

'If I did, do you think I'd be here?'

It's such an obvious answer and I feel embarrassed to have even asked the question. 'Have you tried the hostels?'

'I... well, that is...' Her voice breaks and she clears her throat. 'I don't have a passport or any kind of ID.'

'I don't think that would be a problem.' But I'm not a hundred percent sure and the uncertainty taints my words.

'What if they think I'm an illegal?' She raises an eyebrow. 'I'd rather take my chances on the streets.'

'Promise me you'll think about going to one. Especially if it gets colder?'

She nods. I'm not going to pressurise her. I can't. If I do that she'll probably run. 'You're not going to tell me it isn't safe with a murderer on the loose?' she asks, but there's an edge there, like she's teasing me.

'I assume he's long gone. Probably skipped town, maybe even the country.'

'Is that what you'd do? Run away to somewhere warm and sunny?'

'Probably.' It's what I did the first time I killed on purpose. Went to Greece and drank too much ouzo and tried to forget it had happened.

In the end she refuses my help, but I do manage to convince her to hire a little locker at the train station to store her stuff in instead of carting it around everywhere, giving her twenty pounds to pay for it and make sure she gets some dinner.

* * *

My shift is uneventful; just a stream of smiling children and their rather tired-looking parents, who give me a grateful look as I hand over a little slip of paper to confirm exactly what their offspring have asked Santa for, for Christmas. There are an inordinate number of children asking for something called a wall crawler – I had to look it up and apparently it's some kind of remote-controlled gecko that can climb up walls, it's a little creepy if I'm honest – and plenty of mobile phones, even though some of the kids were barely out of nappies.

After work I walk along the high street, trying to see if I can spot Lena. I don't like the idea of her being out here on her own at night. She's so young, so ripe to be taken advantage of.

There's a white transit van parked down a side street, the back door slightly open so I can see a sliver of light spilling out. A shadow moves down the side of it and I pause. The door opens fully, revealing the shadow to be a man. He looks like he's only a couple of inches taller than me, and he's skinny like a long-distance runner. He looks familiar. Like I've seen him somewhere before, but long ago, in another town, perhaps even in another decade.

I hug the wall as I creep closer to him. *Who is he?*

'I found the weed, sweetheart,' I hear him say as he climbs into the back of the van.

A woman giggles inside. Actually, scratch that, it isn't a woman. It's a girl.

'Shall we get high?' he asks her.

'Sounds good.'

I recognise the voice. It's Lena. Lena is inside this man's van. He's got weed.

Every single fibre of my being is on instant high alert. What kind of a man lures a young homeless girl into his van with the promise of weed? Not a good one, I'm guessing.

Should I walk away? Tell myself it's none of my business, that I shouldn't get involved? Once upon a time I was Lena, only it was a Volvo estate car instead of a van and cheap whisky instead of weed. But still, same same. I creep closer.

'You're very pretty,' he tells Lena. 'Far too pretty to be sleeping outside. Who knows what kind of predators are out there? You should stay with me. I'd look after you.' I can hear it in the tone of his voice. He isn't trying to be altruistic. I think we all know what he's after.

Right, that's it.

I knock loudly on the back door of the van.

'The fuck?' the man says.

I knock again, even more forcefully this time.

'Is it the police?' Lena asks, sounding terrified.

'I'll see. Hold this.' I assume he hands her the blunt so he can tell the police the weed is hers.

I wait for his head to appear and then I grab the front of his top and yank him out. He emits a tiny little scream as he falls into the street.

'Who the fuck are you?' he asks as he looks up at me from his position on the ground.

'Someone you'd better hope not to meet a second time,' I reply, giving him a swift kick to the testicles. He howls and my face breaks into a smile.

'Jessica?' Lena looks at me and then crawls forwards to look out of the van at the man writhing on the floor. 'What did you do?'

'You know what this piece of shit wants, right?' I ask.

'I'm seventeen,' she replies, somewhat coolly. But I can see the fear in her eyes. I think she knew on some level but the reality is starting to hit her as she stares down at him.

'Are you two bitches working together?' he asks. 'I'll fucking take you both on,' he adds in a rather impressive display of bravado for a man whose nether regions are probably still on fire.

'Come on, Lena,' I say. 'We should get out of here.'

He curls into a ball and then manages to stagger to his feet. 'Get out my van, you little slag,' he hisses at her. 'If I see you again...' He trails off and his face morphs into a snarl.

Lena looks at him and then slowly climbs out of the van. Then she looks at me as she weighs up the situation. She turns and runs.

'If I ever see you near her again, I will personally remove—'

'Really?' he interrupts. 'You? Do you honestly think you could take me?' He laughs. As if I'm powerless. As if I couldn't hurt him. As if I couldn't slit his throat with the knife in my pocket and leave him there to bleed out in the street. As if I wouldn't enjoy it.

24

FEARNE

Immy comes home from school, throwing the door open so hard it almost comes off its hinges.

'Hey,' I call out, running to the hallway from the kitchen.

She's crying, fat rivulets streaming down her face.

'Hey,' I say, more softly this time. 'What happened?'

'There's another one,' she eventually tells me, hiccupping slightly as her tears begin to subside.

'What do you mean "another one"?'

'Another van. A blue one. Another creepy guy following us. All the way home from the school gates.'

I reach out to pull her into a hug, but she pushes me away and runs upstairs.

Should I follow her? I don't know and my internal questions are interrupted by a key scraping the lock.

'Hi, love,' Sebastian says as he lets himself in, leaving the front door open while he takes off his muddy boots, fiddling with the laces for so long that all the warmth is sucked out of the house.

'Immy says there's another van.' I don't bother to hide the fear in my voice. This is getting weird now.

'Of course there isn't.' His tone is dismissive as he tries to pry one foot out of its boot.

'We need to take this seriously. Immy says there's now a blue van as well. It followed her all the way home from school.'

Sebastian turns slightly to look out over the driveway in front of the house. I follow his gaze.

'Is that a blue van on our driveway?' I whisper, taking a few steps toward him, seeking his comfort as fear floods over me. Getting older has offered me a level of protection from creeps and weirdos, the catcalling diminishing year by year. But it's still there, the primal fear of a stranger in the night, someone whose steps keep pace with yours, as if they are waiting for the perfect moment to rush you.

'I borrowed it from work.' He sounds proud, like he's puffing out his chest. I turn to look him in the face.

'It was you?'

'What was me?' He takes a step back, looking confused.

'You were the one following Immy.'

'I was making sure she was safe.'

'And you didn't think to tell her it was you?'

The frown of confusion deepens.

'It didn't cross your mind for one moment to text her? Call her?' My voice is rising with each word.

'Hey. Why are you getting upset with me? I was trying to keep her safe.'

'Are you an idiot?' My voice has reached a pitch I haven't used with my husband for many years.

'What?' He takes another step back. He looks almost frightened of me. Good. He needs to feel some of this fear. The terror of someone following you in a vehicle you don't recognise. Mine turns to anger as decades of it flows from me, directed at this stupid man who has no fucking idea.

'You followed Immy home in a van she didn't recognise. You made her think you were yet another creep.'

'But I'm not.'

'BUT SHE DIDN'T KNOW THAT!' I scream the words in his face.

Something clicks into place in that tiny brain of his. 'Oh.'

'You get it now?' I say, returning to my usual voice.

He stares at the toe of his right shoe and squirms a little. 'Yeah. I get it.' Then he thumps the side of his forehead with the heel of his hand. 'Stupid man,' he admonishes himself.

'You meant well.'

'Yeah.' But he doesn't sound convinced. It's always been there, this lack of confidence on his part when it comes to Immy. Like he is never good enough as a dad. Like he is failing her in myriad small ways he doesn't even understand.

'How about you go and check on her. Apologise. Make sure she knows she's safe. And I'll get dinner on.'

He nods and then lunges toward me, scooping me into a hug. 'I don't know what I'd do without you,' he whispers into my hair. I know he only means he wouldn't know what to do with Immy, but for a moment I let myself remember the early days of our relationship when he'd hold me close and tell me I was amazing and beautiful and all manner of other lovely words I haven't heard for a long time.

* * *

The next day I run into Jessica while she's getting a snack from the waffle stand.

'These are absolutely divine,' she tells me with a smile as the teenager working the stall hands it to her. 'Can I get you one?'

'I'm watching the calories,' I tell her, ruefully.

'But you don't need to,' she tells me.

'Christmas in our house is always so food focussed,' I explain. 'There is a literal two-week period where I eat my entire bodyweight in deliciousness every day, so I try to cut down a bit in the run-up.'

'Fair,' she says and takes a nibble from the corner. 'I tend to do it the other way. Eat all the things in the run-up, but then Christmas itself tends to be pretty quiet.' She pauses and then looks at me more carefully. 'You do look like you need a bit of a pick-me-up though.' There's concern tinging her voice.

'I'm just a bit stressed,' I confess. I don't know what it is about Jessica but something makes me want to tell her all my secrets. 'It's Immy.'

'Is she OK?'

'Some guy in a van has been following her and her friends.'

'Oh no. That's terrible.'

'I called the police.'

'You did? What did they say?'

'That they'd keep an eye out for the van. But it sounded like platitudes and nothingness. I doubt they have the resources.' I look up at her. 'I'm just terrified something is going to happen and then it'll all be my fault for not doing more.'

'But what can you do?'

However much I want to tell this woman my deepest darkest secrets, I don't tell her that I've fantasised about taking this guy out by myself. In my dream I'm wearing an all-black outfit and am a little better with a baseball bat than I think I would be in real life. 'I don't know,' I say eventually.

She offers me a gentle smile, as if to say that my impotence is nothing to be ashamed of, even though we both know it is. 'Do you know who he is?'

I shake my head. 'I've seen him, though. And the van. I was able to report the number plate at least. TB64 TRK.' It's so ingrained in my memory that I could recite it in my sleep.

'What kind of van is it?' she asks. 'I'll make sure I keep an eye out too,' she adds.

'It's a white transit. Pretty bog standard to be honest.'

'Any livery?'

'No, nothing like that. There's a big dent on one side though.'

She nods a few times, as if mentally writing down all the details, including the number plate. Not that there is anything we can do with the information.

25

JESSICA

I searched for Lena for hours that night after I found her in the van with that man, but I was eventually forced to concede defeat. I'd walked home in a boiling rage toward him. How dare he? How dare he think he can pick up vulnerable girls and take them to his van with the promise of weed and his 'protection'?

The rage had reduced to a simmer by the morning and I was left with gratitude I was there to stop something awful from happening. But then I spoke to Fearne and learnt that the same man was also stalking her daughter, following Immy and her friends home from school. Catcalling them. Frightening them.

And so now I am looking for Lena again. I need to find her and make sure she's safe. However much I threatened that man, I'm not sure he believed me about what I would do to him if he didn't stay the hell away from her.

The longer I stay out, the angrier I become. Who does that man think he is? The audacity of him. My pot of rage is back with a vengeance, the temperature creeping up and up the longer I search.

I don't find Lena.

But I do find him. And once again I'm struck by how familiar he is.

He's standing outside Ellsbury's only nightclub, staring at the girls queueing up to get in with a hungry look on his face. There's a McDonalds across the street and so I buy myself a coffee and a Terrys Chocolate Orange pie – well, it is the first day of their Christmas menu so it'd be rude not to, even if I'm out hunting creeps – and settle in to keep an eye on him.

An hour later – and with another coffee on the go – I watch as a group of young girls almost fall out of the club. It's only eleven thirty, but judging by the way two of them are swaying and their friends are propping them up, there has been a lot of alcohol consumed this evening.

The man with the van – whose name I really need to learn – begins to follow them. I leave my half-drunk second coffee and walk outside, the cold wind slapping me in the face after the warmth of McDonalds. I keep my distance, the streets are so quiet it'd be hard to lose track of the giggling mass of girls, and I really don't want him to see me just yet.

The girls stop outside a large house and there are a few tense moments when one of them thinks she's lost her keys, although she eventually finds them. How she could lose them in such a tiny little clutch, I'm not sure. It was barely big enough for a credit card and a lip-gloss. They bundle into the house, still giggling, and then there's silence as the door closes behind them.

I watch as the man with the van sighs as if in disappointment and then begins to walk away from the house slowly, dragging his feet ever so slightly. I follow him, hugging the shadows, as he returns to his van. It's still parked on the same street. He opens the back and gets inside. Is he living in it? I move closer, on high alert that the door may open at any moment. But it remains closed as I peer into the front cab section. And there, sitting on the passenger seat, is a letter. It's addressed to a Curtis West of Somerset Terrace in Bristol. I wonder what he's doing in Ellsbury. Well, except trying to snatch vulnerable teenage girls from the streets.

At least now I have a name.

Back at the house, I put on the kettle and change into something warm and cosy. But I can't shake the chill from my bones from being out in the cold and it's far too late to even consider lighting the fire. Instead, I climb beneath the covers on the bed, and flick the switch for the heated blanket.

I wait for five minutes until it gets to work and then I pick up my laptop.

Curtis West has a Facebook account that says he's forty-three and is apparently a labourer. There's a post about how he's off to Ellsbury to work on a house that a mate is trying to flip.

Zoopla shows a listing on College Road, the street where the van was parked. The inside photos of the property are AI generated to give prospective buyers a view of what it might look like. This must be his friend's place.

A Google search reveals that he has previously been featured on an episode of *24 Hours in Police Custody*. That must be where I recognise him from. Honestly, that show is an absolute goldmine to people with my particular predilection. It really shows you all the common pitfalls to avoid, even if most of them are common sense. Like the guy who got rid of the phone he used to order a hit on his brother, but didn't throw away the box it came in.

Back in 2015, Curtis was convicted of kidnapping. He took his boss's daughter and held her to ransom for over a week. She described him as a twisted psychopath. He was given twelve years, so really he should still be in prison. Unless he was released on 'good behaviour'.

I go back to his Facebook profile. It was set up in 2022, so he must have been released by then. He has an eighteen-month-old son called Callum, but he only posts about him on birthdays and Christmas so it doesn't look like he's a hands-on father. Probably a blessing in disguise for both the little boy and his mother.

And so to planning. I head to the living room and switch on a couple of side lamps. It's just after 1 a.m. and I doubt I'm going to get any sleep. Not with a murder to plan. So I light the fire and make the room extra cosy.

I dig out the 'Jessica's Naughty List' pad and carefully remove a sheet before finding a copy of the local newspaper to lean on.

Curtis West. I write his name in bold letters at the top, followed by his crime. *Terrorising vulnerable young girls.* I nibble on a few stollen bites as I think of a potential murder method.

Do I want to make a big statement? A splash as it were. Or shall I do something a bit more subdued, less of a message and more of a quick fix to get rid of someone terrible before he hurts someone else?

Do I want to make it look like an accident? I've never done that before and, to be honest, I'm not sure I have the skills to pull it off, not unless all the chips fall in my favour anyway.

Do I want to make him suffer? My heart says yes. My head says that might be messy.

I fall asleep with the papers on my lap, jolting awake as the newspaper slides off and thunks onto the floor. Perhaps I'll just snooze for a few hours and then head out to stalk my prey?

The light burns my eyes when I wake up and there's a crick

in my neck from the awkward angle I was lying in. But I feel a million times better, my head clear and my spirits buoyed. I'll have a quick shower and then venture out to see what our van-dwelling creep is up to.

The sun is shining and the sky is a brilliant blue, but the wind is cold and I wrap my coat more tightly around myself, stuffing my gloved hands into the pockets. It's only a ten-minute walk to College Road where the van is still parked.

The front door of the house is unlocked and I open it to find the hallway has been stripped back to the bare floorboards, the walls devoid of paper. There's a chemical smell in the air and it's absolutely freezing. I walk quietly through the ground floor, but there's no one here.

'Fuck,' I hear a male voice almost grunt from the floor above. I stand motionless as I wait to hear if anyone else responds. I know I can kill Curtis West, but I'm not sure I would come out a winner against a whole troop of labourers. When I don't hear anyone, I start to climb the stairs, one step at a time, fingers crossed none of them squeak. As I reach the top, I'm met with what may as well have been a gift-wrapped present just for me.

He's balancing on a tall ladder in the room in front of me. It's a kind of mezzanine level, with a balustrade that acts as a barrier against the void space in the living room. The ladder Curtis is on is right up against the balustrade, and he's leaning over it. I take four large strides.

'Hi Curtis,' I say sweetly as I give the ladder a good sharp shove.

Back downstairs I find him lying in a broken pile.

'Oops,' I say.

He's still alive, his eyes flashing daggers at me. I cast around for something to help finish him off.

'Oh, a screwdriver,' I exclaim, picking one up. It's a Phillips head, pretty hefty, certainly not the cheap rubbish you'd buy as a regular person. 'This is perfect.'

I tamp down the urge to get messy with the kill. 'This is for all the girls you've terrified and terrorised over the years,' I tell him as, with a single swift motion, I end his life.

26

FEARNE

I spot the headline as I lie in bed scrolling through the local news and trying to muster the energy to get up.

Man discovered dead in house on College Road.

Isn't College Road just up from the market? I read on.

The victim, who has yet to be identified, was found yesterday by a local resident who discovered the door to the house open during their early morning dog walk. The police are treating the death as suspicious. It follows the murder of Max Kirby, who was stabbed in the Ellsbury Christmas Market last week.

Is there actually a serial killer in Ellsbury? Surely not. That kind of thing doesn't happen in places like this. Ellsbury might be the kind of place where cosy crime writers set their books, but the perpetrators in those stories are always an overzealous priest, or a councilman intent on securing his legacy, or a teacher concealing her past misadventures. And besides, those are fiction. Serial killers do not target quaint market towns like Ellsbury. And a 'suspicious death' could be anything. Aren't all deaths in the home treated as suspicious to start with; a whole 'it might be a murder until proven otherwise' ethos? I don't actually know – all my book research is on the regency period and things were different then – but it sounds sensible.

Yes. I'm sure it's nothing. But I don't think logic is going to help quell the imaginations of my fellow Ellsbury residents. I can see this being headline news for a long time.

I'm needed at the market today, it's been two weeks since we opened and so I'm seeing some of the newbie vendors for a quick check-in. You know, make sure they don't have any major problems etc. I've booked them in to half-hour slots over the day so we can have a coffee and a chat. I deliberately put Alvi first, he's definitely my least problematic stallholder and he promised to bring puppies with him.

But evidently not all of them agree with the idea of waiting for their allotted timeslot. Guess who is waiting outside the hut when I arrive onsite in the morning? Yep. That'll be Bella Donna.

'That's the second murder,' she tells me even though it feels a little unnecessary.

'It's a suspicious death, not a murder.'

'Actually, the police just put out a press release.' She gives me a smile that is somehow both smug as hell and still concerned.

'They did?' I pull out my phone and look for local news. 'Murder inquiry opened for body found on College Road as suspicious circumstances of the death are confirmed,' I read out loud. 'Oh.'

'Oh, indeed. So that *is* a second murder.' She says it like a gotcha.

'Yes, it appears it is.' I'm already tired of this conversation. Especially as I have a suspicion about where it's about to go.

'Energy, Fearne. I can't be more clear about this. The whole energy of the market is off and it's causing all these problems.'

'Do you really think that someone is out there murdering people because your stall is in the wrong place?' I ask, not bothering to hide the sarcasm in my tone.

'Yes.' She claps her hands together like a delighted child. 'I'm so glad you see my point.'

'I'm not agreeing with you,' I correct. 'I'm just checking that's what you're saying.'

'Oh.' Her face falls. 'So you disagree?'

'Bella. The location of your stall has absolutely nothing to do with these murders. And no, I cannot change it. You cannot swap with someone else. You cannot bully and cajole someone else into moving.'

'But it would be in everyone's best inter—'

'No.' I stop her mid-flow. 'I know what this is. This is about you wanting a prime location. Somewhere more central. That's all this is and I'm not going to fall for your bullshit. I have a lot going on right now and I am not dealing with you on top of everything else.'

She takes a step back as if I've just slapped her round the face. 'Wow. Tell me how you really feel.'

I pause. I would *love* to tell her how I really feel. How I can't believe she's putting so much energy into this charade when there are actually big serious problems in the world.

There's a man stalking my teenage daughter.

There might be a serial killer on the loose.

* * *

The next morning, there's a knock on the door and Immy pokes her head into the room.

'Mum?' she stage-whispers.

'I'm awake,' I tell her.

'Is Dad here?'

'He left for the market half an hour ago.'

She almost runs into the room and throws herself onto his side of the bed, wrapping the duvet around her like she's a human burrito. I reach out to touch her shoulder.

'You OK?'

'Have you seen the news this morning?'

'No.'

One hand appears out from the duvet and she thrusts her phone in my face. A picture of the man from the van stares back at me.

'That's the man who was following me,' she says, pulling her arm and the phone back under the covers.

'Why do you have a photo of him on your phone?'

'He was the one who was murdered.'

'Oh. You sound...' I grope for the right word. 'Sad?' I try.

'I... I... well, I don't know... I mean...'

'You know this means you don't need to be afraid any more.'

'Well, not of him. There is kind of a murderer on the loose.'

Yeah, she has a point there.

'Mum?' she asks softly, her voice low and almost timid.

'Yes, sweetheart?'

'The news said he, as in Curtis West, had a string of arrests for kidnapping and sexual assault. Do you think the murderer was actually just taking revenge?'

I think about it for a while. 'Maybe,' I say eventually. I don't know. Not really. I mean, to actually kill someone? To take all that rage and anger and finally let it out against the person who hurt you? 'Maybe,' I repeat.

My blood runs cold. Could it have been Sebastian? Finally doing something, finally getting up off his bum and taking action instead of berating his daughter like she might have made it up? Surely not. I mean, I really doubt he'd have it in him.

'Do you think Max Keogh was killed by the same person?' Immy asks, breaking my thoughts.

'Who?'

'Max Keogh? The guy in the market.' She says it like I'm a little dumb.

'Oh. You mean Max Kirby,' I correct.

'Whatever.'

'The police think that was gang related.'

'There aren't any gangs in Ellsbury.'

'No, but apparently there are some links to bigger city outfits.' I'm trying to be really careful with what I say, trying not to scare her. It's a big bad world out there, but she doesn't need to know that. Not yet, anyway.

'But if a gang killed Max, then who killed Curtis West?'

'I don't know.'

Unless it was someone who knew them both. The same person taking out a thief and a rapist? Some kind of vigilante. Or is that the stuff of thriller novels? Surely it can't be real life.

27

JESSICA

I finally find Lena outside the train station, sitting on the steps looking cold and tired and hungry. A few people have put some coins in the cup in front of her, but it looks like most of them are coppers. Who sees a starving teenager and decides to give them two pence?

'Hey,' I say gently as I approach her. 'You OK?'

'He's dead,' she says, not meeting my eyes.

'Who?' I ask innocently, as if butter wouldn't melt. Or as if I wasn't the one who pushed him off that ladder and then finished him off with a posh Phillips-head screwdriver.

'That guy in the van.' Her voice is small, her words muffled by the neck of her sweater as she tucks her chin inside it.

'Good riddance then.'

'I suppose.'

I pause for a few moments and look around me at the bustle of life around Ellsbury train station. It's a small city but there are still people milling around, going about their business and ignoring us. I'm worried that Lena is just going to get swept away, that she'll be lost in this small sea of people. All it will take is one more opportunist like Curtis West. 'You need to find somewhere safer to stay,' I tell her eventually.

'Yeah, what with this killer on the loose.' She shoots me a look and in that moment I think she knows what I did. 'I still don't have anywhere to go,' she adds.

I buy her a hot chocolate and a bacon sandwich and then head toward the grotto to start my shift. I hate leaving her there, she looks so young, so vulnerable as I walk away. Could I invite her to come to the house? I'm still mulling it over as I reach the staff entrance to the market. I'm sure Hanna would be horrified at the idea of a young woman living on the streets like this. But Hanna might want me to tell someone, social services or whatever.

Then I realise and I stop dead, causing the person behind me to almost walk into me. 'Watch it,' they mutter under their breath, I think it's David Bennett of the food concessions fame.

I can't invite Lena back to the house after my shift.

I can see it in my mind's eye, just lying there on the sofa in plain view of anyone who came in.

How could I have been so stupid? I should have burnt it days ago.

Jessica's Naughty List.

Curtis West.

All the questions I ask myself written out in lovely even block lettering.

Then a cold feeling runs up the back of my neck. What if there's a viewing this afternoon? What if right at this moment there is an overly chirpy estate agent letting themselves and a prospective purchaser into the house, talking animatedly about how quaint the property is, how idyllic the neighbourhood is?

I need to get back there. And I need to do it fast.

But I also need to go to work. I stand motionless, torn

between fear of being unmasked and my duty to my job. The risk of a viewing is low, I understand that, but if there was one then the fallout would be catastrophic. I'm always so careful. So neat and tidy and able to put my extra-curricular activities into a nice little box so that it never spills out into my own life. But now I've broken the one rule. Is this it? The way everything ends? The way I get caught? Just from being distracted and not paying enough attention. And there was me priding myself on being so much smarter than all the other criminals who let themselves get caught.

As adrenaline continues to flood my system I'm hit by a sense of calm, my brain suddenly free to kick back into gear. I could just call the estate agent. Yes, that's a good idea.

I pull out my phone and scroll to the number. A singsong voice answers on the second ring. 'Good morning, this is Timpson and Ward, Becca speaking.'

'Hi, my name's Jessica Williams. I'm the tenant of Hanna Jakkinen. I just want to check there's no viewing planned for today? I've been making a million gingerbread men for the Cancer Research coffee morning tomorrow, and the whole house is in total disarray.' I keep my tone light. Just a ditzy little woman who loves baking Christmas treats and who no one should ever take too seriously. Ha ha ha ha.

'No viewings today, Ms Williams. You take care now though, and if you're passing the office do feel free to drop one of those gingerbread men in.' It's a joke, but I mentally add it to my To Do list. Every tiny thing helps to build the alibi and all that. *'Ms Williams? Oh no, she can't have had anything to do with it. She was baking gingerbread for a charity event all day. She even dropped some round to the office the next morning. What a sweetheart. You know she's Mrs Claus in the market grotto?'*

See, Mrs Claus doesn't kill people.

Mrs Claus doesn't knife thieves through the heart and leave their bodies on display in the Christmas market.

Mrs Claus doesn't stab men through the eye with a Phillips-head screwdriver.

* * *

My shift goes by in a delightful miasma of festive joy, full of awed faces and high-pitched laughter. But unfortunately, not all children believe in the magic of Christmas.

Especially cynical teenage girls.

Lena is waiting for me outside the grotto as I close the door to lock up and head home. I'm so tired my vision is swimming slightly, turning the fairy lights of the market into a kaleidoscope of colour.

'I know it was you,' she says from the shadows, making me jump and drop the keys in the process. The rest of the market is still going, the crowds ramping up their drinking into the evening.

I straighten up, keys in hand. 'Oh, hey, Lena,' I say.

'I know it was you,' she repeats. Her voice is hard and matches her solemn expression.

'What was me?' I ask. But inside I'm scrabbling. She knows. She knows. She knows. But she can't know.

'The man in the van,' she hisses.

'What about him?'

'For fuck's sake.' I blanch slightly at the profanity. 'Are you actually serious right now?' she asks, her voice rising. 'You're going to get all prissy about the f-word when I watched you butcher that man?'

'Fuck,' I whisper under my breath. I guess it's called for. 'Why didn't you say something this morning?'

'I hadn't decided what I was going to do with the intel.'

'And now...?'

'I need somewhere to stay,' she says, pointing to the bags at her feet. The zip on one of them has now broken as I predicted and I can see that it is where she's keeping a sleeping bag and a pillow, which has definitely seen better days.

'I...' I suppose she could stay with me. If she knows anyway, what does it matter if she sees the Naughty List. Although I'll have to destroy it before she decides to blackmail me. 'You could stay with me.'

'Are you kidding? You're a killer. You really think I'd stay with you and risk you slitting my throat in my sleep?'

She might have a point there. Not that I would. I do have a rule against killing people just to keep my secrets. No innocent bystanders and all that. And not even I can do the mental gymnastics to put a homeless teen on the Naughty List. 'OK.' I put my hands up. 'Do you have a better idea?'

She puts out her right hand, palm up. 'I'll sleep in the grotto. You have a key.'

'But...' I start to say but then trail off when I see the look in her eye. She isn't joking or messing around. And, I have to admit, it isn't the worst idea in the world. I'm always the first person on site and the last to leave, locking up behind me as I go. All part of the standard Mrs Claus duties; because even a mythical marriage between magic toymakers with a whole shedload of elves on their staff can't break with the gender norm of the woman doing pretty much everything while her husband gets all the credit.

'It's safe. And warm. And no one would know I'm even there.'

'But...' I know there a lot of reasons this isn't a terrible idea. But there is one huge reason it is. 'I could get fired,' I say softly, the words sounding hollow in my ears.

'Are you seriously worried about that?' she asks. 'You killed someone.' She raises her index finger as if she's about to count off all the reasons why my concerns are ridiculous.

I shut her down. 'Yes. But this is my job. I need this job.'

'And I need a place to stay.' She looks at me levelly.

'Fine. Just please don't get caught.'

Her face breaks into a smile. 'Seriously? You mean it?' And suddenly I see the vulnerable child once more. How can I possibly leave her to live on the streets when there is a warm and safe cabin that no one else will be using? She can lock the door from the inside and not have to worry about falling asleep.

I hand her the key and she smiles as she takes it. Then I fish a few ten-pound notes from my wallet. 'Take this for food,' I say. 'Oh, and get a membership to the gym down the road. They're doing a special deal this month and it'll give you somewhere to shower. You can use the address of the cottage.' I scribble it on the back of an old receipt and tuck it under the cash.

She pauses before she takes the money. 'It's a loan,' she tells me, her features turning serious.

'It can just be a gift.'

'No.' She's adamant. 'It's a loan and I will pay you back. I'm going to get myself a job here in the market. I saw an advert in the *Ellsbury Gazette* this afternoon. That fish and chips place, The Festive Fry, is hiring.'

'You want to work for David Bennett?'

'Who's David?'

'The guy who runs the stall. A few of the food stalls actually.'

She shrugs. 'I need a job.'

'It's just... I've heard some things about him,' I say, nibbling the skin around my thumbnail.

'Any job is better than no job,' she tells me, her voice matter of fact.

'I don't think it's a good idea.' She looks so vulnerable standing there in the cold, like she's literally waiting for someone to pick her up and carry her off to be exploited even more. 'I don't think he's a good boss. He doesn't treat his staff well…'

'I could be a spy,' she says, with a wicked flash in her eye.

'A spy?'

'I could find out what he's really up to. If you think he's dodgy…'

'And then what?' I think I know where this is going.

'Then I blackmail him.' She says it like it's so obvious. Perhaps it is.

'It isn't safe.'

She cocks her head and stares at me with eyes that are far older than her seventeen years.

'OK.' I acquiesce. 'Just promise me you'll be careful.'

'Always.'

I don't remind her that this mess with Curtis West started because she nearly made a very bad decision. I was a desperate kid once too.

28

FEARNE

Sebastian calls me at eight-thirty in the morning, right as I'm sitting down with a large pot of fresh coffee and a blank document to begin the next Cherry Dubois book.

'The council have fucking done it,' he hisses down the phone at me. He sounds mad as all hell.

'Done what?'

'Sent someone. The fucking council have sent someone.'

'To do what?' I ask, but I think I already know and I brace myself for the answer.

'To check up on the market. Apparently these murders are "a threat to tourism". The council have appointed someone to make sure everything is as Christmassy as it can be. They've appointed a Christmas Czar.' He spits the words.

'Have they actually called it that?' Surely not.

'Yes, they have.'

'Do you know who?'

'Apparently they will be here at ten.'

'I'll come in.' I look lovingly at my laptop and the blank

document I was so excited to be starting today. It'll have to wait until tomorrow.

'Thanks love.'

In what feels like a lifetime ago, before I gave up work to help care for Immy, I used to work for the local council. I loved it at first. That rush of walking into the fancy old building with all its history and the scent of floor polish in the air. But over time the excitement wore off, replaced with a deep hatred for all the box ticking and saying no to reasonable requests on ridiculous grounds like incorrect completion of an overly complicated form. It was exhausting and, in the end, I was glad to leave. At the time at least. Until I felt bits of me slipping away as I became a wife and a mother and no one really saw the person underneath any more. That was why I started writing; to have something that was mine and mine alone.

But anyway. My job at the council means I still have a lot of contacts – there isn't a huge amount of staff turnover to be fair – and I've kept abreast of much of the gossip over the years.

I had a text while I was driving, but I wait until I've pulled into my space in the staff parking area round the back of the market to read it. It's from an old colleague.

> Guess who your new Christmas Czar is?

I read as I step out of the car.

But I can already sense her standing behind me. As if she's been waiting for me to arrive.

'Fearne Mahony.' Her voice is like fingernails on a chalkboard.

'Actually it's Fearne Dixon now,' I correct, turning round to face her.

Erin Winters.

Fucking Erin Fucking Winters.

She's wearing a plain dark-grey suit with a fitted pencil skirt and cinched-in waist, with a pale cream blouse, and sheer black tights. She's completed the look with a smart black leather handbag and a pair of stupidly high heels. Her blonde hair – naturally far blonder than mine, like she's some kind of human/buttercup hybrid – is swept off her face into a ponytail. I can't see from here but I imagine she's done that thing where she's wrapped a strand around the hair bobble to hide it. In short, she looks like she works for an uber corporate firm of lawyers or accountants.

She looks like she means business.

She looks like I always dreamed I would when I grew up. I hate her. I've *always* hated her. Even thirteen years ago she would clack around the office in those stupid heels and I would look at her and wish I could be her, even though she bullied the shit out of me.

'What an unexpected surprise,' I say, realising I've been standing staring at her in the car park for a few beats too long.

'Well, when the council needed a Christmas Czar, there was really only one option,' she replies. 'It isn't like anyone in that office has ever been competition for me.' She says it coolly. There was a time we used to compete – or at least I thought we did: for promotions; for training opportunities; for a better parking space closer to the building.

'So we're going to be working together again,' I say, keeping my voice neutral. I really don't want her to see how much she gets to me.

'You're not officially an employee of the market, are you?' She cocks her head to an almost comical angle and makes this stupid face I have to stop myself from punching.

'Well, I help—'

'I mean, surely you can't be dragging yourself away from those little books you write.'

'I've just submitted book eleven to my publisher,' I tell her. *Little* books. It smarts.

'Oh, cute. It's always good to have a hobby. And I suppose you don't really need to work. Although I imagine your husband does appreciate you bringing him lunch. Bit early though, isn't it?' She glances at her watch and raises an eyebrow.

'I'm not here to bring him lunch, I'm here...' But I trail off as she's already turned away and is starting to head toward the market. I jog for a few paces to catch her up.

She pulls her phone from her handbag – which, of course, has one of those organiser dividers inside so everything has its own neat little home. 'Initial observations,' she says into the speaker, holding it flat in her palm. 'Rubbish in the car park, suggests a lack of care from the staff. Faint smell of something unpleasant, to be investigated further. I'm just going through the staff entrance to the market itself. Light out on the string to my left, suggest full review of all lighting. Noise from generator is distracting in this part of the market.'

On and on she goes, making comments about every tiny little thing she sees as if the place is a total dump. As if my husband is not out there with a list every single morning making sure everything is shipshape. As if she could run this place better than he can.

'Overflowing bin by Waffleicious.' She pauses to sniff the air. 'Cigarette smoke detected, suggest a total smoking ban in the area.'

I follow her around, something telling me that knowing what she is really thinking will be useful in the long run. But I can't pretend there isn't an almost morbid fascination in listening to her tearing down everything my family has built for a decade.

'Are you going to show me where the main office is?' she demands as we reach the central drag of the market.

'Oh. Of course, this way,' I motion back the way we came.

She rolls her eyes as if I should have led her there, despite her not asking and seeming like she had her own agenda she was working through.

I knock before I poke my head around the door to the office. 'Erin Winters is here,' I say in almost a stage whisper.

'Erin Winters?' he replies, matching my tone. But he drops the volume for the next part. 'As in Fucking Erin Fucking Winters?'

'Yep. Our Christmas Czar.'

'Fuck,' he says, his face dropping. 'It's even worse than I thought.' His shoulders round for a moment and then he snaps back to ramrod straight. He clears his throat. 'Well, I guess it's showtime.' He winks at me and for a moment I believe that we're a team.

'Erin,' I call behind me. 'Sebastian is ready for your meeting.'

I take a seat by the door, not part of the meeting – I'm sure Erin would remind me that I'm not technically an employee – but able to make notes and observations to share with Sebastian later.

'You know why the council has appointed me?' she asks, but I get the feeling it isn't really a question.

Sebastian obviously thinks so too as he says, 'Perhaps you can enlighten me? Give me the official line?'

'The council is concerned about these murders. They want to ensure that tourists aren't dissuaded from visiting Ellsbury. The city relies on the trade.'

'I'm well aware of that, Erin.'

'Please call me Ms Winters.'

'Right, sorry, Ms Winters.' He sounds like he's taking the piss out of her a little. 'But I really don't think I need a lecture in ensuring the market is a prime tourist hotspot.'

'I've done an initial tour of the market and I'm going to be honest. Standards have slipped. Rubbish everywhere, lights out, the smell of smoke by the waffle stand. Not all of the vendors are open.'

'The market doesn't officially open until ten thirty,' he reminds her.

'Right. Well, I will be here tomorrow at ten twenty-nine then, to make sure everything is perfect.' She smiles at him and I watch his hands curl into fists. 'This is very serious, Sebastian.'

'Call me Mr Dixon,' he says, the petty tone unmissable.

'As you prefer, Mr Dixon.' She pauses ever so slightly after the first syllable of our surname and I watch the vein on my husband's forehead pulse briefly.

He looks like he's about to totally lose his shit.

I have a very bad feeling about all of this.

29

JESSICA

As I have for the last few days, I get to the grotto an hour earlier than I technically need to in order to make sure Lena's awake and the place is tidy before anyone else turns up for their shift. I don't know what would happen if someone knew I was hiding a teen in the grotto. Oh, and that I gave her my key.

So far, every day I've got there to find the grotto neat and tidy with zero evidence she's staying there. There's a colour returning to her cheeks too, and the gym in town's special membership means she's showering daily and you can tell it's boosting her confidence. I even caught her smiling the other day.

But today I approach the grotto to find that new woman with the clipboard and stick up her behind standing outside. Her lips are pursed and she looks like she's struggling not to combust. She's on a call, the phone balanced on the clipboard with the other person on speaker.

'Yes. A vagrant,' she says, clipping each word. She must be talking about Lena. I duck out of sight so I can continue to listen to the call.

'Like a homeless man?' the person on the other end of the line asks.

'Yes. I called the police naturally.' She called the police?

'Did they arrest him?' The person sounds shocked, or like this is the most interesting thing that has happened to them in a long time.

'Her. They've taken her away to the station.'

No! Poor Lena. And – excuse my French – but damn this fucking woman. Who does she think she is, in her fancy suit with her Chilly's coffee cup? Why wouldn't she try to help Lena instead of getting her carted off by the police?

'Is vagrancy a crime still?' the tinny voice asks from the speaker.

'Well, it should be. Anyway, that's not why I'm calling you. Since the aforementioned vagrant was using Grottos R Us property, I needed to bring it to your boss's attention. The council expects something to be done immediately.'

'Right. Well, I'll tell Colin... er, Mr Armstrong... although, what is it that the council is expecting him to do?'

'Take appropriate action. I expect Mr Armstrong to respond by close of play.'

She cancels the call. I can just see a sliver of her profile from where I'm hiding. She's grinding her teeth, her jaw stiff.

I do not like Erin Winters.

There's over an hour before I need to open the grotto so I head immediately to the police station. I ask the desk sergeant if they have a young lady in custody called Lena.

'Surname?' she asks brusquely.

'I don't know,' I'm forced to admit. 'I'm a friend. And I'm worried about her.'

The desk sergeant must pick up on my distraught tone because her whole demeanour softens. I can only imagine the kind of people she has to deal with on a daily basis; I'd be grumpy to start with too if so many of my interactions were characterised by abuse. 'She, the one who's been sleeping rough in the grotto?' she asks.

I nod.

'Do you know why she's on the streets?'

'Only the things she told me. She was living with her uncle but he kicked her out. There was some other stuff too...' I don't want to tell a stranger everything Lena told me. It would feel like a breach of her trust. 'Is she in trouble?'

'Trouble? Oh, not with us. We'll need to contact social services, see if there is anywhere for her to go. But the system is so stretched right now and...' She tails off, shoulders slumping slightly. There's an air of dejection to her. 'Sorry. It's just there's so little real support for these kids and no one really cares what happens to them. And then they end up back here in real trouble a few months later.' She looks like she might burst into tears.

I reach into my bag and pull out a candy cane, wrapped in a red velvet bow, and place it on her desk.

She stares at it. 'What's that?'

'A candy cane. You looked like you could use some sugar.'

'That's so... sweet.' She looks up and forces a grin. 'Normally people just give me shit.'

'This feels like a very tough job.' I motion around.

'It is.' She takes a deep breath. 'I just wish I could do more to help people before they ended up in trouble, you know?'

I nod. 'I've been trying to help her. Lena, I mean.' I pause for a few moments. 'You said social services will be able to do something for her?'

'They'll try.'

'Could she come home with me? I'm not a relative or

anything, but I am a friend... Oh, and I'm DBS checked and everything. I work with children. I'm the Mrs Claus in the grotto at the Christmas market.'

'Oh, I thought I recognised you. I brought my son last week.'

'Ha. Of course you did.' I wrack my brains. 'Toy car and Lego dinosaur?'

'Yes. Wow. You have an impressive memory.'

I don't tell her that it makes it much easier to make sure I remember every tiny lie I tell all day long.

In the end, the police agree to release Lena to my care.

'Someone from social services should be in touch in the next few days,' the desk sergeant tells me. 'But if you haven't heard anything for two weeks, just drop by and I'll give them a chase.'

Lena offers me a thin smile as she comes out of the bowels of the station. 'Thank you,' she whispers.

'No problem.'

She waits until we're outside. 'I didn't say anything to the police. About you. And what happened to Curtis West.'

'Shhh,' I tell her. 'That isn't why I'm here. But thank you,' I add.

'Then why are you here?'

'Because I care about what happens to you.'

'Oh.'

'So, you're going to have to stay with me at the cottage for a bit, OK?'

She chews her lip.

'I promise you're safe with me.'

'You killed that man.'

'Yes. But it was a one—'

'You'd done it before.'

'Yes. But I only—'

'Let me guess. You only kill people who deserve it?'

'Well...' I pause for a moment. It sounded almost childish on her lips, like I was playing at this whole murder thing. But it's true. 'I *do* only kill people who deserve it.'

'You enjoy it. And you've made a whole ritual around it, like you're an avenging angel.'

I feel kind of seen if we're going to be honest about it. Is she right? Am I nothing more than a common killer?

'Don't get me wrong,' she says and stops in the street to let a group of kids from the local school flow around us. She waits to ensure they've all gone before she turns to face me. 'I'm not mad you killed him. He definitely deserved it. But what's going to stop you from deciding that *I've* done something bad?' There's genuine fear in her voice; even though she's trying to maintain steely eye contact I can see straight through her pretence of bravery.

'Why would you do something bad?'

She drops eye contact suddenly, fascinated by something on the floor. 'I... I...'

I put my hand on her shoulder. She jumps a little under my touch, but I don't pull away. 'Lena, look at me.'

Eventually she lifts her eyes to meet mine.

'You are not a bad person.'

'How do you know?'

'I just know. You've been dealt a bad hand in life. But that isn't your fault. I promise that I only want to help you and you will always be safe with me.'

* * *

With Lena safely ensconced at the cottage, I go to work with a clear conscience. I have another glorious afternoon and evening full of Christmas joy and happy little faces. I really do love my job. I even make time on my break to visit Alvi, who has been joined on the stall by an overweight chinchilla called Norris who is extremely friendly and inquisitive. I'm not normally a huge fan of rodents but Norris wins me over in about five seconds.

At the end of my shift, Hanna pops her head round the door of the grotto, just as I'm preparing to lock up. I'm making a bit of a show of doing it all properly and by the book. Big Brother is now watching; Grottos R Us have installed an internal security system. Not that I couldn't take it out at the click of a button, but I don't want people to start asking questions about my illicit tech.

'Hey,' I say softly. She looks terrible. 'Is everything OK?'

'Can we have a quick chat? But not here.' Her gaze flicks to the new camera above the door to the grotto.

I swing my bag over my shoulder and jangle the keys at her. 'Just locking up. I'll meet you outside?'

She's leaning against Waffleicious when I find her.

'What's happened?' I ask her, a feeling of dread in the pit of my stomach.

'Well, Erin Winters reported "the situation",' she says the words with bitterness as she does the quote marks with her fingers. 'Apparently I was "allowing vagrancy to proliferate within the confines of the city" and therefore had to face consequences.'

'Hang on, that's what Erin told your boss?'

'Yeah. I'm being made an example of, apparently. She told him to either fire me or she would see to it personally that Grottos R Us had their trading licence revoked.'

'But she can't—'

'She probably can't. But my boss is a slimy dickhead with no backbone. So...'

'But it's because of me.' The words are out of my mouth

before I realise what I'm saying. 'I'm so sorry. It was me who told Lena she could stay in the grotto. Tell your boss it was me who needs to be punished instead.'

She smiles. 'I knew it was you. You're far too soft for your own good, always looking out for everyone. I can't blame you for giving a vulnerable teenage girl somewhere safe to sleep.'

'I'm so sorry,' I tell her again, guilt biting huge chunks off me. 'This is all my fault.'

'No. It's not. You were trying to do the right thing. I would have done the same.'

'What are you going to do now?' I ask.

'I have no idea. I'd grown to hate this job, but I need to pay the bills.'

She sounds so lost, so dejected, that my heart breaks for her.

So that's two new names for the Naughty List.

Colin Armstrong: CEO of Grottos R Us.

Erin Winters: the wicked witch of Christmas.

30

IN WHICH A YOUTUBER INVESTIGATES (ALBEIT BADLY)...

Eveleigh is an out-of-town shopping centre about ten miles from Exeter; it has a whole castle theme, turrets and all, and is apparently something of a Devon institution. Jessica was employed in the grotto in a costume that left very little to the imagination. Judging by the photos for this current year, it would appear that their 'Sexy Mrs Claus' thing has also become something of an institution.

A quick search of 'Exeter murder 2022' brings up a flurry of results. The homicide department was obviously busy that year. But what catches my eye is a recent result, a YouTube video posted just a few days ago. The thumbnail is your typical clickbait shocked-face picture of the content creator, a pretty young woman with long dark hair and too much makeup, but it's the text over the top that catches my attention.

Rosie Investigates: The Eveleigh Wood Murders. Shocking new information revealed!

Eveleigh Wood. Would Jessica really have killed that close to home? I click the link and wait for the twenty-second advert for some fancy dog food that costs more per month than feeding a whole family to end before the dark-haired woman's heavily made-up face stares seriously at me. She's sitting in a darkened room, illuminated by a single spotlight. I think it's intended to make her look more serious.

> Hi everyone and welcome to *Rosie Investigates*. I'm your host, Rosie Trammel, and today we're going to be talking about something that is very close to my heart.
>
> Back in 2022, there were three bodies found in Eveleigh Wood, which is literally five miles away from where I lived at the time. In fact, it was these murders that originally got me interested in true crime and are why I just had to start a YouTube channel to talk about them.
>
> I'm going to be giving you all the facts and also some guaranteed, never seen before, insider knowledge of what was happening in this area at the time, by a series of actual residents of Eveleigh.

I pause the video. I'm not sure I can cope with just how overly excited this girl is. For all she wanted to look serious, she sounds like she's been sucking on a helium balloon and every other sentence is a question. But is she actually going to have any answers? Or am I going to waste three hours of my day listening to her prattling on without ever getting to anything meaty?

I hit play again and eventually she stops talking and goes to meet one of her so-called 'expert witnesses'.

> Rosie: I'm here on the Eveleigh Estate, just a mile from where the first body was discovered by a poor woman out walking

her dog. Today we're meeting Jane, the woman's neighbour, who has agreed to give us an exclusive interview. Hi Jane, and welcome to *Rosie Investigates*.

Jane: Uh. Hi.

Rosie: So, you lived next door to the woman who found the first body. That must have been absolutely terrifying for you?

Jane: Uh. Yeah.

Rosie: To have something like that right on your doorstep? It doesn't even bear thinking about.

Jane: Uh. No.

Rosie: So, tell us everything that happened.

Jane: My neighbour, well, she's moved now, but anyway. At the time, Sharon lived next door and she had this dog, some kind of terrier thing, who she would walk every evening so he didn't bark all night. She found the man in the woods.

Rosie: And he was dead?

Jane: Uh. Yeah.

Rosie: And how did he die?

Jane: The police said he'd been stabbed.

Rosie: Wow. And did you see anything that night? Anything that might shed a light on the events leading up to that gruesome discovery?

Jane: I was on holiday. I didn't even know there'd been any murders until I came back after Christmas.

Well, Jane turned out to be an excellent witness. Is the whole of '*Rosie Investigates*' going to be as pointless? I fast-forward through the next part, mainly just Rosie talking directly to the camera, before hitting play again when there are five minutes left of the video.

So, to round up what we've seen on today's episode of *Rosie Investigates*. In 2022, there were three bodies found in Eveleigh Wood. All of them male. All of them aged between thirty and forty-five. All of them stabbed. It was clearly the work of a single individual killer. But no one has been found. No one has been charged. There hasn't even been a suspect brought in for questioning. An actual serial killer on the loose and no one seems to care.

But I care. And I'm determined to get to the bottom of this. I promise you all that we will find this killer and bring them to justice.

So if you'd like to help me, like this video and subscribe to the channel.

And I'll see you next time on *Rosie Investigates*.

Rosie Trammel doesn't know who the Eveleigh Wood killer is.

But I do.

31

FEARNE

Fucking Erin Fucking Winters.

She's making my life a living hell.

'She can't just come in and change things!' Sebastian is shouting, picking things up just to slam them back down again.

We're in the kitchen and I'm trying to make dinner, but he keeps getting in my way.

'She's demanding a twice daily inspection of all the stallholders.' The chopping board is picked up and slammed down with such force that bits of cut-up tomato fly off onto the floor.

'And,' he continues, reaching for the lid of the saucepan that is resting on the work surface. I move it from his reach, it's hot and made of glass. '*And* she wants me to ensure I do the inspections personally, sending her a fucking report. Twice a day!' The mortar makes a rather satisfying clunk as he throws it back into its pestle. If he could just stick to fiddling with that it'd be great; it's practically indestructible.

'Who the hell does she think she is?' There's a cracking noise as the ceramic salt cellar becomes a casualty to his rage. 'Fuck's sake.' He looks at it in his meaty hand as if he's wondering how the hell a broken salt cellar got there.

'Please go and sit down,' I tell him, prising the cellar from him. I'm not superstitious, but we all know that spilt salt is a terrible omen. A sign of bad luck to come. I keep that thought to myself though.

He grudgingly releases it. 'I'll get us some wine.'

'That would be nice,' I tell him, even though I suspect I'll be dealing with a smashed wineglass as well in a short while.

I busy myself cleaning up the salt and adding a new cellar to my list of things to buy when I'm next in town. At least it's a good excuse to replace the ugly ones my mother bought us as a wedding present. She didn't really approve of the marriage and she made her feelings abundantly clear by the assortment of terrible gifts she gave us. Gifts that I've been forced to use for years out of politeness and wanting to avoid rocking the boat. Perhaps I should nudge a few other things toward Sebastian this evening, like the gravy boat and the weird plate for putting dirty spoons on.

Sebastian drops a kiss on my shoulder as he places a very large glass of red wine on the counter next to me. But then he stalks to the kitchen table and hefts himself onto one of the chairs. It creaks and groans in evidence that he's still in a foul mood.

'Seriously, though, can she do this? It's my market.'

'It's on council property. And they are the licence issuer,' I tell him, keeping calm. I've done the research, looked for the loophole, the position we can take to push back against her. There's nothing we can do.

'But it isn't fair.'

'No, it isn't.'

'She's going to ruin it all.' These words are almost whispered into his wine. He sounds so sad. A life's work up in smoke because of one self-important bitch.

'I think,' I start, physically bracing myself on the kitchen counter because I know the next words out of my mouth are going to make him angry as hell. 'I think we have to go along with her. For now at least,' I add quickly.

'But—'

'I know her. Erin. She—'

'Ms Winters,' he corrects me with a wry smile.

'Sorry, Ms Winters. She has so much ambition, so much drive to succeed. But really, what can she actually do? She wants, no she *needs* the market to be a success.'

'What are you suggesting?' he narrows his eyes at me.

'Play nice. Do what she asks, or at least make her think you're going to do what she says. Get her on side.'

'Will that work?'

'I don't know. But it's got to be worth a chance.' You know what, I've convinced myself. Maybe spilt salt isn't a bad omen. Maybe it's just spilt salt and everything is going to be fine.

'This is all your fault.' He says it so quietly I wonder for a moment if I misheard. 'You and that woman's petty little feud all those years ago.'

'I don't think she's like this because we had a falling out thirteen years ago,' I say, keeping my tone light as if we're both just joking around.

'Hmm. Well, I suppose time will tell.' He takes a long drink of his wine. 'Is dinner ready yet?'

* * *

The next morning Sebastian gets up at five thirty to get to the market before the crack of dawn to work on the 'formal checklist of Christmas appropriateness' before he sees Erin at lunchtime.

He makes so much noise there isn't a chance in hell I could sleep through it.

'I listened to you last night and I'm going to cooperate with her. At least for now,' he tells me as he rummages loudly through his sock drawer in search of a matching pair. I know I should be glad that he's taking my advice, but it therefore means that it's my fault he's up this early. I can hear it in the edge of his tone.

I pause for a single beat and then sit up in bed, swinging my legs over the side into the frigid air outside the duvet. I swallow down the swearword on the tip of my tongue. 'Right then,' I say instead, with a level of enthusiasm I one hundred percent don't feel, 'let's get you some coffee to take with you.'

'You're an angel,' he says as he heads into the en suite for a quick shower.

'Shall I do you a bacon bap too?' I cross my fingers that he says no.

'When have I ever turned down one of those?'

I feel I've created a rod for my own back. But, still, happy husband, happy life and all that. Besides, now that I'm up, I could kind of do with a bacon sandwich myself. And maybe then I'll finally get to make a start on this new book.

But less than two minutes after Sebastian slams the door closed behind him – with a loud bellow that he'll be home about six this evening in time for us to go to dinner with his mother, the joy. Oh and his cousins from Peterborough who are visiting. Double joy – Immy shuffles into the kitchen wiping sleep from her eyes.

'Why are you being so loud?'

'Sorry, Immy. Did we wake you up?'

She gives me a look that says 'what do you think?' 'Dad was literally shouting.'

'Yeah. Sorry about that.' I wonder for a second why I'm apologising for him. 'He's kind of stressed at work.'

'Who's "Fucking Erin Fucking Winters"?' she asks.

'You shouldn't use that word,' I reply on autopilot. Before I realise that's the name I use. 'She's just someone who I used to work with.'

Immy cocks her head slightly. 'But you don't have a job.'

I don't tell her that writing is a job. And for three months of the year I'm basically Sebastian's assistant slash dogsbody. And that actually being a parent is a job. The pay is shit and the hours fucking ridiculous, but still. 'I used to work for the council.'

'You did?'

'Before I met your dad. And you, of course,' I add quickly.

'Oh. Cool. But that would have been years ago.'

'One of the people I worked with is now working with your dad.'

'Oh. Is this the one Dad said was a "ball-busting bitch"?' She deliberately uses the air quotes so I know it's verbatim from her father and therefore I can't say anything about her swearing.

'She's messing with how your dad runs the market.'

'Dad is seriously not happy.' She says it like it's a piece of brilliant insight and not the most obvious statement in the world.

'No. He isn't.'

Immy chews her lip for a moment. 'Perhaps I'll pop in on him later, after school. We're baking cakes in Food Prep so I'll take him one to cheer him up.'

'He'd like that. And don't forget we have dinner with your grandmother and uncles this evening.'

She scrunches up her face. 'Can't I have ballet practice?'

'You don't want to disappoint your dad, do you?' I hate using Sebastian like that, but he would be disappointed. And probably ranty. At me. Because I didn't warn him about Immy's schedule.

I could do without another reason for him to be mad at me.

32

JESSICA

Hanna and I meet for a coffee on Saturday. I'm expecting her to be a bit of a mess; well, losing your job just before Christmas – there's only twenty-five days to go – when you're a single mum can't exactly be a walk in the park, can it? Hanna's such a sweetheart and I feel so awful for the part I played in all of this, even if she said before it was what she would have done herself.

But she arrives at the cafe looking her usual calmly competent self, albeit a slightly more casual version in jeans and a chunky dark-grey jumper. She flashes me a grin when she spots me already at a table.

'Morning,' she says as she slides onto the seat in front of me.

'Well, you look…' I grope for the right word. 'Perky,' I eventually come up with.

'Ha,' she says and her eyes flash. She has definitely had some good news this morning.

I go up to the counter to order us both a ridiculously delicious-sounding cinnamon spice latte – with added whipped cream and a Speculoos doughnut on the side for good measure

– and then head back to the table. She does have good news, I can see her excitement brimming just beneath the surface.

'Spill,' I tell her.

'Spill what?' she replies, feigning innocence.

'Spill whatever it is that's making you squirm in your chair like an overexuberant puppy.' I raise an eyebrow.

'OK,' she says and leans closer, as if I've finally persuaded her to give up her secret. 'So, there's something I always wanted to do. Ever since I was a tiny girl.' She bites her bottom lip for a moment. 'Just a silly dream, really. Anyway, it wasn't like it could be a serious life choice and so I came to England when I was eighteen to be closer to Mum's side of the family. And I got a proper job, a big shiny career that I thought would give me security.' She pauses as our drinks and doughnuts are delivered. 'This looks amazing,' she tells me, staring at the entire day's allocation of sugar. 'Anyway, where was I?'

'You thought your career would give you security,' I remind her, reaching for my own doughnut with its drizzled icing and crumbled biscuit topping.

'Right, yes.' She snaps her fingers and points one at me. 'But it was all just a lie. When it came down to it, everything I'd worked for, all those hours of overtime, *unpaid* overtime, meant nothing to Grottos R Us. I mean, maybe it's more fool me for thinking my boss actually cared. Or for thinking a company called Grottos R Us could actually be taken seriously in the first place. But, anyway, they fired me without even a second thought. Poof! Ten years and then just nothing.'

'Don't they have to pay you some kind of severance?'

She smiles. 'Well, they don't think so. As far as they're concerned I was fired for gross misconduct. But,' she puts up her hand to stop me interjecting when she sees me open my mouth to speak. 'I spoke to a lawyer yesterday and she's already suggested to them that they would really rather make me redundant, with a nice little package to go with it, rather than risk me suing them for unfair dismissal.'

'Well that's—'

'That, Jessica, is a Christmas miracle. And then this morning I had a phone call from Rovaniemi.'

I raise an eyebrow so she knows to elaborate on what she's talking about.

'It's a city in Finland, the capital of Lapland. It's where my dad's from, where Alvi and I grew up.'

'It sounds cold,' I say.

'Freezing. And dark. In the winter at least. But it's also magical. And it's home.' A nostalgic smile tugs at the corner of her mouth. 'And it's where Santa's workshop is. That's who was calling this morning.'

'Santa?'

'Well, not actual Santa.' She laughs. 'I always wanted to work there. To be one of the tour guides. But it's super competitive to get one of those jobs.'

'That was your dream?'

'It sounds stupid, I know.'

'It doesn't sound stupid. It sounds like utter perfection.'

She smiles. 'It is. And they want me to interview with them next week, but it sounds like it's more of a formality. They're desperate for someone who knows sign language.'

I make a little squeak of excitement. 'That's amazing,' I tell her.

'Yeah. Though in some ways I don't want to leave Ellsbury. Mine and Kelsie's lives are here. Alvi is here. You'll have to look after him.' She looks at me pointedly. 'But I think this could be just what Kelsie and I need.'

'It sounds perfect,' I tell her, my heart almost bursting with happiness for my new friend.

So, given how this has worked out, do I need to take Erin Winters and the CEO of Grottos R Us off the Naughty List?

Hmm. I think I should leave them there, just for a little while longer. You shouldn't excuse bad actions just because the outcome turns out OK.

* * *

I head into work that afternoon still on a high about Hanna's amazing news. I'm just so glad things are working out for her and I'll be keeping my fingers permanently crossed until after her interview next week.

I'm still grinning like a loon as I go to make coffee in the staffroom during my mid-shift break. I've decided to take the CEO of Grottos R Us – Mr Colin Armstrong – off the Naughty List given that he has now agreed to pay up for firing Hanna. I'm a little undecided about Erin Winters. That is, until I'm standing in front of the staff coffee station.

Erin has cemented her position on the list. Her name now written in indelible ink. There's a piece of paper where the kettle should be:

All appliances have been removed pending PAT testing for electrical safety. EW

The wicked witch of Christmas has stolen my coffee.

I'm forced to buy a six-pound gingerbread latte from The Coffee Cabin and I'm just waiting for the barista to add the final touches – toffee sauce and sprinkles in the shape of tiny little gingerbread men – when Lena comes running up to me.

'I got the job,' she says, bouncing on her toes in excitement. 'The Festive Fry. I start tomorrow,' she tells me breathlessly. 'And they're paying proper minimum wage, even though technically they don't have to.' She says this last bit like they're doing her a favour.

'Hang on. So what are they paying?' I'm saying they, but really I mean David Bennett; it is his company who manages The Festive Fry after all.

'Six pound forty an hour.'

That's minimum wage for a young person? I've basically just spent that on a coffee. 'And why wouldn't they have to pay minimum wage?'

'Because technically I'm not "school leaving" age.' She says it like I'm a bit thick. Like I should know the ins and outs of minimum wage regulations in the UK.

Although now I think about it, I might add whoever decided young people should earn less to the Naughty List; the whole thing just reeks of exploitation. But she's so excited and I don't want to burst her bubble. 'That's great. I suppose we need to have celebratory waffles,' I tell her, motioning toward the stand.

'Deal.' She grins and does a dance on the spot.

***

A few days later and the shine has already worn off Lena's new job.

'I stink of fried fish,' she moans, stripping off her uniform fleece in the kitchen so she can put it straight in the washing machine.

'I thought you liked fried fish?'

'To *eat*, yes. But not to smell like.' She wrinkles her nose in disgust.

'I'm making hot chocolate, do you want one?' I ask, already taking two mugs out of the cupboard. I don't think she's ever refused a hot chocolate.

'Please. Do we have any cream or marshmallows?' She turns to me, her expression hopeful.

'Of course. Both.'

'Perfect.' She grins.

'Is there something you want to share?' I ask her. There's a shimmer of energy around her, like she has a secret and she's desperate to tell someone but doesn't know if she should.

'No.' But she answers too quickly.

'Really?' I give her time to contemplate her answer as I get out the mini whisk to make sure the hot chocolate is smooth. I add a healthy scoop of marshmallows to each mug and then a towering swirl of squirty cream.

'Do you remember when you said you thought David Bennett might be up to something dodgy?' she asks.

'Yes.'

'Well... I overheard something today. He was sorting out a delivery and I don't think he realised I was in the storeroom getting more sauces. Someone keeps nicking them off the counter and I have to keep schlepping over to the dry store.' She makes a face. 'Such a pain in the arse.'

'What did you overhear?' I ask, to try to bring her story back on track.

'Right. Yes. So, I was in the storeroom and he was outside with Aleksis. He's the hot one with the short hair?'

I nod. I know who she means. Not that I agree with her assertion on his 'hotness' given he's young enough to be my son, but she thinks he is.

'Yeah. So, David is laughing and joking around, but I can tell from Aleksis's tone that he's not really enjoying himself. And then Aleksis asks if he can take a few days to go back home to Latvia as his grandmother isn't very well. And then David says no, that the market is too busy. So Aleksis says that there's plenty of people to cover his shifts and he'd only be a couple of days. But David refuses.' She sits back in her chair and smiles at me.

'Am I missing something?' I ask.

'David is doing something dodgy.'

'Although I hate to say it, because he *is* being unkind, refusing someone's holiday request doesn't make him dodgy. It makes him a horrible man, yes, but not a criminal.'

'Aleksis isn't asking because he wants a holiday request,' Lena says. 'He's asking because David has his passport.'

'Oh.' Now that makes things very different. And perhaps it helps fill in the gaps with what I heard the twins, Sofia and Valentina, whispering about in Spanish.

'David has Aleksis's passport and the ones for the twins on the Sausage Swing and for one of the guys who works on the Crumble Top. He says he'll give them back if they finish the season on the market and only if they've settled all their debts to him.'

'Why would they have debts to him?'

'They rent rooms in one of his properties.'

'Do you know what he pays them?' I ask.

'Same as me. But their rent is stupidly high.'

'It sounds like—'

'It's illegal,' she interrupts me. 'Taking their passports is illegal. Overcharging on rent is illegal. I looked it up.' She spreads her hands out on the table in front of her. 'See? He's definitely dodgy. And, more than that, if Aleksis doesn't get his passport then he can't go home to Latvia to see his gran. What if she dies before he can make it back? Well, that's not just illegal. It's cruel.'

'What do you think we should do about it?' I ask her as she finishes telling me all the details.

'We need to get their passports back.' She makes it sound so obvious.

'Do you think people like him should be stopped?'

She nods.

'Do you think,' I drop my voice and maintain eye contact with her, 'people like him should be punished?'

I see her pupils flare slightly on the word punish. She nods again.

'And you'll leave this to me to sort out?' I say, my voice serious. 'You aren't to get involved.'

'I could help.'

'No, you can't.' My tone is harsh. I can't make her my accomplice. She can have nothing to do with this.

'Fine. Just promise you'll make sure Aleksis can go home.'

'I promise.'

The Naughty List is getting pretty long this year.

I add David Bennett's name to the very top, in red ink and underlined.

I'm going to enjoy this one.

33

FEARNE

I wake up the next morning to an email in my inbox from the people at the Steamies awards.

> Just checking you received our email concerning your nomination. We're super excited to have you join us this year! Can you let us know how many tickets you need for the event?

I guess I'd better reply and tell them I can't make it. It hurts my soul to have to turn this down. I've seen the full line-up of nominees and the guest list for the gala will be like a 'who's who' of the erotic fiction world. Some of my all-time favourite authors will be there. And I have to miss it.

I get a text from Jessica asking if I fancy an early lunch today. I'm meant to be at the market helping Sebastian but, if I'm honest, I just don't give a shit. I'm directing all my anger about the Steamies toward him – maybe fairly, maybe not; the jury's out – and so I'm hardly inclined to do him a favour.

Fuck him.

> I'm in xx

I message back to Jessica.

A new sushi place opened a few weeks ago on a lane just off the high street. Apparently, it's very good, but so far most of the population of Ellsbury have refused to relinquish their burgers and steaks and so it's pretty quiet this lunchtime. I've been wanting to try it but Sebastian is adamant that 'raw fish gives you food poisoning'.

'They do chicken and even veggie options,' I'd told him.

'Well then it isn't sushi, is it.' Not a question, a blanket statement that he was so correct I couldn't possibly disagree. I remember squaring my shoulders, ready for a fight: sushi is the rice and the raw fish is actually sashimi. But I just couldn't be bothered. And so we didn't go to Sushi Nara.

Jessica is looking particularly radiant this lunchtime; she's wearing a gorgeous dark-green knitted dress with a sweetheart neckline and knee-high black leather boots, her silver hair pulled back into a messy bun.

'You're looking fab,' I tell her as I kiss her cheek.

'Likewise,' she tells me. 'Your hair looks incredible.'

The truth is that I box-dyed it last night to cover up the encroaching greys. I know she has fully embraced hers and I'm a little embarrassed that I'm so vain I feel the need to carry on dyeing mine. So I just mumble a thanks and try to change the subject. 'So, have you been here before?' I ask, motioning around me.

'No. But I stumbled across their Instagram and thought it looked amazing.'

And it is. We order a range of nigiri: amaebi maguro; hotate; spicy salmon tamaki; California roll; pork gyoza; and virgin coladas to wash it down with. It's so good we even stop talking as we shovel food into our mouths like a pair of gannets.

'Best. Sushi. Ever,' Jessica concludes, sitting back in her seat and carefully placing her napkin onto her now empty plate. 'And I have eaten a lot of sushi.'

'You never really talk much about where you were living before,' I say. Normally people like to talk about themselves, they will tell you stories about where they grew up and that time they went to Thailand and how their cousin once licked a frozen telegraph pole for a bet and got his tongue stuck and it was completely hilarious – although maybe not for the cousin at the time. And, if they're new to a place, they will tell you all about the difference between this city and where they lived before, often in excruciating detail. One of the first things I learnt as a novelist was to listen to people, everyone has a backstory and many of them can be mined for characters like panning for gold.

'Oh. It wasn't very interesting.' That's all Jessica has to say.

'Where was it?' I ask.

'Not too far, just a smallish city a few hours away.' She shrugs as if to say there's nothing more of note. 'Shall we have dessert? Apparently their dorayaki are to die for.'

'Sounds good.' I decide not to push her any more about her past. Perhaps there's something – or someone – she's trying to leave behind her. I change the subject. 'And how's the gorgeous Alvi?'

Jessica blushes. She definitely has a crush on him. 'Fine,' she says quickly, but doesn't offer anything else.

I cast around for something else to talk about. But thinking about Alvi has made me think of his sister. 'You know, I haven't seen Hanna for a few days. Normally we run into each other at the market.'

'Erin had her fired.'

'What? Are you serious?'

'Yep. But she's going to Rovaniemi to interview for Santa so it's all turning out OK in the end.'

I pause. I have too many questions and I need to figure out which order to ask them in. 'Do you know why?'

She does this funny little shrug. She probably doesn't know all the details to be fair and I'm sure I can find out the gossip. But she does seem to know about Hanna's plans now so I focus my questions on that. 'Rovaniemi?'

'It's in Finland, right up by the North Pole.'

'Santa?'

'Santa's workshop is in Rovaniemi. She always wanted to be a tour guide there and now they need someone who can sign.'

'Has she already gone?'

'Yesterday.'

But there's one question I don't ask her. *Why didn't Sebastian tell me?*

* * *

'Hey,' I say, poking my head around the door of the office at the market. I've come here straight from lunch with Jessica and I find him sitting alone in the half-light, scowling at two sheets of paper in front of him. One is his own checklist; I recognise the font he always uses – 18 point in Times New Roman, big enough to look like the words should be shouted, but somehow still so dull you could cry. The other page is covered in dense text, a row of small neat boxes down the side – I can only assume this is Erin's list. 'You didn't tell me Hanna got fired.'

'Hanna?'

'From Grottos R Us?'

He looks confused. 'What are you talking about?'

'I just ran into Jessica. Mrs Claus,' I add for context. I don't tell him we went for sushi when I told him I was too busy to help him earlier. 'She said that Hanna got fired.'

'Hanna?'

'Yes. From Grottos R Us.' Jeez this conversation is going nowhere.

'Got fired?'

'Yes. You didn't know?' This feels odd. It's exactly the kind of thing he *should* know.

He picks up his phone and angrily jabs at the screen. 'I need to speak to Colin Armstrong.' It's a demand and not a question. 'No, not tomorrow. I need to speak to him now.' He rolls his eyes at me in the exact same way Immy does.

The wind picks up around me, reminding me it's the middle of winter and I'm not wearing a proper coat. I step fully inside the office and close the door behind me before sinking into one of the chairs.

Sebastian puts the call onto loud speaker so I can hear everything.

'Hello, Colin Armstrong speaking.' Now, I have met the CEO of Grottos R Us and he is a complete twat. Self-righteous, thinks he's God's gift to business, more than a little misogynistic, you know the type.

'Colin. Good afternoon. It's Sebastian Dixon.'

'Sebastian Dixon...' Colin sounds like he has no idea who my husband is and I watch as Sebastian bristles.

'From the Ellsbury Christmas Market?'

'Oh. Yes. Of course.' He doesn't actually sound like he has any idea who he's talking to though. I sat next to him at a Christmas gala last year. He said a whole three words to me. 'Pass the salt.' It was fun.

'I've heard through the grapevine that there's been a change in personnel.'

'Right.'

'A change at your end, that impacts the way the grotto here at Ellsbury might operate.'

'Right.'

'I understand that Hanna is no longer with your company.'

'She is not.'

I can feel Sebastian's anger rising quickly. 'Well, I need to know the potential impact this will have on my operation.'

'I'm afraid I don't understand.'

I reach out and touch his hand gently. A subtle note of warning that he needs to keep his cool. He shrugs me off. 'Mr Armstrong. I can tell you're not understanding. We have a contract. One that stipulates how Grottos R Us will operate to ensure everything at the market runs smoothly.'

'I do understand that, Mr Coxon.'

'Dixon.'

'Apologies. Now, Mr Dixon, the grotto will continue to operate as it always has. Your boss has already been informed of our plans and I have apologised for the behaviour of my rogue employee and ensured the situation has been dealt with.'

'My boss?' Sebastian asks. My heart sinks. I know exactly who Colin Armstrong has been talking to.

'Yes. Erin Winters. She's got some spunk that one, I can tell you.' He laughs, rather more raucously than is strictly necessary in my opinion.

'Erin Winters is not my boss,' Sebastian replies through gritted teeth.

'Yes she is.'

'No. She. Is. Not.'

'Oh. She sounded pretty confident that she was in charge of

things over in Ellsbury. I suggest you schedule a meeting with her to get the full download.'

Sebastian hangs up the call and sits frozen with his finger held just above the screen. He stays like that for a full thirty seconds. I count them, waiting for him to react.

'That. Fucking. Woman,' he says eventually, enunciating each word carefully. 'How dare she? How dare she come in here and pretend that she can run this place better than we can.'

The use of 'we' takes me aback for a moment. 'She has no idea,' I say. I decide to test the idea of 'we' in this endeavour. 'We've been doing this for years.'

'Exactly.' He slaps the desk. 'Sorry,' he apologises when he sees me jump in my seat. 'We need to do something, Fearne. I can't play nice if she's going to act like she's my boss and then withhold important information from me.'

'We'll think of something,' I promise.

'Will we?' He doesn't sound fully convinced.

'We always do.'

He smiles at me. 'You're right. We make a good team, you and I.'

On the one hand, it feels good to form a united front with my husband. A bit more like the old days.

On the other hand, Erin Winters is seriously starting to piss me off.

34

JESSICA

Lena has taken on some additional shifts doing food prep in the Hot Eatz warehouse kitchen on the industrial estate. This is where David Bennett has his office, literally one of those places with a mezzanine room and a window so he can look out from his ivory tower at his workers below. She left at nine this morning, promising to return home with more dirt on him. She thinks we're accomplices, that we're in this together.

But she is a seventeen-year-old girl and I will not drag her into the actual details. It's bad enough that she is a side witness to murder; actually, it's bad enough that she's being forced to already confront the seedy realities of our world. She should still be going to school every day and her biggest worries should be having a crush on a boy in her class and whether she wants to carry on with hockey because it's a massive time thief and comes with a risk of getting hit by someone's rogue stick. Those are seventeen-year-old girl problems. Not being homeless and then witness to a stranger murdering the guy who tried to abduct you and who you are now living with temporarily while she plots how to murder your boss.

I need to get this kill done. And quickly.

So, with Lena out all day, once again I take out the 'Jessica's Naughty List' pad and carefully remove the next sheet.

David Bennett.
Exploitation.

It's the best word I can think of for what he's doing, but I don't quite feel it captures the true disgracefulness of his crimes. Of the human impact of his actions.

I chew the top of the pen as I think about possible methods. David Bennett is fairly well respected, at least by other influential types. He's one of those guys people will mourn and call 'a top bloke' and a whole load of other monikers that sound positive but are really just empty platitudes. His death will be noticed. I need to dig into his life a little more, see what else he spends his time doing.

And I think I need to take this one away from the market.

It turns out – not that I'm really surprised – that David Bennett has a girlfriend who is creepily young by comparison to him. She's beautiful too, although her eyes look sad as she stares at me from my screen. I've found her Instagram and it's full of images of her posing in their huge house, their huge *white* house. Seriously, everything is white, including the kettle and the toaster and the walls and the floor and even the sofa – which just feels like a mulled wine disaster waiting to happen. Her outfit is the only real colour in any of the pictures, a splash of red silk, a swirl of green wool. All that white with just a tiny pop of colour makes her Instagram grid almost mesmerising.

Luckily for me, she's just posted about heading back to the US for a week to visit her parents. So at least I don't have to factor a live-in girlfriend with an artistic eye for a good social media aesthetic into the equation.

Something about her grid makes me keep scrolling. And then I find blue. Ooh. They have a swimming pool. An *indoor* swimming pool no less.

I've never staged an accident before. Could I pull off making it look like he drowned in his own pool? Or is that a bit passé?

Hang on. I scroll a little further and find a picture of the hot tub in their garden. *'Davey and I just love relaxing in the tub after a hard day's work'*, the caption says. I look through the comments.

PeachPieGal
Super jell. I'd be in there every night.

EllsburyElla
We are! Davey pretty much lives out there.

Interesting. Perhaps he shouldn't drown in his own *pool*. Perhaps the hot tub is a better option?

I take a walk. First, I head to the industrial estate and the warehouse where Lena will be hard at work slicing onions for a pittance. I'm proud of her though, she's got grit and determination and I think, with the right opportunities, she's going to go far in life. Anyway, all I want to know is if David Bennett is also inside the warehouse. His car – a Porsche 911, just to be the ultimate mid-life crisis cliche – is sitting in his own designated space. David Bennett: Hospitality Mogul, the little sign says.

I keep on walking. The Bennett house is only a few streets away, certainly close enough for him to walk to work, but then he wouldn't be able to show off the fancy car he bought by paying poverty wages to desperate teens and overseas workers whose passports he steals.

All the houses on Fairway Drive are identical, all huge but utterly soulless newbuilds, thrown up over the last few years by developers looking to make their fortunes from people with money but absolutely no taste. Their gardens overlook one of Ellsbury's three golf courses. But – luckily for me and unluckily for Mr Bennett – it's the least expensive of them all and the company that owns it doesn't bother much with security or fences. In fact, I can walk onto the course via a footpath and then make my way directly into his garden through the scraggly looking plants along the border, which I think he's hoping will one day grow into a lovely thick hedge. This is almost too easy.

The hot tub sits on the decked area behind the house, it's a covered one but I can see a tiny wisp of steam around the edges so I know it's definitely switched on. An empty bottle of what looks like Jack Daniels lies on its side on the ground beside the steps so he obviously uses it regularly. Hmm... now that gives me an idea.

There's an outdoor bar, complete with tall stools and what looks like a thin fire pit built into the top. It's like he went to some kind of expo for influencers and bought everything he saw. There's an array of bottles lined up behind the bar, everything from flavoured vodkas to Malibu to Jägermeister. But no Jack Daniels. I open the cupboards underneath and find the extra stock. Literally bottles and bottles of the stuff. How much does he drink? The answer is evidently *a lot*. Probably enough that it's a known problem amongst his friends and family. Possibly enough that people might not ask too many questions when he gets hammered and drowns in his own hot tub.

But the question remains as to how I can get him to drink enough to drown him without leaving a trace?

Or is there another way? I think back to the little stash I swiped from Max Kirby before I killed him. Would people buy it if David Bennett was dabbling with recreational drugs on top of all that whiskey?

* * *

I return to the Bennett house after my shift that evening. No time like the present and all that. He's exactly where I hoped he would be. Facing towards the house, lazing into the corner with both hairy arms draped over the sides of the hot tub. A bottle of whiskey in one hand. He's not even bothering with a glass. His head lolls a little as I watch him, like he's struggling to support the weight of it.

Hmm... a drunk man in a hot tub. Whatever could go wrong here?

There's only a tiny sliver of amber liquid left and I wait until he realises the bottle is basically empty. 'Good evening, Mr Bennett,' I say as I walk up to him. He twists in the hot tub to look at me.

'What the fuck? Who are you?'

I'm wearing plain black leggings and a matching jacket, my features concealed by the hood I've pulled up. Oh, and gloves, of course. I'm not an amateur.

'Get out of my garden.' He starts to stand up, but then swiftly sits down again. I guess 'Little David' is out.

'Hey, don't be mean.' I stick out my bottom lip into a pout. 'I brought you a present.' I hand him a 'new' bottle of Jack Daniels, even though it's really one of the ones I swiped earlier.

'Hang on, I recognise you,' he says, as he takes the bottle. 'You work at the Christmas market.' He points a finger at me.

'I'm Mrs Claus in the grotto.'

'Oh. Cool,' he says and nods a few times as if his brain is trying to process the information. 'Umm. Thanks for the Jack. My favourite.' He seems to have decided I'm not a threat at all, even if perhaps he has realised that it's rather bizarre I'm here in his garden with whiskey for him.

'Aren't you going to drink it?' I ask sweetly, looking pointedly at the bottle.

For a moment I see the indecision in his eyes. He isn't sure if he should drink the gift or run for the hills with 'Little David' flapping in the wind. He makes the wrong choice and twists the cap off the Jack Daniels before taking a large slug.

'Good?' I ask.

He nods.

He didn't notice the bottle wasn't brand new. He didn't notice any change in taste from the ground-up tablets I put inside. They were small and blue and from the stash I took from Max Kirby. I'm assuming some kind of benzo, like diazepam or something. He takes another huge drink and when he's finished I notice almost a quarter of the bottle has gone. This guy can really drink.

'So, who are you again?' he asks, his head lolling forward. He blinks a few times as he tries to regain his composure.

'I'm your day of reckoning,' I tell him.

'The fuck?'

'Your day of reckoning.' I don't like that he's made me repeat it. It kind of ruined the effect if I'm honest. 'I need the code to the safe where you keep all their passports.'

'Safe?'

Did I give him too much? To be honest I assumed we'd have a bit of time for a chat before the effects of the booze and drugs took hold. But, then again, I didn't expect him to gulp it down like a man finding water in the desert.

'Where do you keep the passports for the people who work for you?' I speak slowly, carefully, trying my best to make sure he understands what I'm asking.

'Desk.' He lifts his hand and points toward a window on the second floor of the house. His home office, I guess. Then the hand falls into the water with a splash, as if he no longer has the strength to hold it up. 'I feel...' but he trails off as he slumps forward.

I grab the bottle before it hits the water.

He tries to sit up again, but he can't. He keeps sliding back under the surface.

I put the lid back on the Jack Daniels; I'll take this bottle home with me to destroy the evidence that the benzos were mixed in. I head over to the bar and get a fresh bottle, open it and then pour about a third out into the small sink. Then I put it over by the hot tub as if he was drinking this one just before... well, we all know what's going to happen to him.

He's still struggling. Not quite ready to give up entirely. I glance at my watch. It's getting late and I want to get home and have a glass of wine and read a couple more of the great anthology of Christmas stories I've been enjoying these past few days.

It takes him another few minutes before he stops moving and the water closes over his head for the last time. What a way to die: in your hot tub with your 'Little David' out, high on benzos and full of Jack Daniels.

I admire my handiwork for another minute or so and then I head into the house to get those passports. Everyone has an individual locker in the staffroom at the market and I'm sure there's enough of a gap around the edge to slide each one inside. It'll be a Christmas miracle for everyone involved and I'm pretty sure no one will ever say a thing to the police about it.

35

FEARNE

The Sausage Swing is still boarded up when I head into the market for ten in the morning. Normally there's the smell of bratwurst roasting to entice me into a second breakfast, but today there's nothing except a rather bored-looking Valentina – or possibly Sofia, I still struggle to tell them apart – leaning against the stall.

'Everything alright?' I call out to her.

'Mr Bennett is late.'

'That's not very like him.'

'He is *never* late.' She puts a strong emphasis on the never. It's true. There is so much money to be made at the market and David Bennett makes sure he can squeeze out every single penny. Which includes being open on time every day, with a stack of freshly cooked items to tempt the punters coming in.

'Maybe he's sick?'

'I hope not,' says a voice behind me. I turn to find the other twin. Ah, so it was Sofia I was talking to before, Valentina has slightly longer hair than her sister.

'If he doesn't open, he won't pay us.' Valentina looks distraught at the idea.

'We have spare keys in the office. Do you know how everything runs?' I ask.

'Of course. But we have no float or anything.'

'Let me see what I can do.'

Twenty minutes later and all food concessions run by David Bennett are open and the staff are prepping for the day ahead. A few other stallholders have chipped in to make up a big enough float to get them going, and I'm just putting up some handwritten signs to request card payments where possible.

'You can't have a handwritten sign.' Her voice is shrill in my ear and the hairs on the back of my neck immediately stand up on end.

'Good morning, Erin,' I say, turning to face her.

'Ms Winters,' she corrects.

I merely raise an eyebrow at her. Is she serious that she wants me to call her *Ms Winters*, after all this time?

'You can't have these signs up. It looks like a shambles.'

'It was either this or no food stands,' I tell her simply.

'But it looks like a mess.'

'It looks better than having four of the chalets closed.'

'I'm going to file an official report of non-compliance,' she says and takes out her phone to take some photos of the offending items. 'In fact, I think I will make it even clearer that there are explicit rules to be followed in terms of the way this place looks. With significant penalties for people who breach them.'

'You're going to fine David Bennett?' Erin works for the Chief Executive of Ellsbury Council. David Bennett is his brother-in-law. Personally, I probably wouldn't piss off my boss like that.

'Of course not.' She smiles this saccharine grin at me as she puts her phone away. 'I'm going to fine *you* for putting up the signs. Do have a good day, Mrs Dixon.' And then she walks away, leaving me staring at her.

She can't do that. *Surely* she can't do that.

* * *

Two hours later, I hear Sebastian swearing in the office and so I hurry to find out what's wrong.

'That fucking woman has issued new rules. With fines for my stallholders if they don't comply. *My* stallholders. I'm going to ring her boss. This has gone too far.'

He calls the council offices and demands to speak to the Chief Executive.

He hasn't put it on speaker so I can't hear the person on the other end of the line. But I can tell from the vein on my husband's forehead and the way it's starting to bulge, that he's getting fobbed off.

'Yes. It is urgent,' Sebastian says. There's a pause as he listens to the other person again. 'Yes. It is important. I'm from the Ellsbury Christmas Market and there's a serious issue at hand.' Again, a pause. 'No. Erin Winters cannot deal with the problem. I need to speak to the Chief Executive.'

I can feel his blood pressure rising from here.

'Right then. Well, I understand. If you could get him to call me as soon as possible. Yes. Thank you.' He hangs up the call and turns to me. 'Apparently the Chief Exec isn't at work today. Some kind of family emergency.'

'Did they say which part of the family?' Sebastian looks at me blankly. 'He's David Bennett's brother-in-law,' I explain. 'David also didn't come to work today.'

'Do you think they're connected?'

We're interrupted by a loud rapping on the office door.

'I need to talk to you, Fearne.' It's Bella Donna. Of course it is. I really don't have the energy to deal with her today.

'What is it?'

'The notice.'

'What notice?' She's already testing my patience.

'In the staffroom. About non-compliance.'

'She fucking better not have,' Sebastian mutters under his breath as he stands up. 'I'll go and see,' he tells me, leaving me alone with Bella.

'I have been extremely patient about the whole energy being off here.' She's lying. Or perhaps she's just forgotten that huge scene she caused when I was trying to enjoy a quiet afternoon gin and tonic. 'But only because I've been able to work around it with the changes I made to the layout of my stall.'

She's referring to the way she has strung up a million of her stupid crystals across the front, in total violation of the aesthetics guidelines but something I convinced Sebastian to turn a blind eye to. 'Right,' I say, hoping she's going to get to the point quickly so I can send her on her way. I really need a coffee.

'So, if I can't have my crystals to realign the energy around the stall, then we are back to having a problem.' She taps her foot a little as if I'm meant to jump in with an answer to her woes and I'm being tardy in my response.

'Well, I don't...'

'Not good enough.' She turns and stalks out of the office.

* * *

A little after 4 p.m. – and just as I'm debating if I can slope off to get a coffee and do more work on my new Cherry Dubois book –

two uniformed police officers arrive at the market. Sebastian leads them into the little office and offers them a seat.

Neither of them look particularly comfortable, and the shorter of the two looks like this might be his first day of work after leaving school. But the taller one clears his throat and then removes his hat, tucking it under his arm. I'm instantly more alert; he's obviously here with some kind of terrible news. My brain spins as I go through a whole series of potential what ifs and awful situations.

'Is Immy alright?' Sebastian blurts out, having obviously landed on the same terrible scenario as I did.

'Immy?' The shorter one pulls out a notebook and begins to flick through the pages. 'I... who...?'

'Immy's our daughter,' Sebastian tells him. 'Has something happened to her?' There's an urgency in his voice, intertwined with a tone that I can only describe as 'papa bear'.

'Oh. No. Sorry,' the taller officer says. 'Um. This is about one of your stallholders. We regret to inform you that they were found dead this morning.'

'David Bennett,' I say under my breath.

'Yes.' The young one snaps his head round to stare at me. 'How did you know that?'

'He didn't come into work. It was unusual. That's all.'

'Oh. Well, that makes sense.'

'What happened?' I ask.

'It looks like an accident. He was found in his hot tub.'

The news spreads through the market like wildfire and instantly David Bennett's untimely demise becomes all everyone is talking about. I take a little walk through the stalls, making sure everything is running smoothly while Sebastian starts to make some calls to see what happens now. David Bennett didn't have a second in command, no one to instantly step into his

How to Slay at Christmas

shoes and keep everything running, and so Sebastian is getting worked up.

'We are literally not talking about this,' I tell Bella Donna the moment I see her, even going so far as to put up my hand as if that would physically stop her.

'I don't think you're taking me seriously,' she says.

Yeah, no shit.

36

JESSICA

So far, so good. The whole 'poor David had an accident' thing looks like it's sticking. No one yet has mentioned the fact he was naked. Or that he'd taken any drugs. But then I suppose those aren't the details the family will want to be disclosed to the gossipy general public.

I didn't tell Lena what I did. I figured it was better for her to have proper culpable deniability.

'I know it was you,' she tells me through a mouthful of Coco Pops.

'What was me?' I ask innocently.

'David Bennett.'

'He drowned after drinking too much,' I say, turning round to butter my toast the second it pops up. There's nothing like a slice of sourdough toast with lashings of slightly salted butter melted onto it.

'How did you do it?' she asks and I can hear the excitement in her voice. I really do need to nip this fascination with death and destruction in the bud. I could save her from a life like mine. Not that I don't like what I do. But it's not exactly a respectable pastime is it? When people ask what you do for fun, it would be far easier if you could say you like reading or building Lego or whatever, rather than killing scrooges.

'I promise I didn't kill him.' I hate lying to her but, really, what is the alternative here?

'You're lying. I'll figure it out eventually,' she tells me before cramming another huge spoonful of cereal into her mouth.

I decide to try to distract her with the offer of a trip into town. We're both starting our shifts later today so there's plenty of time to take her shopping this morning to get a few things. She needs new trainers for work and a couple more jumpers and another pair of jeans. Not to mention another few pairs of underwear and socks.

'I'm honestly fine with what I have,' she tells me.

'You're having to put a wash on every other day,' I point out.

'But—'

'It's my treat,' I tell her. My own finances have been taking a bit of a battering recently but I'm going to dip into my emergency savings. I'm sure I'll be able to get myself back on track in the spring when I start playing poker again.

'Hush money,' she says without emotion.

'More just that I'd like to live in a house that doesn't smell of damp clothes all the time,' I reply. But she was right the first time.

We head into town and beeline toward the new Stradivarius store that opened a few weeks ago. I did some research this morning and apparently that is where all the teenagers are shopping, even though I thought it was a make of violin. Their stuff is quite nice, but I'm not going to tell Lena that.

She quickly finds an armful of things to try on: jeans, jumpers, a couple of t-shirts, and we head toward the changing rooms. Fearne is standing outside, waiting for someone with a bored look on her face and her phone in her hand.

'Fearne,' I say as we get closer.

'Oh, Jessica, hi.' She smiles and puts her phone back in her pocket. 'I see you got roped into shopping too.' She looks at all the things Lena is holding. 'You must be Lena?' she says, imbuing her voice with kindness. 'Jessica has told me lots about you.'

'Uh. Hi,' Lena replies a little awkwardly. 'Um, I'd better try these on.'

'How's she getting on?' Fearne asks once Lena has vanished into the bowels of the changing rooms.

'OK. I think. It's tough. I just don't know what happens next. All I want is for her to have a normal life but I don't know how to make that a reality.'

Fearne gives me an encouraging smile. 'Well, I'm here if there's anything I can do to help.'

'Thank you,' I reply. A large group of teens barrels past us, one jostling into me so I step closer to Fearne.

'School inset day,' Fearne says. 'Hence all the kids. I don't think I've ever seen the town this busy.'

We move on to chat about nothing in particular for another ten minutes. Just as I'm growing impatient, Immy beats Lena out of the changing rooms by a matter of seconds.

'Ooh, that jumper is lush,' Immy says when she sees what Lena is holding. Then she takes a step backwards and scrutinises Lena. 'Hey, I think I know you.'

Lena narrows her eyes at Immy.

Then Immy pulls her long hair back from her face and twists it into a bun.

'We used to do classes at the same dance school,' Lena exclaims. 'I recognise you now.'

'Yeah, I look totally different with my hair down.' Immy shrugs as if this is a lifelong affliction. 'Are you getting that jumper?'

Lena nods and the four of us shuffle off to the tills.

'Can we go to Serendipity?' Immy asks when we've paid. Fearne nods and Immy and Lena head off at a speed far greater than mine.

'We'll catch you up,' I call after them. Then I turn to Fearne. 'What is Serendipity?' I ask. I'm so out of touch with teenagers. Little children I can do, but kids are a whole different ballgame once they hit twelve and it only gets worse from there.

'A makeup brand. They do the little cases you can slot everything into,' Fearne explains. 'Some influencer model-type person that Immy loves, I think she's called Tori? But, anyway, she does all their ads and Immy is obsessed.'

'Sounds...'

'Expensive? Yeah.' She nods ruefully. 'But what can you do?'

We catch up with the girls who are squealing with delight over some new shade of mascara 'that's just dropped'. I make a mental note to get one of these PALETTES Makeup Systems – which sounds like pure marketing speak – for Lena for Christmas.

'Jessica and I are going to the cafe next door,' Fearne tells the girls. 'Come find us in there when you're done, OK?' They both nod. Fearne turns to me. 'They put Baileys in the hot chocolate if you ask nicely.'

'Well, that's me sold,' I say and we link arms as we make our way there.

'You heard about the guy who runs the food concession?' Fearne asks me as we sit in the warmth with our drinks, which have so much Baileys in that I'm very glad I don't have to drive later.

I nod. 'Imagine drowning in your own pool.'

'Hot tub,' she corrects me. 'Couldn't have happened to a nicer person,' she adds quietly, making it very clear she did not feel particularly sympathetic to the dead.

'You didn't like him?'

'He was a weasel. Sebastian tried to block his application for such a large concession, but the Mayor himself insisted David Bennett got a whole ton of the stalls.' I remember Hanna telling me about bribery and corruption, she'd intimated that Sebastian was in on it, but maybe he wasn't. 'How's Lena taking it, she's been working on The Festive Fry, hasn't she?'

'Oh, she's OK. I don't think she's given him too much thought to be honest. I'm not sure he was the best boss in the world.'

'Oh, trust me, I could tell you some stories. I won't though,' Fearne adds quickly. 'You can't besmirch the dead, and all that.'

'Can't you?' I ask, with a raised eyebrow.

'All I'm going to say is that sometimes people get what is coming to them and I'm not sure I'm going to actually shed a tear for David Bennett.'

I wonder what she'd do if she knew it was me. Would she hate me? Or would she raise her mug of Baileys-laced hot chocolate and offer me a toast?

37

FEARNE

Sebastian and I are having a day off. We have a plan to drive the hour or so to Brighton where we'll walk by the sea and have lunch and then do some shopping. Every year, once the market is up and running smoothly, we go on a little day trip and take the opportunity to make up a hamper of tasty treats for Sebastian's mum and her friends in her retirement village. Despite all the issues this year, we've decided to honour the tradition. Well, Sebastian is nothing if not a creature of habit.

Just as we've settled into the car, we're blocked in by a black sedan. 'Fuck's sake,' Sebastian mutters as he undoes his seat belt to get back out and ask what the hell these people think they're playing at.

They are both wearing suits, the man in dark blue and the woman in smart pinstripe. He's older, probably mid-forties, with mousy-brown hair trimmed close to his head. She's probably only thirty and carries herself with the quiet confidence of a woman who knows she is brilliant, her hair pulled into a neat bun like a ballet dancer, no wisps in sight. I step out of the car.

'I'm DC Jenkins,' the man says, reaching out a hand for Sebastian to shake.

'And I'm DS Krishnan,' the female officer adds.

'Sebastian Dixon,' my husband replies. 'And my wife, Fearne.'

'Can we speak inside?' DS Krishnan asks, but with enough authority that it isn't really a request.

We head back into the house and I put the kettle on. I guess we aren't going to Brighton. Which means I will have to go on my own tomorrow to buy everything for the hamper. Which I'll then get completely wrong. Which will then mean I'm blamed for ruining my mother-in-law's Christmas. The joy.

'We regret to inform you that another body has been found at the market,' DC Jenkins tells us.

Another body? Oh, for fuck's sake. What is Erin Winters going to say? And Bella Donna is going to have a fucking field day.

But I don't say any of that out loud. Instead I ask, 'What happened?'

'We don't have all the details yet. It looks like an accident.'

'You don't sound sure,' Sebastian says.

'Well. There have been a lot of bodies in Ellsbury recently,' DC Jenkins says. DS Krishnan shoots him a look, one that tells him firmly that was not part of the agreed script.

But he does kind of have a point.

'Do you know who?' I ask and feel a rush of shame that my first thoughts were of how this would affect me and not the poor person who has died.

'Um. Can we?' DC Jenkins looks at DS Krishnan. She nods.

'Gloria Symmonds,' he reads from his notes.

Sebastian and I exchange blank looks. 'I don't know who that is,' my husband says.

'She was one of your stallholders.'

He shakes his head. 'No. There isn't anyone by that name. I know everyone who works at the market.' It's a point of pride for Sebastian.

'Gloria Symmonds,' DC Jenkins repeats again, as if repeating the same name will somehow jog Sebastian's memory.

'No.'

'Do you know what stall she ran?' I ask. But there's a tiny dawn of realisation. There is one stallholder who I always presumed was using a nom de plume.

'Crystals and Gifts.'

'It's Bella Donna,' I say.

'The crazy—' but Sebastian cuts himself off before he finishes the sentence. It's probably not the time to be slinging names around.

'Do you have any more information?' I ask quietly, the news not really sinking in yet.

'Not much,' DC Jenkins says and shifts his weight in his chair, glancing at his colleague who gives a tiny nod as if to say he can tell us a little more. 'She was found by one of the other traders this morning. We believe she may have slipped and hit her head. Her body was suspended upside down in a mesh of wire holding up a range of her crystals.'

'Would there have been any reason for her to be up on the roof of her chalet?' DS Krishnan asks.

'Absolutely not,' Sebastian answers quickly. 'That would be against all our Health and Safety protocols. I take things very seriously at the market.' He has jumped into defensive mode and for a moment I want to scold him for being an unsympathetic brute, given we're talking about a dead woman here. But, in reality, if Bella Donna was killed in an accident on the market, this is going to be a major headache for him. And if there is even the merest suggestion that it was the market's fault then that fallout could be a thousand times worse than a simple headache.

Criminal negligence.

Is that a real thing? Or is it one of those urban myths or Americanisms – because everyone in the US tries to sue for even the smallest of things. Is there a chance that Bella Donna's death could be Sebastian's fault?

'We're not here to apportion blame,' DS Krishnan says, but there's an edge to her tone. They might not be actively trying to pin this on someone, but they also aren't *not* trying. If that makes sense. 'We're just attempting to establish what exactly happened, why she was up on that roof, and put together a picture of the hours previous to the accident.'

'We have CCTV,' I say. 'Lots and lots of cameras scattered across the market.'

Sebastian shoots me a look. *What if it looks like it's my fault?*

I shoot one back. *It won't. But it will look super suspicious if you don't offer them the tapes.*

Fine, his eyes reply. 'We should be able to access the files from here,' he tells the officers. 'Although we have had a few teething issues with the system: it was only installed this year.'

'I'm assuming it was installed after Max Kirby's murder? There wasn't any footage of that.'

'Well…' Sebastian looks a little pained. 'There was an issue with the cameras on that night. The WiFi had been glitching all evening and unfortunately nothing was filmed as a result.'

'Right. Well, let's hope that wasn't the case for poor Gloria Symmonds.' DS Krishnan makes it sound almost like an accusation. Like last time Sebastian turned off the cameras and perhaps he did it again.

We troop upstairs to the office and gather around Sebastian's computer screen. We watch in silence as he fast-forwards through yesterday to the end of the market and everyone closing down their stalls for the night. Then he continues to speed things up as the whole place is silent. It isn't until six in the morning when a figure moves through the gloom toward Crystals and Shit. It's Bella Donna, dressed in her usual attire of a long flowing skirt and massive puffer jacket.

On screen she climbs onto the roof of the chalet, using the window ledge as a step and wriggling her body up. It's highly undignified and I have to stifle the urge to laugh. The woman is dead and it really isn't the time. Suddenly she slips, her feet flying from underneath her. There isn't sound on the tape but I can imagine the sickening thunk as her head meets the wooden frame and her neck twists to an unnatural angle. Then her body slides, slowly, so very slowly, until she's tangled in the mesh she'd used to string up the lights, her head toward the ground and feet in the air. A rogue gust of wind whips at her skirt, revealing her underwear.

What a terrible way to die.

What a terrible way for your body to be discovered.

* * *

The police depart and Sebastian heads into the market but I stay home. I just can't face the idea of seeing where it happened, the video is so seared into my brain. And what I still don't understand is why she was up there in the early hours of the morning.

Idly I rewind the video, sending Bella Donna sliding back up the roof and onto her feet, the whole accident shown in reverse as if time was going backward and she could still be saved.

I watch her climb down and open the shutters to the stall. Her final customer walks backwards with their purchase of something shiny. Other customers crowd in, looking at her selection of gifts. It's three in the afternoon according to the timestamp in the top corner, the winter sun weak, when I see her.

Fucking Erin Fucking Winters.

She's pointing up at the crystals strung along the top of the stall. I pause the recording, freezing Bella's expression on the screen. She looks furious, her jaw set at an unusual angle, like she's grinding her teeth. Hard.

Was Bella up on the roof because Erin told her to remove the crystals?

In which case, did Erin Winters essentially kill Bella?

Or was it my fault because I didn't tell her to take them down earlier? Has my own laziness, my desperate avoidance of conflict, caused someone to fall to their death?

38

JESSICA

Just so we are really clear, that last death had nothing to do with me. I did not kill Bella Donna, even though I'd heard rumours on the grapevine – well, from Fearne – that she was a tad on the difficult side. Which means that – unless there are two killers in Ellsbury and that seems unlikely – what happened to Bella was just a tragic accident. And I would certainly not wish that kind of death on anyone; it was probably painless and over before she even knew what was happening, but being found with your underwear on show is hardly the most desirable legacy to leave.

Fearne comes to find me in the staffroom during my break. She looks exhausted, her eyes rimmed with red and her skin pale.

'Is everything OK?' I ask her gently.

'It's just...' Her bottom lip wobbles. 'Bella,' she whispers eventually. 'I feel so guilty. Like I wished bad things on her and then this happened.'

'You know it wasn't your fault though?'

She nods. 'I know. It's just... she kept pestering me about the "energy impact" of where her stall was and I dismissed her because she was just a bit of a loon. And that's why she put all that stuff on the roof in the first place.'

'But she didn't have the accident because she put the stuff up there,' I tell her, keeping my voice nice and neutral. I don't want to feed her irrationality here.

'No.'

'She was up on that roof last night because she was told to take them down.'

She nods.

'And who told her she had to take them down?' I ask.

'Fucking Erin Fucking Winters.'

'Exactly. Now, how about we meet up when I finish my shift, have a drink or two?'

'That'd be nice.' She smiles at me and her whole face brightens. 'Shall we just go to The Apres-Ski, I could do with the kind of measures Mr Usman pours?'

'Sounds like an excellent plan.'

Her phone beeps and she pulls it out to look at the message. 'It's Sebastian.' She grimaces slightly. 'Apparently, those guys, Max Kirby's friends, are back making trouble.' The grimace deepens. 'Something else I could really do without today. I'd better go.'

'I'll see you in The Apres-Ski,' I tell her as she turns to leave and rescue her hapless husband from actually doing his own job.

* * *

I watch Max Kirby's friends from the window of the grotto as they stalk around the market. You'd think that, after one of their group was murdered, they might have learnt some manners. But no such luck. And especially Z, he still has the strut of a man who knows his father, the Mayor, will always have his back. Who doesn't have a care in the world. Who thinks he's untouchable.

One of the elves tells me that they've been spraying graffiti onto one of the stalls. 'And definitely not of the family friendly kind,' he adds, raising his eyebrows.

More rumours filter through to the grotto over the course of the next few hours. Tales of more petty theft, more vandalism, more disruption.

I get ready to meet Fearne in The Apres-Ski for that quick drink after my shift and for once I'm very glad to take off my costume and slip into something more comfortable. I'm in a foul mood and I hate it.

'Cheer up, love, it might never happen,' some slightly drunken lout shouts at me as I pass the burger stand. I shoot him a look and he shrinks away as if I've slapped him. I smile – inwardly at least – at the flare of fear I saw in his eyes. Sometimes it's good to let the beast rise a little closer to the surface, especially around the kind of men who come up with such unoriginal lines to shout to women they don't know.

But I do genuinely cheer up when I order a double gin and see the way Fearne's face lights up when she sees me. Normally when I'm in a new city each year I don't socialise much. It's so much easier that way. Easier to get away with murder. Easier to leave after the Christmas season is over. Easier to walk away and start again somewhere new the next year. But it's been nice to make friends in Ellsbury. Hanna and Fearne and Lena. For the first time I actually think I'll be sad to move on come January.

A man in a checked shirt at the other end of the bar raises his glass to me. Alvi. This time there's a chihuahua sitting on his lap. I wave to him then turn my attention back to Fearne.

'Sebastian told Erin he was calling the police about Z and his friends,' Fearne tells me. 'And she told him not to. Said having even more police round here wouldn't exactly help with visitor numbers.'

'So, they are just going to get away with it?'

'She told him to deal with it himself.'

'And how exactly is he meant to do that?' I ask. I mean, I have a few ideas, but they might be slightly disproportionate to the crimes involved.

'I have no clue,' she says and sighs loudly. 'He's just been called to the council for a meeting, though, so hopefully someone has an idea.'

I motion to Remi to pour us another round. Today is definitely feeling like a two large gin and tonic kind of day. Especially because they are serving the gin from The Ellsbury Still and it's surprisingly good, clean and strong with a subtle hint of citrus.

Suddenly there's a commotion outside and a ripple of rumour starts to fan across the tables of revellers. Something is happening.

'I should probably look,' Fearne says wearily. 'No doubt it'll become my problem at some point,' she adds dryly.

Outside we find an apoplectic Z being held by the scruff of his neck by Connor Harvey from The Ellsbury Still stall.

'Put me down.'

'Not until you apologise,' Connor says. 'And promise to clean it up.' He turns and spots Fearne. 'Is your husband around?' he asks her hopefully.

Fearne shakes her head. 'He was called to the council for a meeting.'

'It's eight-thirty in the evening.'

'Erin Winters,' Fearne says.

There's a flash of understanding on Connor's face. 'Fair enough. Say no more.'

Z, still being held by the scruff of his neck like a recalcitrant kitten, struggles slightly. 'Put me down.'

Connor tightens his already vicelike grip. I can see the muscles on his forearm twitching. 'This little shit has graffitied Crystals and Gifts,' he says, before leaning in a little closer to Z. 'Tell them all what you wrote.'

'It was a joke,' Z says. 'Don't get your knickers in a twist.' He laughs but Connor most definitely doesn't join in.

'Tell them.' Connor's voice is little more than a growl.

'Only disgusting dirty slags die with their pants on show.'

There's a gasp from the assembled crowd. Z has definitely crossed a line.

I know you might find this hard to believe, but I do believe in the sanctity of human life. And I especially believe in the fact that innocent people deserve to live their lives in peace and to have their deaths dealt with respectfully.

The anger I've felt all day rises.

I only kill people who deserve it. I only kill people who ruin life for others. I have rules. I need to have rules. Rules keep things orderly. Keep things neat. Keep things... bearable.

But I want to kill. The beast is rattling at the bars of the cage and I want to let her out.

I need to let her out.

He deserves it.

Is it enough of a reason? Does a man deserve to die for some graffiti? He hasn't ruined a life. But he has ruined a death.

He deserves it.

Without rules, I'm just as bad as them. Worse than them.

Please.

39

FEARNE

Bella Donna's death hits me in a way I'm not expecting. I mean, I know I didn't particularly like the woman. She could be a total pain in the arse. But I didn't want her dead. Not seriously, anyway, even if I might have thought it a couple of times in that tongue-in-cheek way we all do. But no one actually thinks other people deserve to die for their transgressions, do they?

'Why don't you take Immy to Brighton?' Sebastian asks on Saturday morning. It's the first weekend of December. 'You look like you could use a break.'

My hand goes instinctively to my face, a finger swiping under each eye to check for rogue mascara. 'Do I really look that bad?'

He smiles. 'Of course not. But you didn't sleep much and I think it would do you good to get some fresh air.'

I reluctantly agree and, once I've been able to crowbar her out of bed, Immy even more reluctantly agrees to come with me.

'You can help choose stuff for your grandmother's hamper,' I tell her.

'Great,' she replies in a tone that says it is anything but.

'I'll let you pick where we have lunch.' I waggle my eyebrows.

She narrows her eyes. 'What if I choose somewhere fancy?'

I slide a piece of blue plastic from my back pocket. 'Your dad gave me his credit card...' I grin.

'Yasmin said there's a seafood place in the marina that is the best she's ever been to.'

'Who's Yasmin?'

'Seriously? Yasmin went to my school? Then she married that footballer? She's on Instagram?'

I have no idea who she's talking about. 'Oh, that Yasmin. Of course.' I smile.

'You're sure Dad'll be OK with us going there?' Her father isn't always renowned for his financial generosity.

'Of course,' I reply brightly. I'm assuming somewhere that impresses a footballer's girlfriend turned influencer will be extortionate, and so I'll end up paying for it from my Cherry Dubois money and it'll be my little secret.

* * *

Lunch isn't just extortionate. It's almost three hundred pounds. And that's without any drinks as I'm driving and Immy's underage. Three hundred pounds! It's good though and the look on Immy's face when she spotted some other influencer at the next table was worth the hefty price tag.

'Perhaps don't tell your father how much it was, eh?' I tell her.

'Won't he see the statement?'

'He won't bother checking.'

She sits back in her chair and stares at me. 'I know, Mum,' she says, somewhat enigmatically.

'Know what?'

'Oh, come on. You're not that good at keeping secrets, you know.'

'What secrets?'

'Cherry Dubois,' she whispers under her breath.

I feel all the blood rush to my face. How can she possibly know?

'Why don't you tell Dad about those books?' she asks.

'I... uh... um...'

'I'm kidding. I get it. And I would never tell Dad. I know it's really Cherry Dubois paying for lunch.' She smiles at me. 'I'm really proud of you, Mum.'

I spend the rest of the afternoon with a warm glow in the pit of my stomach. Immy is proud of me. I always hoped she would be, but I never thought I'd do anything to earn that pride. Perhaps I need to just believe in myself a little bit more.

'You probably should tell Dad, you know,' she says as we push open the door to Baumann's, home of the best artisan chocolates in town. 'About the pen name,' she clarifies.

'He wouldn't understand.'

'Why not? Because it's porn?' She says it so innocently.

'It's not porn. It's erotica.'

'Old ladies' porn,' she says. 'And don't worry, I haven't been reading it. Not my jam. At all.' She shakes her head.

'Well, I'm glad.' And relieved. So so so relieved. My Cherry Dubois stuff is definitely not something I want my teenage daughter reading. I feel sick at the mere thought of it. 'But your father wouldn't approve of me writing it.'

'Even though you're making bank.'

'I'm not making bank.'

'You left your laptop open the other day. I saw the page for your pen name and you're like number ten on the entire of Amazon.'

'Were you spying on me?'

'Not spying. *Snooping*.' She says it like snooping is a much lesser crime. 'I wanted to see your order history for Amazon so I'd know what I was getting for Christmas.'

'You know that isn't much better?'

She shrugs. 'You were logged in on a different account though.'

'Ms Dixon. If you continue to snoop on me, then you won't be getting *anything* for Christmas,' I tell her with a raised eyebrow.

She looks at me and grins. 'Chill. I didn't find anything.'

'Except that I write under a pen name.'

'Well. Yeah. So I didn't find anything except that you're a damn rockstar.'

Oh, she's good. She's very very good. I go from anger to blushing with pride in under a second.

'You cannot tell your father.'

'Your secret is safe with me.' She mimes zipping her lips, locking a padlock and throwing the key behind her. It's the same thing she would do when she was little. Not that I encouraged the keeping of secrets from Sebastian, but he didn't always need to know we'd had ice cream in town or I'd bought her a new dress for a party.

She loops her arm through mine. 'Now, let's get this shopping done. Is this the place with all the samples?' She grins as she looks up at me.

We get through half a tray of samples as we build the ultimate box of chocolates for Jennie and her cronies. Peppermint creams. Champagne truffles dusted in chocolate powder. Langues de chat. Pralines. Little milk chocolate trees filled with gooey salted caramel. The finished thing weighs almost a kilo and the girl behind the counter wraps it in tissue paper and ties a large red ribbon round it. It looks like a work of art. And so it should, for the price tag. But Sebastian's mum is the one person he's always happy to treat.

The next shop sells vintage sweets and an array of festive-shaped biscuits and I buy enough shortbread to sink a small battleship. Immy keeps picking up everything she sees and asking me what it is.

'Uh, this stuff is like pink?' she says, brandishing a box close to my face.

'That's coconut ice,' I tell her. 'We used to have it sometimes when I was a kid.'

She makes a face. 'Sounds gross. What about this?' She holds up a clear gusseted bag filled with little purply red balls, a ribbon twisted around the top to seal the contents.

'Aniseed balls? Surely you've had aniseed balls before?'

She shakes her head. 'Is this actual honeycomb?' She squints at the bag she's holding.

'It's called honeycomb, but it's more like a kind of toffee. In the US it's called Fairy Food.' I shrug. I don't actually know if that's true or the kind of urban myth bullshit my big brother used to feed me when we were kids. 'It's what you get in the middle of a Crunchie.'

'All this stuff is weird,' Immy decrees, motioning around the entire shop.

'All this stuff is retro,' I correct.

'Weird.'

We finish up in the sweetshop and then head a few metres up the cobbled high street to a small stall selling hot chocolate with cream, marshmallows and a striped candy cane sticking out of the top. I try not to be 'cringe' and hide how much I baulk at the eight-pound price tag. Each. This isn't about the money; it's about making memories with my daughter.

* * *

'How was it?' Sebastian asks, looking up from the laptop he's working on at the kitchen table.

'Good,' I reply. 'I think we managed to get everything.'

'Even the cherries in kirsch?' he asks. I forgot those one year and there was hell to pay for about three months.

'Two jars. And some peaches in brandy.'

'Courvoisier?'

'Of course.' I wouldn't dare get any other; Sebastian gave me a list of all the allowable brands the year after the forgotten cherries in kirsch incident.

'Mum'll like that.' He smiles. 'You look a lot happier. I guess it worked to take your mind off the whole Bella thing.'

And, with that, reality crashes over me like a tsunami. I've spent a fabulous day spending a fortune with my beautiful daughter and that poor woman – irritating as she was – is dead. Dead, just weeks before Christmas. Did she have a family? Children? Husband? Parents? Siblings?

Could I have stopped it from happening? Or perhaps it wasn't my fault and I should be placing the blame more firmly at a certain Christmas Czar's feet.

Fucking Erin Fucking Winters.

40

JESSICA

It's Sunday and Lena has a day off. She's arranged to go into town to meet Immy for a bubble tea. It's kind of sweet to see them making friends. Plus, it gives me the cottage to myself; it's been feeling a little claustrophobic with both of us living here and getting under each other's feet all the time.

Oh, and I really need to do some research without worrying that Lena is looking over my shoulder and either judging me or getting ideas.

I lay in bed – well, on the sofa – this morning and, as the sun rose, I made my decision. What Z did wasn't enough. My head has to rule my heart. Otherwise all of this is over. I'll get reckless and I *will* get caught and that is not an option.

So there are two possible paths.

The first is to leave Z be. To let him carry on doing whatever other petty crimes he thinks he can get away with.

The second is to find more evidence that prove he does actually deserve it.

It doesn't take long before I'm forced to concede defeat on the digital research though. Z is clever enough not to document his crimes on Instagram or TikTok and his daddy is influential enough to stop the press from talking about his misdemeanours.

I don't have enough information to build a case against him, so I'm going to have to go on a little field trip. Hawcroft House – because yes, the Mayor of Ellsbury did name his house after himself – sits in a secluded spot to the north of the city and so I borrow one of the bikes from the cottage's shed. I'm assuming it was Hanna's once upon a time, but it's been carefully maintained and it'll be far easier than walking.

When I was Lena's age, breaking into people's houses was tricky. Especially the kind of big posh houses belonging to people who had something worth taking. They had CCTV systems and alarms and it could all get pretty messy pretty quickly. But then we invented WiFi. We installed 'smart doorbells' and 'smart cameras' and all other kinds of 'smart' technology. All of it runs across WiFi, just like the security network at the Christmas market. I bought this jammer when I went to Las Vegas in the spring. It's tiny, smaller than my phone, and super discreet so you'd think it was a battery power pack from looking at it. Highly illegal here in the UK, but only if I get caught.

With the entire security system taken out, I'm free to do whatever I want without fear of someone watching and recording me. I start with a good old recce of the place. There's a large house with views out over the rolling fields to the rear, a few outbuildings and a garage with a dormer window that makes it look more like an annexe.

Now then, if I were a twenty-three-year-old manchild who still lived at home with my parents, where would my room be? I think I would choose the annexe. Convince myself I was an independent adult rather than a kid who couldn't do anything without his mummy being close by.

There's one of those key safes beside the door to the annexe like you get sometimes with an Airbnb. I try 1234 as the code and it pops open right away; so far, so predictably poor at home security. There's a key inside and so I let myself into the annexe.

It's immediately clear that my assumptions about Z were correct and this is indeed his domain. It's an absolute pigsty and the stench of Lynx hangs heavy in the air. There's a small kitchenette and a living area with a sofa and a big TV. I count three pizza boxes from three different establishments, and at least ten empty beer bottles scattered around. There's a pile of clothes on a small armchair and some weed paraphernalia on the coffee table.

In the bedroom I find a full gaming set-up. Two screens, a headset, keyboard, mouse. All top of the line and no doubt a gift from the Bank of Mum and Dad. There's probably three thousand pounds' worth of kit here. I wiggle the mouse and a screensaver pops up. A single click on the mouse and the screensaver is replaced by his desktop screen. No password. He plays Grand Theft Auto. I'm not surprised, I can understand how a game based on stealing cars and wreaking havoc would appeal to him.

I pull up a chair and sit down ready to have a dig through his digital footprint.

And what I find does not disappoint.

Zachary Hawcroft may be known as Z to his dumb little friends, but online he also goes by TruthTeller69. And ThatRedPilledGuy. Project_Z42. ExpressLaneToHell.

Well well well, it appears Z is a very busy boy.

All these different handles are troll accounts. He appears to spend hours online, hunting down vulnerable young people and messaging them with hate-filled bile. Bullying. Cajoling. In more than a few he makes threats of violence toward his victims. Or he tells them they should kill themselves. I stare at the messages with my mouth open. How can someone think these things? Write these things?

I was looking for an excuse to add him to the Naughty List. I just found it.

With bells on.

* * *

I go to work feeling an odd mix of anticipation and sadness. I feel for all those people whose lives have been harmed by Z and his spite-filled words. But at least this evening I am going to do something about it.

'Fancy a drink?' Carl asks me as we finish for the evening. He isn't allowed to drink onsite because he still looks exactly like Santa even without the outfit. 'We could go to a pub down the road.'

'Sorry, I have a ton of chores to do at home. Christmas feels like it's really coming up quick this year.'

'It does every time,' he laments. 'And then it'll all be over for another season.'

'How about tomorrow?' I ask instead. I don't want him to think I don't want to share a few glasses of wine, he's such a sweetheart, but I do have other business to attend to this evening.

'That would be delightful,' he replies with a twinkle in his eye.

* * *

I wait for Z in the shadows behind the garage. I've already jammed the WiFi again to make sure there's no CCTV footage of me skulking around the Hawcrofts' property. It's just gone ten when he finally comes home and I breathe a sigh of relief that soon I can get warm again, my toes are freezing. He's had a few beers and he sways slightly as he walks up the stairs to the annexe. I count to thirty and then follow him. No doubt he's about to log in as ThatRedPilledGuy or TruthTeller69 and spew some terrible words at some innocent teen out there in the world.

I stay in the kitchen out of sight as he settles into his leather gaming chair, a beer at his elbow, fingers poised over the keyboard. 'Fuck's sake,' he says as he realises there's no WiFi. He picks up his mobile and goes to call his dad to sort out yet another of his life's little problems. But the jammer is flawless and so he can't call either. 'Fuck's sake!'

'Having problems there?' I ask, stepping from the shadows.

He jumps out of his skin. 'Who the fuck are you?'

I smile, a slow and languid smile and for a moment his bravado cracks.

'I said who the fuck are you and what are you doing in my house? You... you...' He grasps for an insult and I brace myself for something vile and misogynistic. He doesn't disappoint. 'You crazy whore.'

'Well, you're half right.' The languid smile becomes a wide grin. 'I am crazy.'

Killing him feels good.

It feels like justice.

It feels like therapy.

Oh, who am I kidding?

It feels like fun.

41

IN WHICH MORE MURDERS COME TO LIGHT…

In 2021, Jessica Williams was the Mrs Claus at a shopping centre on the outskirts of Leeds. But here's something interesting; there was no uptick in unsolved murders, no new police taskforce created to look for a potential serial killer.

Am I wrong about her? *Has* everything I've found so far just been coincidental?

I widen my search and begin to look for other deaths around that time. Eventually I stumble on a series of articles in the *West Yorkshire Gazette*.

West Yorkshire Gazette – 12 December 2021
Body Found in Morley

Residents of the delightful area of Morley have awoken to horror on their doorstep. The body of a man was discovered by early morning dog walkers in Hembrigg Park. He was found with drug-related paraphernalia and it is believed his death may have been caused by a "bad batch". Police are urging any witnesses to come forward.

West Yorkshire Gazette – 16 December 2021
Second Body Found in Morley

Residents of Morley have once again awoken to a nightmare. Another body has been discovered, this time by a pre-dawn jogger in Lewisham Park. As with the Hembrigg Park death, there was evidence of drug taking. Pharmacological testing has yet to be confirmed, but sources close to the *Gazette* suggest a strong link between the deaths and further corroborate the theory of a "bad batch" of an illegal substance blighting our streets.

Now, two dead drug addicts does not show signs of a serial killer. Until I find an article written by one of the men's wives.

West Yorkshire Gazette – 20 December 2021
My Husband Was Not An Addict

The wife of the man found dead in Hembrigg Park last week has come forward to lambast the public view of her husband. 'He was not a drug addict,' she told members of the press at a conference earlier today. 'He liked a drink, of course he did. But that was all he ever did. He wasn't sitting in parks injecting heroin. That just wasn't him.'

Is the best way to get away with murder for there never to have been one? It would make sense.

Is that how she's eluded capture for so long?

42

FEARNE

Every year, on the second Wednesday in December – and I'm realising now that for someone who kind of hates Christmas, I have a lot of 'traditions' – I help the local residential care facility bring festive cheer to the young people they support. I mentioned it to Jessica the other day and she was super quick to volunteer her time as well.

'Can I come?' she'd asked.

'Of course.' This is always a 'the more, the merrier' type situation.

'As Mrs Claus?' she'd asked.

'Umm. Yes, please. They would love that.'

'Yay!' she'd exclaimed, jumping up and down and reaching out to squeeze my upper arm. 'This is going to be so much fun.'

I normally think of the day as a bit of a penance, a way to rebalance the scales after I was given so much. Gosh, that makes me sound like a douche. Like an utter twat who, even when she's doing something nice for someone else, is still only thinking of herself.

I need to be more like Jessica.

And so this morning I put on a big smile and pick up the bag of gifts I've been collecting over the year for the residents. There are twenty-four in total, and so I pick up a couple of presents each month to spread the cost. This year, though, I think there'll be far more excitement about actual Mrs Claus delivering them than the gifts themselves.

Northgate Manor is on the outskirts of the city and so I pick Jessica up as I pass her house. She looks utterly perfect and she's even added a white faux-fur stole and muffler to the ensemble to make herself look even more like Santa's wife.

'Non-regulation addition to the costume,' she says, touching the stole. 'Don't tell Erin Winters.' She giggles and I immediately feel my mood lift. What is it with her that always makes me feel so much lighter?

We have an incredible time with the kids and they are absolutely overjoyed to get a visit from the real Mrs Claus. We sing carols and eat too much cake and talk about all our favourite holiday traditions. Jessica – not that I'm surprised – has an almost encyclopaedic knowledge of Christmas movies and so we play a game with the children acting out little scenes while she guesses which film they are from. But, all too soon it's time for us to leave and head back to normality.

Jessica and I head into the market and she peels off to go to work. I wander through the stalls toward the office to find Sebastian.

Hmm. Now that is weird.

There's a man I don't recognise with a tape measure at Bella Donna's stall. He has a tiny nubbin of a pencil behind one ear and the air of someone who knows what they're doing.

'Hi,' I say, stopping in front of him.

'Hi,' he replies, his eyes darting left to right. *Who the fuck are you?* his demeanour says.

'I'm Fearne Dixon. Sebastian is my husband,' I say brightly, thrusting my hand toward him.

'That's... nice.'

'You've met Sebastian? He runs the market?'

The man shakes his head. 'I'm dealing with Ms Winters.'

Of course he is. 'Oh. Right. And you are?'

'Trying to work.' He turns away from me. What a twat.

I bump into Erin – not Ms Winters – on my way to the office. 'Umm... who is the guy at Crystals and Gifts?' I ask.

'Crystals and Gi—' She cuts herself off. 'Oh, you mean Artisanal Ellsbury?'

'Artisanal Ellsbury?'

'The new vendor will be here tomorrow. Teddy is just being a darling and getting a head start on the new stall.' She smiles at me as if to say *is that all and will you fuck off now*.

'Sorry. Artisanal Ellsbury?' Sebastian and I had a long conversation last night about what to do with Crystals and Gifts. We can't really have an empty stall, and so it should go to the first person on the waiting list. Which would be Huber Wood Carvings.

'Yes, Artisanal Ellsbury.' She says it slowly, as if I might not be all there mentally. 'It's a stall selling local food and drink. All artisanal. All very exclusive.'

'But who appointed them?'

'I did.' She gives me a smug smile.

'But we have a process. A series of vendors who are lined up to act in reserve if something goes wrong and someone has to pull out.'

'Don't make such a big deal out of it.'

'But it *is* a big deal.' I can feel myself burning with anger. She has no fucking idea what she's doing. 'Sebastian spends ages every year working to get the balance of the market just right.

The perfect mix of products and a wide range of price points so everyone can afford to participate.' Sometimes I hate my husband and his pernickety ways. But this is one occasion where I understand why he's so painstaking in his selection. Every single person who comes to the market finds something they are interested in, something they can afford, something they will look at with fondness, even if it's only a miniature bottle of gin or donation sticker from the rescue centre.

Not that Erin Winters gives a shit. 'Look.' She puts up her hands as if to say what is done is done. 'I'm just doing what I'm told.'

'By whom?' I ask.

'We all have our bosses, Fearne.' She smirks. 'I was your boss once.'

And don't I know it.

It was December 2011. Funnily enough – not that it's actually funny, but you know what I mean – Christmas was upon us then too. Perhaps all my memories of Erin Winters are destined to be held against a backdrop of fairy lights and tinsel and hangovers from a constant stream of events interspersed with justifiable day drinking.

I was in the office early, desperate to put the final finishing touches on the presentation I was going to give as part of my final stage interview. I was still riding a high from an amazing date the night before: Sebastian surprised me with a trip to the theatre for our two-month anniversary. He asked me, in stuttered words to convey the magnitude of the request, if I might like to meet his toddler daughter soon. It was a huge deal to him. It was a huge deal to *me*. It meant this was serious, this was *something*.

Anyway, I was working away when I felt a presence behind

me. 'Oh, sweetheart. You're not working on that for the interview, are you?'

I turned to face Erin who was wearing this concerned look but it was hiding a huge grin. Like she had a secret. A guilty secret. But one she was desperate to share.

'My interview is at eleven.'

'Except...' her face twisted into a grimace, but still the grin remained in the background.

She was right. My interview was cancelled and guess who was offered the job? The rumours flew around the office and they weren't exactly complimentary about Erin. Or about what she may, or may not, have done behind the locked door of the Chief Executive's office.

A year later and I couldn't take it with Erin any more.

'Just quit,' Sebastian told me.

'You make it sound so simple.'

'It is. Any job that makes you feel like shit isn't worth doing.'

'Yeah, but you're forgetting that I need to pay my rent.'

'You could move in with me.' He'd said it so quietly I thought I might have misheard. I waited for him to say something else, but he didn't. The silence yawned between us. 'But only if you wanted to,' he added after what felt like an aeon.

'Are you being serious?'

'Do you really think I'd joke about something like this?' He had looked up then, his eyes piercing my soul. 'I love you, Fearne. And Immy does too. We want you in our lives.'

'I... I...' I stammered, my brain trying to catch up with what this might mean. I was not quite thirty, but inside I still thought I was twenty-three. Spoiler alert: I'm still convinced I'm in my twenties and that fate is just playing some kind of cruel stunt on me by making me look like I'm mid-forties. Was I ready to take on a whole ready-made family? A serious relationship with a man and a child. What if I changed my mind? I'd end up breaking both their hearts and it wouldn't be fair. I loved this man. And I loved Immy. But what if it didn't work out? What if I ended up hating him? What if I ended up shackled to a bore of a man?

It took two years for the cracks in mine and Sebastian's relationship to really show, or at least for the cracks to become impossible to ignore any longer. But by then Immy was calling me Mummy and I would have laid down my life for her. I had no way to leave Sebastian without losing Immy. And so I stayed. Stayed and created a nemesis for myself in the form of Fucking Erin Fucking Winters. If only she hadn't stolen that promotion from me. Then none of this would have happened.

Fair? Probably not.

Justifiable? Absolutely.

And now, even as I've made my peace with the shreds of my marriage and the hope of a better future once Immy is older, she's threatening to shatter my fragile harmony. Fucking Erin Fucking Winters ruined my life once. I'm not going to let her screw me over again. The rage I suddenly feel toward her takes me by surprise. I knew I hated her. Blamed her. But I didn't know just how ferocious I was capable of feeling.

'You're a bitch, Erin. You just can't help yourself, can you? Is your life really so shitty that you have to fuck with everyone else's? Does it make you feel better? You're a fucking evil witch and I wish I'd never met you.' It spews forth from my mouth as if I'm unable to stop it, even though I know it isn't proportional to her current crime; but thirteen years of hate has to go somewhere.

43

JESSICA

Lena has to go into work a couple of hours before me. She texts me about fifteen minutes into her shift to tell me that Fearne and Erin are the subject of all the gossip.

> LENA
> Apparently it was the mother of all blowouts.

> JESSICA
> I'm sure it was just a little argument.

But when I get to the staffroom to change into my Mrs Claus costume, I find the Romero twins from the Sausage Swing chattering away in Spanish. I'm slightly hungover from having drinks with Carl last night – he might look harmless, but he can sink a pint like you wouldn't believe – and it's a struggle to keep up with their conversation.

'Honestly, I thought there was going to be a proper fight,' Sofia says.

'A proper catfight,' Valentina adds.

One of the Waffleicious guys who was making coffee goes

over to them. 'You talking about the big fight?' he asks the twins. I don't know if he speaks Spanish or if he's just made an assumption and it really is all anyone can talk about.

They both nod in unison.

'I was waiting for someone to throw in a whole bucketful of jelly. Make it a real wrestling match.' There's a lewd wiggling of the eyebrows in case no one else had understood the implication. Gross.

'Apparently,' says a voice from behind a locker. I think it's one of the barmen from The Apres-Ski. 'Or at least this is what I've heard on the old grapevine.' He pops his head round the locker as if to check for eavesdroppers. 'Erin Winters is demanding a public apology from Fearne. Like she wants a whole big show so Fearne can say she didn't mean it.'

'What was it she called her?' Sofia asks.

'A "fucking evil witch",' the Waffleicious guy replies.

'Brilliant. Good on Fearne,' Valentina says. 'I hope she sticks up for herself. Erin Winters deserves it.'

* * *

No one sees Fearne all day. I ask Sebastian where she is when I bump into him on my break.

'She's at home,' he tells me through gritted teeth, as if he's been asked the question one too many times already today.

'OK. Well, just tell her I'm thinking of her and I'm here if she needs anything.'

He looks at me kind of blankly and then narrows his eyes as his expression turns to one of suspicion. 'Why are you being so nice?'

'Well, I am Mrs Claus,' I say and drop into a small curtsy. It's meant to be a joke. It's meant to make him laugh. But, instead, his frown deepens.

'Seriously?'

'Umm... Well, we're friends,' I stutter.

The look on his face tells me he's not convinced at all. I wonder if she's just never mentioned me to him. It kind of stings if I'm honest. I *thought* we were friends. Maybe I was just reading far too much into a casual acquaintanceship?

The thought sits with me through the second part of my shift. But, no; it doesn't feel right to say we're just acquaintances. I might not have the most practice at this kind of thing, but Fearne and I are *definitely* friends.

And so I do what friends do when my shift is over. I head over to her house to check on her, armed with a box of chocolates and a bottle of a nice red wine I think she'll like. It's called 19 Crimes and the name tickles me a little in the off licence. Apparently it's been aged in old rum barrels for a fuller flavour; it sounds right up her street.

The Dixon house is on a street of similar size properties. All with a wide driveway and a built-in double garage. The kind of house that I once dreamed of living in, before I realised that would require the compromise of domesticity and likely come with some kind of banker husband who probably wouldn't approve of my 'hobbies'.

The whole street has taken Christmas decorating very seriously, with outside lights and wreaths and stencilled window displays. All of them except for the Dixon house, which stands out like a sore thumb, a dark spot in a sea of twinkling colour.

The house is on the end of the row, so has a modicum more privacy than some of the others. It's always struck me as a little bizarre that wealthy middle-class people pay a fortune for a house with a garden their neighbours can see directly into.

Surely you should get more for the three-quarters-of-a-million price tag that these command?

From the street I can see that both the living room and the dining room are empty. The kitchen must be round the back and that must be where she is. Unless she's already gone to bed of course, but it is only nine thirty.

I ring the doorbell. There's no response. I can hear music in the kitchen and her car is on the driveway.

A scream rips through the night.

Was that Fearne?

Is she hurt?

I ring the bell again, but still no one appears.

I need to check on Fearne, I need to make sure she's OK.

There's a gate next to the garage that looks like it leads to the back garden. I test the handle and it swings open without complaint. I must remember to have a word about security with Fearne. This is a nice area, but leaving an unlocked gate to the garden is just asking for trouble.

Oh, actually, I'll take that back. The first gate leads to an area around the side of the house where the bins and recycling are stored. This looks to be a serious endeavour in the Dixon house. But there's a second gate into the garden. And this one is locked.

I cast around looking for a key, but of course Fearne is clever enough not to leave a key on a piece of string or anything like that. That's what my dad used to do. I wouldn't recommend it. Not after what happened.

I didn't bring my lock picks with me. I mean, I was expecting to find Fearne and have a drinkie while she tells me her woes. I take a step back and look at the gate. I need to get inside. So I do it the old-fashioned way. I pull one of the bins over and climb on top, using it to help me get over the gate, dropping to my feet the other side. My back makes a scream of complaint. I'm still pretty fit, but I'm definitely not the eighteen-year-old girl who used to practically parkour her way across a city.

But at least I'm in the garden. I hug the shrubbery around the edge to make my way toward the house. Light spills out onto the patio. I duck as I approach the window, crab-walking to a central position before poking my head up to look inside the room.

As I'd expected, it's the kitchen I'm looking into.

And there, standing in front of the kitchen island, is Fearne.

She's holding a knife in one hand. Blood drips from it.

My eyes follow one of the drops and then I see it.

Her.

Erin Winters.

In a pool of dark red.

Fearne has killed Erin Winters.

Fuck.

44

FEARNE

I don't think I've previously appreciated just how much a knife wound can bleed. I've seen it on TV of course, but I think most of those murder shows are dialling it back in a bit. Because holy crap.

There is just so much of it.

Pooling beneath her.

Spattered up the otherwise pristine white walls.

It's on my hands and in my hair and even smeared up my leg.

I look at her lying there, her eyes staring at me without seeing. The knife glints in my hand, blood reflecting off the burnished silver handle. My mother-in-law gave us these knives as a wedding present. They were a family heirloom apparently.

It doesn't feel real. Like she's an actor and the house is a set and everything is just a prop.

But it is real. The stench of pennies in the air is unmistakable.

But, before I can fully contemplate my apparent psychotic break, I notice movement in the garden.

Fuck.

Someone is out there, skulking around on the patio.

Fuck.

My brain fires into gear.

Fuck. This is bad. This is very very very bad.

The person in the garden accidentally trips one of the security lights and the whole lawn area is illuminated. I get a good look at their face. At her face. It's Jessica.

What do I do?

But before I can think about it too hard, my hand – the one holding the knife, blood still dripping – rises as if it belongs to someone else. My other hand beckons to Jessica.

She stares at me, her mouth a perfect 'O'.

I beckon again, this time making my movements more exaggerated. Perhaps she can't see me properly.

Fuck.

Why is Jessica standing in my garden?

I need to talk to her. To explain that this isn't what it seems. That I didn't *mean* to kill Erin. Becoming friends with Jessica has been one of the highlights of this Christmas season and I don't want to lose her now.

I think I might be concentrating on the wrong thing here. *What if she tells someone?*

I'll go to prison. I'll go to prison for a long, long time and I'll lose Immy and none of the last decade will have meant anything, it will all be for nothing. I can't lose Immy.

I need to talk to Jessica. But she's still standing open mouthed in my garden staring at me. Why is she ignoring my beckon?

Although, to be fair, I'm not sure I would approach a woman holding a bloody knife with a body on the floor. Can she see Erin? Or is the angle all wrong from where she's standing?

I stay still and debate my next move. She looks like she's doing the same thing.

But, then I'm striding toward the patio door, turning the key and sliding it open. The cold air hits my face.

The outside light blinks off and plunges the garden into darkness.

'Jessica,' I call into the black. 'I know you're out there.'

I hear the words as I say them and I know I sound ridiculous. It wasn't deliberate but I put some kind of ominous tone to the sentence. Like it's a threat.

Jessica is silent. Did she hear it as a threat? It wasn't. But perhaps it *could* be a threat. If I was that way inclined – although, judging by the way I feel about the sight of that much blood in the kitchen, I'm definitely not that way inclined.

I can see my breath pluming in the cold. The outside light flashes on again and I watch as Jessica takes a few tentative steps toward me. 'I guess you weren't expecting to see me...' she trails off, sounding almost contemplative.

I shake my head. Where is she going with this? I feel the muscles in my legs tense as I prepare to run from her.

'Ah. Screw it. Do you need a hand?' she asks.

'A... a hand?' I squeak. Is she asking if she can help me?

'With her.' She points toward the body. 'I doubt you want to spend the next twenty years in prison.' She flashes me a smile.

'Why would you help me?'

'I thought we were friends.'

'Yes, but...'

'Isn't this what friends do?' she asks.

I've always seen those necklaces and mugs and what have you, 'gifts for your bestie' – there's normally someone on the market selling them – and so often I've seen this sentiment of having a friend who you'd do anything for, even bury a body. I always thought it was hyperbole. And I never thought I'd have a friend like that.

But here we are.

Jessica's demeanour changes and she takes control of the situation. She touches my elbow and turns me back toward the house. 'Come on then,' she says, in a similar way to how you might talk to a slightly confused elderly relative. 'So how about you make me a cup of tea and tell me what the hell happened. And then we'll make a plan?'

I make tea – squeezing the bags hard to make the brew as strong as possible – and then hand a mug to Jessica.

'Well, then,' she says. 'I guess you'd better tell me what happened.' She turns to look pointedly at Erin's inert form.

'I didn't mean to.'

'Well, obviously.' She smiles at me and I feel her calming presence soothe me.

'I... I...' but I trail off.

'Just start at the beginning,' Jessica says softly.

I take a deep breath. 'So, Erin and I had a bit of an argument. Um, at the market. And I maybe said a few things that I shouldn't have.'

'She probably deserved them.'

I glance at Erin's body. It feels wrong to be mean about her now. 'So, I was going to clear the air. I asked her to meet me for a coffee earlier but then she didn't show up and sent me some bullshit message about a meeting or whatever. She never liked conflict. I know that's kind of hard to believe, but she liked to bully and cajole and she could only do that if she was right. And she knew she was wrong this time. The argument was about her renting Bella Donna's stall out, something that she definitely didn't have authority to do, and she didn't follow the process. Anyway,' I shake my head. 'Sorry to go off track.'

'Just take your time,' Jessica reassures me.

'Then she turned up here. She was in this hideous mood. I don't know exactly what happened but I think she'd been pulled up by her boss. Sebastian made a formal complaint about her. She was so pissed. She kept saying that she would ruin us. Just saying it over and over again, spitting the words in my face. And I know her. I know how petty and vindictive she can be.'

'And she wouldn't stop?'

I shake my head. 'She just kept saying it, over and over, getting in my face. And I... I...' I motion toward the body. 'I didn't mean to.'

'Of course you didn't.'

'Um. Can I just ask...' I trail off. What do I actually want to ask her?

'Why I'm helping?' she offers.

I nod, slightly dumbly.

Jessica pauses for a moment and then considers me over the top of her mug of tea. I feel like she's looking into my soul and judging what she sees, as if she's weighing up if I'm worthy to receive the truth or if she should just make up some bullshit. 'You saw me,' she says eventually, with a nonchalant shrug.

'But why? Why were you in my garden?'

She puts down her mug carefully, the motion slow and controlled. Then she leans back a little. A tiny laugh escapes her lips and sends a shiver up the back of my neck. 'Because I was worried about you. But none of that really matters. We should get started.' She pauses for a moment. 'With her.'

'You sound like you know what you're doing.'

'Perhaps I've just listened to a lot of true crime podcasts,' she says with a twerk of her eyebrows. She suddenly reminds me of Immy, who is also a fan of those podcasts. 'Grab her feet,' she instructs.

'What are we...'

'You have a chest freezer?'

'In the garage.'

'Perfect.'

Even with the two of us, it's hard work to get her into the freezer. A human body is surprisingly heavy, especially when it's a dead weight.

'Lucky this isn't full,' Jessica observes as I lift the lid and wisps of freezing air escape.

'I emptied it last week so there was space for all the festive goodies.'

'Smart woman,' she replies with a proud smile.

'How long can a body stay in the freezer?' I ask, staring at her face.

'Indefinitely,' Jessica says. 'Just make sure you don't have a power cut.'

A shiver runs up the back of my neck. There have been a number of storms already this year and I know a few people who've lost power, sometimes for days.

45

JESSICA

Once the body is in the freezer, I make Fearne another cup of tea.

'I think I might need something stronger,' she says softly, her eyes trained on the patch of blood still staining the kitchen floor.

'I think you need a clear head because we still need to finish.'

'Yes ma'am,' she says and gives me a funny little mock salute. 'Sorry. I get weird when I'm...' she shakes her head a few times. 'I don't know what I am...'

'You're probably in shock.'

'Yes. Probably.'

I let her finish her tea, even though she grimaces at the amount of sugar I added to the brew. 'Right then,' I say as soon as she puts down the cup. 'Let's get cracking. Where's your bleach?' I head to the cupboard under the sink before she replies.

'Under the—' she stops mid-sentence when she sees I'm already there and pushing bottles of every other cleaning product under the sun out of the way to get to the bleach toward the back. 'Am I really that predictable?' She sounds sad.

'Everyone stores their bleach in the cupboard under the sink. Well, unless there's a baby or toddler in the house, then you'd probably keep it somewhere a bit more secure.'

As we clean up the rest of the blood and make sure every tile in the kitchen has been bleached to within an inch of its life, I can sense her sneaking glances at me. She's wondering how I know what to do. Why I'm so calm. Why I haven't asked her more questions about exactly what happened.

You remember earlier when I was worried that perhaps we were only acquaintances because she hadn't told Sebastian about me? Well, I think that ship has sailed and we are firm friends.

'How did she get here?' I ask, just as we're finishing up.

'She walked.'

'You're sure?'

'Yep. She arrived on the doorstep a little sweaty, having a moan that it was further than she'd thought, as if it was my fault she couldn't use Google Maps. Apparently she'd forgotten her phone, left it in the office.'

'Her phone is in the office?' I ask quickly.

Fearne nods.

'And she walked here?'

Fearne nods again.

'Who knew she was coming?'

Fearne shrugs. 'I don't know. She was meant to meet me earlier but she didn't show up. I sent her a text message... umm... expressing my opinion of her.' She makes a face.

'You called her a...'

'Bitch. Yeah. And something else too.' She looks down at the floor, twisting her hands in front of her. 'We knew each other once and...'

'What did you call her?'

'A fucking evil witch.'

'Ouch.' I'd heard the gossip but hearing the words from her own lips gives them a certain kick.

'Yeah.' She pauses for a moment. 'That's why she came here. To have it out in person.'

'Do you think she would have told anyone else about this? A boyfriend maybe? Sister? Best fri—' I cut myself off on the last one. Erin Winters hardly strikes me as the 'girly gossiping over lunch' kind of woman.

'She's single. No kids. No siblings. No one who looks like a particularly close friend,' Fearne tells me. 'I might have done a little social media stalking when she first showed up at the market.'

'Good. That's good. So her phone isn't here and she probably didn't tell anyone either.' I'm thinking out loud, trying to put together a plan to get Fearne free and clear from all of this mess, my words slow and thoughtful. 'So that means we can make an alternative narrative for the situation. I've got it.' I smile at her, probably a little maniacally, but it's too late to hide the crazy now. I snap into efficiency mode. 'I won't be able to get into her phone. But she might have a MacBook, or an iPad.'

Fearne looks at me as if she isn't quite understanding.

'I won't be able to use her face to unlock the phone.' I put up a hand to stop her from interrupting, I know what she's going to say and I know it won't work. 'Even if I went and got the phone, by the time I'm back here the facial recognition will fail. You can't use a frozen body to unlock an iPhone.' She doesn't ask me how I know. 'But I can take something to unlock her other devices.'

'I...'

'I need her index finger. From her dominant hand.' I wrack

my brain to remember if I've seen her write something and which hand she used. It would be just my luck to take the finger from her right hand and then discover she's a leftie.

'She's right-handed.'

'You're absolutely sure?' I ask.

Fearne nods. 'I'm a leftie. I read something once that lefties live two years less than righties and it's always fascinated me since.'

'That's...' I trail off. It's the kind of thing that interests me, but I guess now isn't the time.

'I think it's probably skewed by industrial accidents and things like that. Everything is designed for people who are right-handed so I guess it's more dangerous if you're a leftie.'

I blanch slightly at the thought. There are some things I'm oddly squeamish about and people getting crushed by large machinery is one of them.

I try not to look at Erin's face as I open the freezer. She looks slightly grey, but she could still just be sleeping. Perhaps just following a huge blowout and feeling the ravages of a hangover nipping at her heels. Her hand is cold and I can feel the change in skin texture. She's been in here for forty-five minutes and she's starting to freeze. It's a blessing in disguise as there isn't much blood as I saw through the bottom joint, twisting in the final moment to complete the dislocation. I grab a little sealed baggie of ice cubes from the freezer and pop it inside.

'Are these for cocktails?' I ask, brandishing the bag of ice.

'Yeah. The perfect amount for a Manhattan on the rocks.'

'And perfect for carrying a finger.'

Fearne turns slightly green. 'Well, I guess I'm never drinking a Manhattan again.'

Erin's coat is a size too big for me but it'll do. I wear it to leave the house, pulling a hat over my hair. Her handbag is slung over my shoulder.

I take the most direct route I can from Fearne's house to Erin's office, deliberately keeping my head down as if I'm bracing myself against the cold. I even use her scarf to cover the lower part of my face. That way, if any CCTV cameras pick me up, they will just assume it's her walking back.

Her office has a security access system and her pass makes a rather satisfying beep as it unlocks the door. Again, I try to hide my face as much as possible. There's every chance there are cameras in the office too. I'm quick as I go to her desk, following Fearne's exact instructions as to where it is. Not that it's hard to spot. The other desks in the open-plan area are covered in trinkets and empty coffee cups and pictures of family. But not Erin's. Everything is perfectly aligned at ninety-degree angles, all in matching shades of dark blue. There are no personal items, no photos. This desk could belong to anyone, but everything about it screams Erin.

Her phone is in the top drawer of the pedestal under her desk. Of course she's the kind of person who wouldn't have her phone out to distract her from her mission to ruin Christmas through endless lists.

Her work computer is an ancient Lenovo desktop. There's no way I can break into that without it looking hideously suspicious so I leave it well alone and get myself out of that office as quickly as possible.

Erin's flat shows just as many signs of her being the worst type of anally retentive. There is nothing inside, no personal things at all. If you think of the home of a serial killer, you'd probably imagine something similar to the sterile box I find when I unlock the door using the keys from her handbag.

She has a MacBook. *Hallelujah*. The finger works perfectly to unlock it.

And double hallelujah. She's such a workaholic that she has access to her work emails and calendar from this MacBook. I find the meeting with Fearne she had put in her diary for earlier that day, the one Erin didn't show up to because she got called into another. From the looks of it, that one was with the Chief Exec, evidently where Erin got a major ticking-off from her boss. She put a block in her diary from six pm. *Visit FD*. She marked it private so other people looking at her diary wouldn't see what she was doing.

I could delete it. Tell Fearne to pretend Erin never went to the house. But then what if she had told someone? Or a clever dick in some forensic IT centre is able to recover the private appointment. No, better to leave it that Erin did go to Fearne's. That they chatted, had a cup of tea. And then Erin walked back to the office, picked up her forgotten phone and went home.

I spend half an hour looking at nice hotels within about an hour's radius of here. I book a three-night stay at The Brixley Manor using her credit card. Then I put on an out of office message saying she has a few days off and she won't have access to email over that time.

I turn off the phone and take it with me.

Tomorrow I'll come back to the flat and switch it back on while I'm standing close enough for anyone who tracks the phone to think she's at home. And then I'll head toward The Brixley Manor, throwing the phone out the window at some point on the trip. It'll take a while for anyone to realise she's missing. And when they do it will look like she decided to take a trip but never made it to her destination.

It's not a perfect plan by any means. Normally I don't kill my victims willy-nilly and then have to try to pick up the pieces afterwards. I plan, and plan some more, and make sure there isn't a shred of evidence to tie me to a murder. But this is messy and uncertain and I don't like the gnawing feeling in the bottom of my stomach that I'm making a right pig's ear of all this and it'll come back to bite me.

46

FEARNE

There's an atmosphere in the house, like the air is charged, like there's a bomb just waiting to go off. I need to stop myself from going into the garage and opening the freezer every five minutes. Immy and Sebastian never go out there, the chest freezer is the domain of forgotten batch cooking and other terrible things, all the good stuff like ice cream is in the smaller freezer in the kitchen. But they'll soon get suspicious if I'm out there constantly.

I'm making a chilli, occasionally stirring the pot on the stove as I make a list of all the things I still need to add to the Christmas food shop now it's only two weeks until the big day, when suddenly there's an ear-splitting alarm filling the kitchen.

'What the fuck was that?' Sebastian comes into the kitchen.

'I... I...' I try to talk but my heart is in my throat, all my fear instincts on high.

The alarm goes off again and Sebastian stares at the phone in his hand, which appears to be the culprit.

I breathe and laugh, a short sharp bark, as I feel the whoosh of adrenaline leave my body. 'Did you set an alarm for something?'

'I didn't set an alarm.' He peers at the screen and I make myself a mental reminder to book him an optician appointment. 'It's some kind of alert.'

My phone is on charge by the kitchen table and I cross the room to get it. I have an alert too.

Severe Alert
Issued by the UK Government

A RED warning for wind has been issued in your area. Extremely strong winds are expected to cause significant disruption from 8pm this evening (Saturday 13 December 2025). Strong winds can cause flying debris, falling trees and large waves around coastal areas, all of which can present a danger to life. Stay indoors if you can. It is not safe to drive in these conditions.

The storm may damage infrastructure causing power cuts and disruption to mobile phone coverage. Consider gathering torches, batteries, a mobile phone power pack and other essential items you already have at home.

Stay up to date with the weather forecast for your areas and follow advice from emergency services, network operators and local authorities. For more information search online for 'gov.uk/alerts' or Met Office warning and advice.

'Oh,' Sebastian says, and there's a hint of disappointment there. 'It's just a weather warning.'

'It sounds pretty severe,' I reply. 'I mean, enough for them to message everyone.'

Sebastian's face falls. 'You're right. I'll probably need to go to the market.' He cracks his neck to each side and then sighs deeply. He looks tired. Actually, he looks more than tired, he looks bone weary, as if everything is pressing down on him, squashing him. 'I need to speak to Erin,' he says. 'No doubt she'll have some bullshit protocol all worked out that I'll have to follow.' He scrunches his face up in anticipation.

'Don't you already have a process?' I ask gently. I know he does. Even though we've never had a government alert before, we've still had milder storms and I've even helped lash down bits of awning myself when we first started out.

'Ah, but you see,' he tells me, 'it isn't Erin's process.' He lifts his phone and squints at the screen.

'What are you doing?'

'Calling her.' He gives me a funny look as if to ask what the hell else I thought he'd be doing. He stares at me while it rings. I try to arrange my face into an expression that says I don't already know she won't answer. Although my stupid brain immediately jumps to a *what if she does answer* scenario, as if we were in the middle of a horror film.

'Fuck's sake,' Sebastian says as her voicemail clicks in. He listens to her clipped words about being unavailable and then leaves a message. 'Erin. Sebastian here. I presume you've had the government alert and are already devising a procedure. Please advise what you want me to do so that I don't fall foul of your rules.' His tone conveys his exhaustion with her. I just hope that the borderline rudeness won't make him a suspect, that the police won't think that perhaps he hated her enough to kill her. Surely not.

'What are you going to do?' I ask him.

'Wait for her to call,' he says simply.

'Umm...'

'What?'

'It's just...'

'What? Just tell me, Fearne. I'm really not in the mood for this right now.' He stares at me for a few moments and I can feel his irritation rising. 'For fuck's sake. What did you say to her this time?'

'I didn't say anything.' My voice sounds whiney and a bit pathetic in my own ears.

He gives me a look that says he's thoroughly disappointed in me. 'I know you two have history, but I have to work with her now and you're making things more difficult than they need to be.'

'I promise I didn't say anything.'

'But you *did* something?' He raises an eyebrow.

'I think I need to show you something,' I tell him.

I lead him through to the garage, the cold air hitting me in the face as I open the adjoining door from the kitchen. In four steps, I'm in front of the freezer, my hand resting on the lid.

'I really don't have time to talk about the preparations for Christmas dinner right now,' he says. He's still standing inside the kitchen, watching me from the warmth of the main house. 'And if you're worried about the power cut messing with the freezer, we have insurance.'

'It isn't that,' I whisper. 'Please just come here, Sebastian. You need to see this.'

He chunters something under his breath but lumbers over to me. I lift the lid and a curl of freezing smoke lifts into the garage. I suppress the urge to make some kind of 'ta-da' announcement as I push aside some bags of frozen peas to reveal the body.

'Is that...?' He reaches out a finger as if to touch her, but pulls it back before he gets too close. She looks different, ice encrusting her skin and dusting her eyelashes. She doesn't look real. Although the stab wound on her chest absolutely does. Sebastian turns to look at me, his expression unreadable.

'It was an accident,' I say. His face doesn't move. 'I promise. I didn't mean to kill her. It just happened. I... I...'

But still he's impassive, giving nothing away about how he feels.

'Please say something,' I beg softly.

Nothing.

'Honestly, I didn't want to kill her. It isn't like I planned this. I just...'

He raises his hands and rests them gently on my shoulders. And then his face breaks into a smile. 'You killed the witch?' There's awe in his voice.

I nod.

'You absolute fucking beauty.' In a flash he leans in to kiss me, mouth open, teeth bashing, his tongue in my mouth. It's the most erotic kiss we've shared in... well... years. I feel myself respond to him. But... hang on. We're standing in front of the body of the woman I kind of accidentally murdered.

I push him away.

'Sorry,' he says, a little sheepishly. 'I just...' He shakes his head as his smile broadens. 'You got rid of her. For me.'

Who said my husband wasn't romantic? I'm being sarcastic, obviously, it isn't like un-aliving our enemies is our love language. And, to be fair, I didn't do it for him. I did it for me. Because she was a bitch and she ruined my life and I wasn't going to let her ruin it again. But, of course, it was an accident. I think.

'When did you...?' he asks, looking back at her.

'Two days ago.'

He nods a few times and then it morphs into a jig. He's like an excited kid on Christmas Day.

'You seem to be taking this well,' I remark, my tone dry.

'Ding dong, the witch is dead.'

'Yes. But two things. Number one.' I put my index finger up. 'You won't be getting a new process from Erin about dealing with the storm.'

'So, I can do what I need to do without worrying about her interfering.'

'But you can't make it known that you know that. So, you'll have to act as if you're preparing for her interference.'

'Fine.'

'And number two.' I raise my middle finger to meet my index one. 'What the actual fuck do we do if there's a power cut to the freezer?'

'Oh.' His face falls. 'That is a pretty good question.'

'I know.' I'm not really in the mood for his condescension.

'So, what was the plan for the body? I mean, she can't live here permanently.'

'I don't know. Jessica is think—'

'What?' He sounds seriously pissed off. 'Someone else knows?'

'Jessica.'

'Jessica?'

'Mrs Claus.' My voice is small. 'She came round just after it happened. She helped me to clear up and stash the body. Showed me how to bleach the floor to get rid of all the blood.'

'And you trust her?' He raises an eyebrow.

'I... I... we're friends.'

'You barely know the woman. Jesus Christ, Fearne. What the fuck were you thinking? What if she goes to the police? They could be here any moment.' He looks around and I can feel his panic. He slams the lid down on the freezer. 'We need to hide her properly.'

'Please calm down.'

'You told a stranger that you killed someone.' He enunciates each word carefully.

'You don't have to talk to me like I'm stupid.'

'You don't think this was stupid?' he counters.

'We can trust her. She's part of this too. She helped me. If she goes to the police now they'll have plenty of questions for her as well.'

He sighs. Once. Twice. Three times. A tad overdramatically, as if he were a put-upon lady in one of my regency romances. 'Call her. Ask her what to do about the freezer if there's a power cut. Put it on speaker. I want to hear her, get a feel for what she might be scheming.'

'She isn't schem—' I cut myself off when I see the look on his face. 'Fine.' I start to head back toward the warmth of the kitchen. 'My phone's inside,' I tell him over my shoulder and he trots behind me.

'Hey, Fearne,' Jessica says as she answers the call. I look at Sebastian to make sure he can hear her clearly. He nods.

'Hey, Jessica. Umm. Did you get the government alert?'

'Yeah. Almost frightened the life out of me.' She laughs.

'Well... it's just... what do I do if there's a power cut?'

'We can't talk like this...'

'I know, it's just... I'm really worried. If the freezer starts to defrost and she—'

'I know it must be a worry about the *Christmas dinner*. And I know you're busy and it's only natural to worry that things will go wrong. But I'm sure it'll all be fine.'

'I'm not talking about Christmas din—'

'You have a big chest freezer, right? They can stay cold for hours. It'll be fine.'

'But—'

'For fuck's sake, Fearne.' I physically take a step back. I've never heard her swear and certainly not so forcefully. 'We can't talk like this on the phone.'

'Sorry.' I make my voice as small as possible. 'You're right. I just... I panicked. But I'll try to stay chill.'

'Have a glass of wine and relax, OK?'

'Yeah. See you tomorrow?'

'Sure.'

I hang up the call and look at Sebastian. 'See. She isn't trying to trap me, or trying to gather evidence against me, or anything like that. She's helping me.'

'I don't know if I trust her.'

'We don't have a choice,' I remind him. It's all well and good to sit there and pontificate on the reliability of our accomplice, but the fact is she knows far too much and there is nothing I can do about it except to believe her.

'I could do some digging about her...' Sebastian says, trailing off as if it's just a casual thought.

'You sound like we're in one of those true crime thingies Immy loves so much.' I don't really understand the fascination with them. Why would you want to spend your free time thinking about murder and death and all the bad things in the world? Everything is shit enough without adding other people's problems into the mix, like solving crime is a participation sport.

'I just think it might be worthwhile knowing a little more about the person we're putting so much trust in.'

'She's my friend.' I'm adamant.

'Maybe. But it's always worth doing some due diligence, don't you think?'

47

JESSICA

I could hear someone else in the background of Fearne's call. Someone breathing, fairly rapidly, as if they were pissed off.

It must be Sebastian.

So, she told him.

Fuck.

What will a man like that do with that kind of information? I think that, for all his flaws – and there are many, he does actually love Fearne and the life they have built together. He won't want to put that in jeopardy. He'll want to help her. But what does that mean for me?

* * *

The electricity goes out at nine that evening, plunging the living room into darkness. Lena is in the bedroom and I hear her let out a howl.

Running up the stairs in the pitch black with my heart in my mouth, I try to prepare myself for what I might find. 'What happened?' I ask as I throw open the door.

'The Switch wasn't charged.'

'Oh.' I suddenly feel stupid – not a feeling I particularly enjoy – and I take a step into the dark room. 'But you're OK?'

'Of course. It's just a power cut.'

'Come downstairs and I'll light the fire,' I tell her. 'I've got a battery pack you can use to charge the Switch.'

'You do?'

'Yep.'

'You're always so prepared. Like a... a...' She gropes for something suitable. 'Umm... a Boy Scout?'

'Dib dib,' I say, doing the salute, although she won't be able to see it with all the lights out.

She laughs. 'You are so weird.' I can hear the eyeroll in her voice, but also the affection and my heart swells for a moment.

Five minutes later, she comes into the living room. I've lit the fire and already the room is getting warmer, the flames blazing in the grate as the larger logs start to catch. She's holding the Switch and I motion toward the battery pack I've laid out on the sofa for her.

'What are you doing?' she asks, motioning at the fact that I'm sitting on the floor with a deck of playing cards laid out in front of me.

'Playing Solitaire.'

'Do you know any games for two people?'

'Um. Well, there is one that I used to play with my brother and his friends.'

'Cool. Can you teach me?' she asks, putting down the Switch to come and join me.

'Sure.' I pick up the cards and begin to shuffle. Lena looks almost shocked. 'I play poker,' I tell her. Her mouth opens wide. 'You're surprised?'

'It's just... you're so...' she trails off. 'I don't know. You don't seem like you'd gamble. Like you follow the rules and things.'

'Do I need to remind you of the other thing I do?'

She blushes. 'Well, no. I guess you kind of have a point there.' She grins. 'I kind of like this version of you. You seem cooler.'

'I'll have you know that I am the epitome of cool,' I reply with mock incredulity.

'Seriously?' Her gaze is rather withering in that way only teenage girls can pull off.

'No. I know I'm not cool. But I can play cards.' I add further flourishes to my shuffling of the deck before dealing us nine cards each, three face down, three face up on top of them, three for the hand.

Lena looks at the cards in front of her. 'What game is this?'

'This is Shithead.' I'm definitely breaking my no swearing rule today, that must be at least the third time.

'Shithead? But I don't know how to play.'

'I'll teach you. It'll be fun.'

And it is. She takes to the game quickly, not that it's hugely complicated to begin with, and is soon beating me on her luckier hands.

'Shithead!' she exclaims with relish as she beats me a third time.

We raid the snack cupboard for crisps and chocolate and miniature slices of stollen. Soon the cards are slightly tacky, something that would normally irritate me irrationally, but with Lena it just reminds me that we're having a good time.

'You keep looking at your phone,' Lena says.

'I'm not.'

'You are. Are you waiting for someone to call?'

'No.' The truth is I'm waiting for Fearne to message me in a panic because her power is also out and she has a body in her freezer. Given how she was acting on the phone, I'm surprised I don't get a flurry of texts from her. But there's nothing. Radio silence.

Something doesn't feel right. And I'm normally pretty good at figuring out when things have gone sideways. How else do you think I've managed to avoid any kind of suspicion all these years?

There's a gnawing sensation in the pit of my stomach.

Something is wrong.

Disaster is coming.

I can feel it in my bones and I am never wrong.

* * *

There's a soft knock on the door a little before ten, just as Lena's starting to yawn and say she's ready for bed.

I open it to reveal Alvi on my doorstep with a pair of huskies.

'Hey,' he says. 'I was walking these two,' he motions at the huge fluffy dogs who are literally staring at him with something I can only imagine is pure love. 'And then the power went out. I wanted to check you're OK.'

'Oh, we're fine,' I say. But then I see just how earnest he looks, how concerned. I guess it wouldn't hurt to make him feel like he's helped rescue a damsel in distress. And I've been reading a few of Fearne's Cherry Dubois books recently and they've made me feel like I might enjoy playing the damsel, if only for a short while. Those damsels seem to have a *lot* of fun.

'Would you like to come in?' I ask and move aside so he can step over the threshold.

Lena mumbles something about leaving us alone and heads to the bedroom.

'Take a husky for warmth,' Alvi calls after her. 'Storm, go find her.' The dog runs up the stairs after her and Lena squeals softly in delight.

'Drink? I can't do anything hot obviously.' I motion around at the flickering candles and firelight to demonstrate the lack of power. 'But I have alcohol. Wine, sherry, port, Chambord, cherry brandy.'

'That sounds like the contents of my English grandmother's Christmas liquor stash,' he says softly.

'I do love a festive liquor.'

'Shall we have a port? I feel like it's that kind of evening.'

I pour one for both of us, using the special small crystal glasses with the holly pattern I found last year in a charity shop. We sit on each end of the sofa and Shadow, the other husky, climbs up between us, curling himself into a tight ball and falling instantly asleep.

'I like what you've done with the cottage,' he says, looking around at the veritable winter wonderland I've created in the living room. Some of it's older stuff, things I've accumulated over the years, like a pair of vintage porcelain candle holders with built-in snuffers. Some is new. Every year – no matter how tight the finances are – I make sure to set myself aside a budget to buy more decorations. It's one of the highlights of the season. You know, amongst some of the other activities I allow myself to enjoy. This year's pièce de résistance is one of the gonks from James's stall on the market. I chose a medium-sized one in a little green outfit and he's so ugly he's positively charming, especially in the soft glow from the candles.

'We had Christmas Day here one year,' Alvi says, voice full of nostalgia. 'Hanna and I and our parents were meant to be flying back to Finland, but there was this huge snowstorm and Heathrow was closed. The farmhouse was being renovated and so we all ended up here. Mum and Dad and Granny and Grandpa and Hanna and me. All six of us crammed in here. My poor granny had to magic up a Christmas dinner for us all from a small turkey crown and a kitchen with only a tiny oven. It was chaos.'

'It sounds like fun.'

'It was. The next year, the whole family went to a rented villa in Italy and all we did was moan about it not being as fun as the previous year squashed into the cottage. I think my Finnish grandparents were kind of pissed off actually, given they'd paid for everything. But expensive doesn't always mean better.'

'Very true,' I agree.

'So how about you? Tell me one of your Christmas stories,' he says leaning forwards. Shadow huffs gently and wags his tail so Alvi reaches out to stroke his fur. The movement is absent-minded, as if he's on autopilot to always seek a dog to pet.

'Oh. Um... well...' My mind goes to *that* Christmas. But, of course, I can't tell him that, can I? Nothing is more guaranteed to break the romantic mood than the story of a masked assailant and blood. So much blood.

'You can tell me, you know. I promise I'm a good listener and I never judge. The dogs taught me that.' His voice is soft. As if he really cares.

I want to tell him. But I know he'd run a mile. So instead I tell a made-up story about my cousin telling me that Santa wasn't real.

'What a bastard,' he exclaims.

'I was heartbroken.'

'I bet.'

'But then his parents, my aunt and uncle, told him that if he didn't believe in Santa then he wouldn't get any presents.'

'I bet he changed his story pretty smartish.'

'You bet he did.'

He smiles and for a few moments I debate just leaning forward and kissing him. But I can't get involved romantically with anyone. Not now. Not here.

I'm going to be lucky to make it through 'til Christmas before I have to cut and run. There have been too many murders. Not mine, mine will never trace back to me. But Fearne's might. I always thought the worst fate was to spend the rest of my life in prison for murder. But it would be far worse to spend the rest of my life in prison for a murder I didn't commit. That's just unthinkable.

I'll have to take Lena with me when I run.

Or find her somewhere else. Could she stay with Fearne? Be a sister to Immy?

* * *

I dream of him that night. Of big strong arms holding me tight against all the rubbish in the world. Of kind eyes telling me I'm special and brilliant and that he will always look after me. Of words whispered in the night that he sees me, really sees me, and loves me anyway.

48

FEARNE

I lie awake in bed and pray for the electricity to come back on. I've obsessively googled how long the items in a chest freezer will last for and the general consensus – thanks Mumsnet for finally being useful instead of a cesspool – is twenty-four hours. There are a few sites that claim forty-eight hours if the freezer is full – as mine definitely is – but they seem to be mainly insurance companies who I have an instant distrust for. After all, if you were on the hook to pay to restock people's entire contingent of frozen foods, you'd probably err on the longer side too.

What none of these estimates take into consideration, though, is exactly *what* I have sitting in my freezer threatening to defrost. It isn't a few bags of sweetcorn and some oven chips I'm worried about.

'Will you please try to sleep,' Sebastian grumbles next to me. 'I can tell you're awake.'

'You're awake too,' I point out.

'I'm thinking about her.'

'Erin?'

'Jessica.'

How to Slay at Christmas

Oh. I'm not sure I like the way he says her name. He's spent most of the evening on his phone researching her, all the while moaning about how this will rinse his data package for the month. But, despite his efforts, he really hasn't found very much. Jessica Williams doesn't have a big social media presence, just a Facebook account set up a few years ago and giving very little away about who she really is or where she comes from.

'Don't you think it's suspicious?' he asks, rolling over to face me and somehow letting in a blast of frigid air from outside the cover.

'Not everyone lives their lives online,' I remind him for what feels like the hundredth time this evening.

'You do.'

'I have an author Instagram account. My publisher says it's important for discovery.' Again, we've already had this conversation.

'You have Facebook too. And TikTok.'

'I don't use TikTok.' It was set up a few years ago when I was having a crisis of confidence about my writing career and thought I needed to do more myself. I vowed to post to TikTok every single day for three months to see what happened. I lasted four days before I ran out of content and lost the will to live. Sometimes I get an urge to try again and then I remind myself just how painful it was and have a large glass of wine instead.

'What if Jessica Williams isn't her real name?' he says and sits bolt upright in bed.

'If you don't stop letting all the cold in, you can go and sleep on the fucking sofa,' I say through gritted teeth, pulling the duvet back toward myself and tucking it around me. 'It's freezing in here.'

'No. Hear me out.' He sounds like an excited little kid. 'It would explain why I can't find much about her.'

'There are a hundred things that would explain that.' I'm starting – talk about an understatement – to get bored of this.

'Whatever. What if she *is* using a fake name?'

I take a deep breath. He isn't going to let this go, is he? Which means I'm going to have to talk through the logic with him, make him realise just how fucking ridiculous this all sounds and that we have bigger things to worry about than Jessica. Like the actual fucking dead body slowly thawing in the fucking freezer. 'Fine,' I say, turning toward him slightly. 'What if she is?'

'Then it would be suspicious.'

'Suspicious of what?' I ask.

'Well… I don't know. Just suspicious.'

'You can't just say it's "suspicious". You have to be more specific.'

'I'm not sure I do.' He's a little petulant.

'In this case, I think you do. So, what if Jessica is using a fake name? What would that suggest about her?'

'That she can't be trusted,' he says, huffily.

'Or that she can't trust other people. Perhaps she's running from an abusive ex? Or she's in some kind of witness protection thing.'

'That only happens in films.'

'I'm sure it happens in real life too.'

'Hmm.' He doesn't sound convinced. 'I still think it's weird to use a fake name.' He flops back down onto the pillows, causing the entire bed to shake as if there's been an earthquake.

'She might not be using a pseudonym,' I remind him.

He's quiet for a few minutes and I feel myself gradually relaxing as I nudge toward sleep. But suddenly he sits up again. 'What if she's running some kind of con?'

'A con?'

'Yeah. What if she goes place to place and finds some poor

naive person to latch on to.' It is clear from his tone that I am the 'poor naive person' in question. 'And then she waits and watches and then, when they fuck up, she swoops in.'

'You think Jessica made friends with me so she could wait for me to accidentally kill someone?' I inject as much condescension into my tone as I can so he can truly understand the lunacy of his suggestion.

'Not specifically a murder. It could have been anything. Just something you wouldn't want the world to know. And then BAM!' He claps his hands together, causing me to almost jump out of my skin. 'Then she whips out the blackmail demands.'

'It doesn't sound very likely. And it really doesn't sound like Jessica.'

'Maybe not the Jessica she's been pretending to be, no.' He flops back on the pillows. 'I think I've cracked it,' he says with more than a hint of pride. Then he turns away from me, dragging as much of the super-king duvet as he can with him. 'Night, Fearne. Love you.'

'Love you too,' I reply on autopilot, rolling on to my other side so we're back to back.

I'm still trying to sleep ten minutes later when I have a sudden thought.

What if Jessica *is* using a fake name? Not to con me, or because she's running from someone who hurt her.

How did she know exactly what to do with the murder scene?

Why was she so calm and collected as she mopped up all that blood?

How did she have the stomach to remove one of Erin's fingers so she could access her laptop?

What if Jessica is running because somewhere in her past there's another body. Someone she killed?

* * *

The electricity is back on by the morning and I breathe a huge sigh of relief as I check Erin and find there are still ice crystals in her eyelashes.

Sebastian heads off to the market to assess the damage. 'I'll call when I have more info,' he tells me as he grabs the flask of coffee I made him from the kitchen counter. 'Is this tea?'

'Coffee.' I should have waited to ask him before I bothered.

But he surprises me by leaning in to kiss my cheek. 'Even better,' he says.

He calls an hour later to tell me we've been lucky and there's almost no damage to the market from the storm.

'Or certainly nothing that the team and the vendors can't fix within an hour or so,' he says.

'That's great news.'

'Oh, and I've been thinking more about the whole Jessica thing.'

'And?'

'Well, I can look at her CV. Try to piece together a bit more about her from that.'

'But she's a Grottos R Us employee.'

'I still interviewed her. There's a printed copy of her CV in one of the filing cabinets in the office. I'll look for it when I get home tonight.' I can almost hear him rubbing his hands together in glee at the thought of continuing his sleuthing.

'Great,' I say. 'And don't forget you promised your mum you'd pop in and see her on your way home.'

He makes a noise, which I think is a muffled groan. 'I'd forgotten. I'll be home about eight. Love you.'

'Love you too,' I say but I'm already heading up the stairs toward the office.

It takes me fifteen minutes to find Jessica's CV in the midst of my husband's chaotic filing system. I'm not looking for evidence that Jessica Williams is some kind of fake name. If it is, she's been using the same one for long enough to get references from a few of her last employers. No, what I'm looking for is something else. Anything that might help to answer my questions from the middle of the night.

Jessica Williams has experience with murder.

But just how much?

* * *

Sebastian is acting like a complete lunatic. He's obsessed about Jessica and what she might be up to.

'You have to stop,' I tell him. 'You'll make yourself sick, churning through all of this.'

'I'm fine,' he snaps back at me.

'You're clearly not fine.'

'You don't understand. We don't know who she is and what else she's done.'

But he's wrong. I do know what she's done. I've been doing some digging of my own and discovered a string of unsolved murders in every place she's been a Mrs Claus for the past five years. It's too much to be a coincidence. She's a murderer. And, judging by the fact that she's never been caught, she's an extremely good one.

'You have to let me help you here, Fearne,' he says, his tone serious as he swivels in his office chair to look at me. 'I need to protect us. I need to protect you. To keep you safe.'

There's something about the look in his eye that I can't reconcile to the husband I know. Is there a chance he's found the same breadcrumbs I have? That he's started to put two and two together and might come to the same conclusion about Jessica's history? I think she's kind of a superstar, a woman who has dedicated her life to taking out the trash, getting rid of some of the truly shitty people out there. But I doubt Sebastian would think of it like that. He would think her a cold-blooded killer. And then what might he do?

49

IN WHICH THE EVIDENCE CRYSTALLISES…

There's a new episode of *Rosie Investigates*, the thumbnail a clickbaity image of her doing a shocked face, her hands on her cheeks like a parody of *Home Alone*. The headline promises 'revelations that will blow your mind'.

I really don't have the time or the energy to sit through the entire episode and I fast-forward, tapping my fingers while I'm forced to watch an advert for pet-friendly hotels in the Cotswolds before I can watch the final few minutes.

So, to round up what we've seen on today's episode of *Rosie Investigates*. It turns out that none of the men whose bodies were found in the woods were particularly nice guys. I know that all the tributes say they were, but that's what everyone says, isn't it? I mean, I'm not saying these men deserved to die… but the streets are definitely a bit safer with them gone.

But here's the really interesting part. Two different witnesses recall seeing a stranger in the vicinity of the woods on the evenings the men were killed. Both witnesses describe her as being a fairly petite woman, probably in her early thirties, and wearing a thick woollen hat. And I know there will be a lot of you out there, a lot of my male viewers in particular, who won't believe that a woman could be the killer. But that's only because you've been trained to think like that. Take the blinkers off, people.

So, here's the big question. Are we looking for a killer to punish? Or are we looking for a vigilante to praise?

I'm determined to find the answer. If you'd like to help me, like this video and subscribe to the channel.

And I'll see you next time on *Rosie Investigates*.

That's it. Enough. I could keep searching for a thousand hours, find a hundred more possible examples and still nothing would give me actual concrete proof. She's too clever for that, and besides, if she was leaving evidence that linked her directly to the murders then the police would have smashed down the door by now.

Jessica Williams is a killer.

She moves from town to town each year, leaving a trail of bodies in her wake.

50

JESSICA

Lena wakes me up at 8 a.m. on Monday, thin light coming through the curtains that I only half closed last night. I feel terrible, like I drank far too much wine and ate too much salty food last night, which just feels rude given I drank exactly nothing and only ate a salad for dinner. My neck feels like it needs a good old crack, evidently sleeping on the sofa is doing me a whole load of no good.

'We should swap,' Lena says. 'You should have the bedroom and I'll sleep down here in the living room.'

I wave my hand dismissively. 'Of course not. You're a growing teenager who needs a ton more sleep than I do.'

She pauses for a moment as if she's thinking through the veracity of my argument. 'Fine,' she acquiesces. 'But today I have a treat planned for us. To say thank you for everything,' she adds quickly. 'You've been... well... amazing. And I can't thank you enough.'

'Anyone would have done the same,' I reply. But we both know it's a lie. Most people would have walked past the girl starving on the streets without a second thought. Most people wouldn't have stepped in between her and a man trying to lure her into his van. Although, to be fair, most people wouldn't have traumatised her either by subsequently killing him and then dragging her into other murder plots. So, you know, balance and all that.

Apparently we're going to a wreath-making workshop later at one of the small independent bookshops in Ellsbury town centre. It's opposite a particularly cute cafe, one I long to go to but usually avoid because it's pretty pricey. It was once an apothecary shop and the myriad drawers and bottles lined up on every surface give it a proper 'olde worlde' feel, like you've stepped back to the Georgian era. I like to imagine this was the place you bought hemlock or nightshade to sort out all manner of problems from nosy neighbours to boorish husbands.

We head inside the cafe and I stand in awe. It's just so perfect. 'I think I was an apothecary in another life,' I tell Lena.

She rolls her eyes. 'I don't think they would have called you that,' she says drily. I shoot her a quizzical look. 'They would have called you a witch.' She's so matter of fact about it. Should I be offended? But she's right. If I had been born a few centuries ago and pursued the same interests I do today, they would have called me all manner of things; witch would have been almost a compliment.

Lena orders us these fancy festive brunch platters. 'Like an afternoon tea, but in the morning,' she tells me with a smile.

I know she's doing this for me. That she's spent a long time thinking about exactly what would make me happy and then planned the day around it. And so I try to put all the other stuff from my mind for a few hours. No thinking about death. Or bodies in freezers. Or the hot guy I can't have. Or the fact that soon I'll have to ask Lena if she would like to come with me to the next place, carve out a life on the run with me.

The food is amazing: mini sausage sandwiches in the shape of fir trees; bacon, brie and cranberry puff pastry bites; stollen mini muffins; tiny mince pie brownies. And there's an amazing cinnamon spice latte that is literally Christmas in a mug.

Bellies full, we head over the road to make the wreaths. The bookshop smells like a pine forest and an instrumental version of 'Feliz Navidad' is blasting. It isn't quite midday but I spot a cauldron on one of the tables and cross my fingers it's full of mulled wine.

'It's so festive,' I say to Lena, whispering in her ear.

'That's why I picked it. I know how much you love Christmas.'

'Welcome,' a woman in a reindeer-festooned apron says as she approaches. 'You must be Lena and her mum?' But she doesn't wait for the correction. 'Fabulous. I've put you over here,' she waves toward the same table as the cauldron of – fingers crossed – mulled wine.

We work well together. Luckily the main portion of the wreath has already been made for us and so really the focus is on decoration. There are pinecones and cinnamon sticks and sprigs of small crimson berries that we wrap thin wire around and then twist onto the wreath base. Lena takes some thick red ribbon and ties it into the perfect bow while I look on, impressed. Then she cuts the ends into points.

'So it doesn't fray,' she tells me.

'How do you know how to do that?'

'Ballet,' she says and smiles. But the edges drop quickly and a shadow passes across her face. I want to give her that life back, the one where she snipped the edges of her ballet ribbons to stop them fraying. But I don't know how.

By the end of the workshop, we have produced something I'm genuinely proud of. 'It will have pride of place on the front door,' I tell Lena, bumping her hip with mine. 'This was such an amazing idea. Thank you so much.'

She smiles at me. 'Thank you.' She pauses for a moment. 'For everything. I really mean it.'

* * *

I'm still riding the warm fuzzy wave of a morning well spent in Christmas pursuits when I head into work. Alvi is on his stall, chatting to a well-dressed couple with a greyhound in a fancy matching Barbour coat. He waves as I pass and I wave back. He blushes and returns to his sales spiel.

The staffroom looks like a bomb has exploded, with coffee cups and takeout containers on every surface. Some of my fellow market workers are worse than students, and with less than a week left of the market it seems they've lost the will to even pick up their own rubbish. A big sign has been put up on the pinboard, the words written in red marker pen and capital letters.

THIS PLACE LOOKS LIKE A PIGSTY. CLEAN IT UP!!!

I'm not normally one to agree with a passive-aggressive message, but I kind of think Sebastian has a point this time, the place really is disgusting. Luckily, I keep a spare mug in my locker, one I know that someone else hasn't used and then failed to wash up properly.

Hmm, that's weird.

There's an envelope inside my locker. Someone must have slipped it through the gap around the door. The envelope is posh, the paper almost creamy, the kind you might use for an expensive greetings card. My name is written in block capitals on the front.

Inside is a card, a wintry scene depicted in decoupage; I think it's probably one from the Scissors Sisters stall. It must be a Christmas card from them. That's sweet.

But then I see the words written inside and my blood runs cold. The writing is small and neat. Careful. To conceal the scribe perhaps?

> *I see who you really are... meet me tomorrow evening after you finish work... ribeye.stereo.mountain*

Is that a What3Words location? I pull out my phone and bring up the app. The pin shows a place not far from here, maybe two miles or so.

It's a stretch of woodland in the middle of nowhere. Isolated.

I look back at the words. Someone knows who I really am. *What* I really am.

How have they found me?

Fuck.

Fuck.

Fuck.

Is it Sebastian? It must be Sebastian. He knows that I helped Fearne with her predicament. Did he go looking after that? Dig and dig into my past like the pedantic little fool he is, peeling back the layers of my life until he found a thread to pull.

I can feel my heart beating in my neck. Thump thump thump. As if at any moment my carotid artery will explode, like a bomb going off.

But I swallow it down. There is a queue of small children already lining up to meet Santa and his wife. They need to see the calm and collected Mrs Claus who will give them comfort that the presents will all be wrapped in time and delivered on Christmas Eve, ready for the big day. They do not want to see some maniacal-looking woman who thinks the gig might truly be up this time.

I find Fearne in the office on my break. She's on her own, no one else within earshot. 'You told him,' I hiss at her as I approach. She physically recoils.

'I had to. There was a body in my freezer and the electricity had just gone off.'

'It came back on a few hours later,' I remind her.

'I didn't know that at the time.'

'He sent me this.' I hand over the card.

'You think this is from Sebastian?' She looks up and then I see the fear in her eyes.

I nod. 'The address is some remote wood somewhere.'

'But why would Sebastian...' but she can't bring herself to finish the sentence. She reads the card again, mouthing the words silently. Then she looks up at me again. 'What do we do?'

How do I tell her?

The only logical thing here is to kill him.

'He promised me he wouldn't do anything.' Her voice sounds small and far away. 'He promised me he would take our secret to the grave.'

I think that might be exactly what he's going to do. He will take our secret to the grave. It's just that his grave is going to be a shallow one in the woods and he's going to be occupying it pretty soon.

51

FEARNE

Sometimes you have to make a choice in this life. A choice between yourself and someone else. I'm sick of putting myself second, or third, or just generally last. It's time for me to put myself first. To look out for number one.

Jessica knows what I did. Knows all the details of exactly how we covered it up.

Jessica knows what she's doing, she has experience. Lots and lots of experience.

There are only two ways this ends.

And so I'm going to help her go up against the person threatening her.

Even if it is Sebastian.

* * *

The police arrive at the house the following morning, just as I'm getting ready to head down to the market to keep an eye on Sebastian who went in at the crack of dawn.

DS Krishnan looks the same, in that perfectly polished way.

DC Jenkins on the other hand looks like he's sporting a bit of a hangover, his hair slightly mussed and his shirt crumpled underneath his jacket.

Oh shit.

'Is this about Bella Donna? I mean Gloria Symmonds?' I ask, trying to sound super casual.

'No. It's about a missing person. We're trying to track down her last movements and we're struggling. Someone at the market said you knew her more personally so we thought we'd drop by for a chat.'

'A missing person?'

'Erin Winters?'

Fuck. It was only a matter of time before the world knew she was missing and the search began. I paste as neutral an expression as I can muster on my face. 'Erin? What happened?'

'That's what we're trying to ascertain.'

I nod a few times, as if I'm trying to process the information. 'I'll make tea,' I say to buy myself more time to fully compose myself. Jessica and I already talked about what happens if – or rather when – the police turned up.

'Keep it simple. Keep it honest,' she'd said. 'Obviously not too honest,' she'd added with a chuckle and a wink. Her whole reaction at the time makes so much more sense now I know the truth about her.

'Erin and I used to work together, back in the day,' I tell the police. 'It wasn't wholly amicable, we were kind of rivals and then she became my boss and so I ended up leaving the council.'

'And then she became the...' DS Krishnan pauses to check her notes. 'Christmas Czar? Is that a real job?'

'The council wanted to make sure that tourists weren't being put off visiting Ellsbury because of the murders at the market. Her job was to make sure everything was as enticing as possible.'

'But that caused tension?'

'She clashed with my husband. And then she started to do things which were outside of process. Like bringing in a vendor to replace Bella Donna without going through the proper channels.'

'And that was why you argued?'

'Yes.'

'And this was the day before she went missing.'

'It was last week. Thursday, I think.' I can feel that my palms are sweating and I try to wipe them on my jeans without DC Jenkins and DS Krishnan noticing.

'Erin was booked into The Brixley Manor for the day after, but she never arrived.'

'Oh. What happened to her?'

DS Krishnan looks a little bored. 'As I said before, we have no idea.'

'Right. Yes. Sorry. It's just, this is a bit of a surprise. I mean, you hear about people going missing in books. Not that I really read thrillers, I'm more of a love story person myself. I'm a writer. An author. I write regency romances.' I'm talking way too quickly, my words falling out of my mouth in a jumble.

'You seem kind of jittery,' DC Krishnan observes, putting down her little notebook to peer at me more intently.

'Just...' *Fuck*. 'I mean... there's been these murders and then Bella Donna's accident. And now this...'

'It's a lot to get your head around,' DC Jenkins says with a friendly smile. 'I think the whole city is on edge and you've been closer to everything than most.' He sounds almost sympathetic.

'Yeah. Normally Ellsbury is so quiet and now...' I spread my fingers wide on the kitchen table.

DS Krishnan picks up the notebook and scans her list of

questions. 'The main thing we're trying to understand is if she left of her own accord.'

'Like she just walked out on her life?' I ask.

'It's surprisingly common with missing persons. Sometimes people just have enough and walk away.'

'That doesn't sound like Erin.' I mean, it would be super convenient if the police concluded she just packed her bags and left everything behind to start a new life in Bali or whatever, but no one will believe it. Or at least, no one would believe that I would believe it. And that might be enough to arouse suspicion.

'No. Her boss at the council said the same.'

They ask a few more questions but I apologise and say I have nothing else to give them. 'We were never really friends and I've barely seen her for the past thirteen years,' I explain as I show them out. 'I'm sorry I couldn't be of more help.'

But as soon as I close the door behind them, I feel my legs buckle and I slide down the wall until I'm sitting on the floor. 'Holy fuck,' I whisper under my breath. That has to be the most stressful thing I've ever been through.

I'm still sitting on the floor in the hallway when Sebastian pops home an hour later.

'What are you doing?' he asks from the doorstep.

'The police came. About Erin.'

'Oh. What did they say?' He comes inside and closes the door behind him, eyes darting around the hallway as if he's half expecting the police to still be here.

'She's officially missing. They don't have any leads. They don't think she just walked away from her life.' I'm deadpan as I list them off.

'Do they suspect you?'

'No. Or at least I hope not. They gave me no indication anyway.'

'Phew.' Then he reaches out to give me a hand to stand. 'I mean, that all sounds OK. For now, at least.'

'For now?'

'They'll be back.' He sounds very sure. 'Especially if Jessica decides to fuck us over.'

'I really don't think—'

'Just stop defending her. Please. Come on, you know she's a fucking liability.' His anger is quick to erupt and I take a step back from him. 'Just leave it with me, OK? I'm going to sort this whole mess out.'

I don't tell him that his plan will not work. That Jessica has already shared the note with me and that she has a plan for him. His idea of silencing Jessica is going to end very differently from what he expects. I'm going to help make sure of that.

'What are you planning?' I ask him. The more I know, the better prepared I can make sure Jessica is.

'The less you know, the better. Just trust me.'

I try asking him again before he heads back to the market but he's so evasive.

'I need to go out this evening,' he tells me before he leaves.

'Oh.' I try to stay cool. 'Are you meeting someone?'

'No.'

'Oh. So...'

'It's nothing important. Just leave it, OK.'

I put my hands up in a position of surrender. 'Fine. I'll be out this evening anyway. It's book club night.'

'I know.'

But what he doesn't know is that I am not going to book club. Because of course I can't 'leave it'.

* * *

Ellsbury has been trialling one of those electric car rental schemes where you can borrow a car for a few hours for a small fee. Well, I can hardly follow my husband in my own car, he'll spot me a mile off.

I wait for him in the staff car park, a cap pulled over my hair and some fake glasses from one of Immy's old school plays to disguise myself. At six fifteen I watch him walk across to his Volvo. There's a nervous energy emanating from him, I can feel the crackle of it in the air.

He turns left out of the car park and I hang back so he doesn't realise I'm following. I don't really know what I'm doing but I'm sure this is what I've seen on TV. Aren't you meant to stay about three cars behind so they don't immediately spot you and get suspicious?

Ten minutes later and he pulls onto our own driveway. That's odd. Why is he back here? Or did he just forget something? The door to the garage begins to rise slowly. We both have a dongle thing for it in our cars, but we so rarely use it for anything other than storage of junk. It isn't like we park in there every night or anything. The door sticks about halfway up. He should have fixed it years ago, but he didn't and so he has to get out and raise it manually the rest of the way. He gets back in the car then carefully pulls his car inside the garage, closing the door behind him.

What the hell is he up to?

Ten minutes later, the door opens and he drives back out. He has to scurry back to close it manually and once again I curse him for never bothering to fix it. I'm worried he'll turn round and see me staring at him from behind the wheel of the hired electric car. But he pays me no attention and soon he's reversing off the driveway.

I follow him as he weaves through the evening traffic,

keeping far enough back that he won't notice me. But then the traffic thins and we're driving into a more isolated area, away from civilisation and toward a large area of woodland. He turns up a track on the left but I don't follow him. I know where he's going.

A few hundred metres up the road, I pull into a lay-by and take out my phone.

It's him, I message to Jessica. I'm so sorry.

52

JESSICA

Is it wrong to kill in the spirit of self-preservation? I don't know.

Actually, scrap that. I do know. No one deserves to die because they might expose me. I always knew there was a risk of getting caught, however careful I've been all these years. Despite how hard I've worked to cover my tracks and ensure no one ever finds out the truth. So, of course it's wrong to kill someone to save myself.

Aha! But what about killing to save someone else? Surely that isn't wrong? That must be some kind of loophole, surely. Not *loophole*, that's the wrong word, like I'm looking for an excuse. Like I *want* to kill him.

Just like I wanted to kill Zachary.

Be quiet, I hiss to that voice. I don't need their opinion right now.

But what about her?

Shhh.

But... maybe the voice does have a point. If Sebastian tries to expose me, he will expose his wife. There is no way round it. Someone will look at my activities, my journey around Ellsbury on the day Erin Winters went missing and they will find me at Fearne's house at the same time that Erin was meant to be there.

So. Is it wrong if I kill him to save Fearne? I don't think it can be.

If I were to write a Naughty List entry for him, what would I put as the grounds? Is trying to fuck over your wife the week before Christmas enough to make him truly an enemy of the festive season?

Should I write a Naughty List item for him, make sure I'm getting the kill just right? Or am I overthinking this? It doesn't need to be avant garde or impressive. I will just go to meet him at the designated place and stick a knife through his heart.

Simple.

Easy.

I've done it a dozen times before.

I've enjoyed it a dozen times before, the voice in my head whispers and I can see her licking her lips at the prospect.

And then what happens? Once the life has drained from his eyes, then what?

Run. Run as far as the wind will take me. That's what every fibre of my being screams. Except... that means leaving Ellsbury behind.

Ellsbury.

And Fearne.

And Alvi.

And Lena.

Can I really get away with killing him? Can I bury his body somewhere no one will find him? And will Fearne ever be able to look at me again? It's one thing to turn a blind eye while someone murders the husband you're not sure you even like any more, but it's quite another to want to be friends with the killer.

This is all such a mess.

* * *

I change into a simple outfit of dark jeans and a black hoodie. I tuck my hair under a charcoal-grey beanie hat and stuff a pair of leather gloves into my pocket. The woman staring back at me from the mirror looks nervous. She looks like she's never prepared for a kill before.

Am I really sure I want to do this? I could run now, get as far from Ellsbury as possible, hope that Sebastian isn't as stupid as he looks and is able to keep his wife's secrets. Change my name and allow Jessica Williams to disappear without a trace. She didn't exist until 2019, she can vanish again.

But then what happens to Lena?

I stare at the woman in the mirror.

We're doing this, I tell her.

She nods. *Then let's fucking do it.*

I cycle to a spot about half a mile from the *ribeye.stereo.mountain* location and hide my bike behind a tree so you can't see it from the road. And then I proceed on foot, creeping through the shadows and thanking my lucky stars there's an almost full moon. A Cold Moon this one is called. It feels somewhat fitting given what I'm about to do.

You don't have a choice.

My hand strays to the small waist bag I'm wearing. It's the kind of thing women wear if they enjoy jogging. I personally hate jogging, but fitness is important and needs must. Plus, it is a very useful place to keep the knife I've chosen specially for the occasion. It's a Japanese santoku knife, designed to slice effortlessly through basically everything but a little shorter than a standard chef's knife, for added precision.

About fifty metres from the spot in the woods I pause and pull the gloves from my pocket, slipping them on and flexing my hands a few times so they're perfectly fitting. I crack my neck to the left and then the right, then roll my shoulders forwards and backwards a few times to get the blood flowing. You don't rush to a scene cold, you arrive warmed up, ready for anything. Because you never know what you're really going to find. Or how prepared your target may be.

My phone vibrates and I pull it out of the bumbag to find a message from Fearne.

> It's him, I'm so sorry.

What does Sebastian think of me? What does he think I'm capable of? I'm assuming he has grossly underestimated me, that he thinks I'm a slightly dozy woman who he can both outsmart and overpower.

He's wrong, obviously. On both counts. He may have a height advantage and the natural musculature of a man, but I have trained: I'm quick and strong and I know exactly how it feels to plunge a blade into human flesh. He will pause at the crucial moment and give me a window to take my own kill shot.

I can hear him breathing on the other side of a thick wall of bushes. A warm glow emanates from the centre of the clearing in front of me, the light diffusing into the surrounding trees. He keeps rustling something, it sounds almost like cellophane. Has he come prepared with a plastic sheet for easy disposal afterwards?

I take a few deep breaths. In for the count of eight. Out for another eight. In. Out. Nice and slow; I feel my brain clear, the voices quietening, until there is nothing left but peace. This will soon be over and then I can go home and decide what to do with the rest of my years. Can I really have a life here, in Ellsbury?

The answer is waiting on the other side of the bushes.

53

FEARNE

I take the electric car to the drop-off point and then drive my own back home. I feel numb. My husband is about to try to kill my friend.

I sit on the driveway in the car for an hour. Waiting. Although that has never been my strong suit. Every minute I pick up my phone to check that Jessica hasn't messaged me with an update.

I stare at the house. At my home. At the life Sebastian and I built. The one that is about to come tumbling down when Jessica kills my husband to save the both of us.

How did it come to this?

I can't go into the house. If I do, that will be it. The end of it all. And I can't bring myself to do it.

Headlights catch me unaware as a car swings onto the driveway next to me.

It's Sebastian's car. But who is driving it? I can't see in the dark.

The driver's door opens and someone gets out. They stretch, as if they've just been performing some kind of hard labour. I would recognise that motion anywhere, especially the odd way he thrusts his hips slightly; the main reason I've never invited him to join me at a yoga class.

Mud covers his clothes.

What did he do? Where is Jessica? Two people met in the woods and only one was ever intended to come back. But he is the wrong one.

He opens the garage door and drives in, closing the door behind him. He never even looked at my car, never noticed that I was sitting waiting. Watching.

I feel like I'm on autopilot as I get out of the car and close the door as softly as possible. I don't lock it; he's still inside the garage and I know he'd hear the clunk of the lock and possibly see the flash of the side lights. I don't want him to know I was outside. I creep into the house and head straight up to the bedroom.

Ten minutes later, he knocks on the door. 'Are you awake, love?' he asks as he peers into the room.

'Sorry, I was just having a nap. Time must have run away with me,' I say as I switch on the bedside light. I'm still dressed, I didn't want to risk him bounding up the stairs to find me trying to shimmy out of my jeans.

Besides. He was meant to be dead. Instead he killed Jessica. I'm not sure it's news I can bear to hear in my pyjamas.

'I need to show you something.' His voice sounds big and heavy, but there's a hint underneath the sombre, something almost gleeful.

I follow him down the stairs, each step drawing me closer and closer to a truth I don't want to know.

Once we're in the kitchen, he takes my hand and leads me into the garage.

'Open it,' he says and motions toward the chest freezer. This must have been what he was doing in the garage. Making space to put Jessica's body in there with Erin's.

'No,' I say. I can't bear it.

'I did this for you.'

'But...' I stand frozen in the doorway. This wasn't meant to happen. 'How are you here?' I whisper.

He turns back to face me. 'What?'

'How...' but I don't finish the sentence. With a rush of bravery – or stupidity, I can't decide – I walk toward the freezer and place my hand on the lid. One quick breath in and I open it, bracing to see Jessica's face staring back at me.

The freezer is empty.

'Where is she?' I ask, taking a step backward.

'I found a place to hide Erin.'

'Not Erin. Jessica? Where is she?' I step forward again and look deep into the chest freezer, as if it might be possible that Jessica is in there but I just missed her on my first look.

'Jessica? What are you talking about?'

'You killed Jessica. Where is she?' My voice is high pitched, the words almost ragged as I feel reality starting to twist and fold. This isn't right. None of this is right.

'Hey. I didn't kill Jessica. What are you talking about?' He takes a step toward me, but I move away, desperate to keep some distance between us.

'You went to meet Jessica. You sent her that note.'

'What note?'

'The card from the Scissor Sisters.'

'What?' He shakes his head. 'You aren't making any sense.'

'You bought a card from the Scissor Sisters, or used one of their samples, I don't know, that bit isn't important. But you gave it to Jessica. Inside you'd said that you knew who she was. You told her to meet you in the middle of the woods.'

'So, you think I went to meet her and killed her?'

'She was meant to kill you.' I clamp my hands over my mouth but the words are out before I can stop them.

'Jesus Christ, Fearne.' He says it on an outward breath. 'You thought Jessica was going to kill me this evening? And you... you...' He looks at me as the realisation hits him. I was going to let him go to his death. 'Do you really hate me that much?' he whispers.

'I... I...'

'I promised you I would keep your secrets.'

'But the note?'

'I didn't send the note. I don't—' He cuts himself off, raising his hands to his face as if he wants to claw off his own skin. 'Jesus Christ.' He bends at the waist, his hands migrating to his hair. 'You thought... You thought she was going to kill me instead. And you just...' He straightens up, his whole body a ball of energy. 'You let me go.'

I don't know what to say. Seeing him here, the vulnerability of him, the pain on his face and the hurt in his eyes. Did I really think he was trying to lure Jessica to her death? Did I really think she was going to kill him instead?

'I love you, Fearne,' he says softly as he crumples to his knees. 'I love you, but you... you...' He draws in a deep raggedy breath. 'You hate me. And it breaks my heart.'

'I don't hate you.' But the words are hollow. He's right, I was going to let him die tonight.

'Have I really been that bad? I know I'm difficult, and grumpy, and a bit old fashioned. But I love you. With all my heart.'

He looks up at me, his eyes red rimmed and filled with tears. 'If you really hate me that much, just tell me. I'll let you go, you can take everything. I only want you to be happy.'

I look around me, at the detritus of our life held in the garage, the bits of junk interspersed with all the nostalgia. The old suitcases we used to take on trips away when Immy was a toddler. The swing-ball set we bought one year but never used. The lumpy plant pot I made in a ceramics class when I was bored and seeking fulfilment through creative endeavour, but it was so bad it's only ever been used to store random screws and other bits and bobs.

My marriage hasn't always been bad. Once upon a time we were happy, once upon a time we made an effort for each other and filled our days with creating memories. But somewhere along the way we lost each other, we lost the sense of what was important.

'I feel like you take me for granted,' I say softly. 'I feel like you treat me as a maid and a nanny and an assistant. I feel like all I do is the cooking and the laundry and the food shopping and the hoovering and the dusting. I don't feel that you treat me as a person any more. And I certainly don't think you see me as a partner.'

He stops sniffing and wipes his face with the sleeve of his jumper, leaving a smear of mud across his cheek. 'I've been a shitty husband and a shitty father.'

Does he want me to disagree with him; to tell him that of course he hasn't, that he's not that bad? I fight down the urge to tell him that everything is fine and to apologise for overreacting. I've always been a people pleaser, trying not to rock the boat, taking accountability for other people's shortcomings to keep the peace. Well, no more.

'Yes. You have,' I tell him decisively. 'And I know I've not been perfect either, but—'

'You are perfect, Fearne,' he interrupts. 'You're perfect to me, and I've been a fucking idiot. I'm sorry.' He looks up, his eyes imploring. 'Please forgive me. Please let me try to make it up to you.'

'I... I...'

'Please don't say it's too late.' He shuffles toward me on his knees and buries his face against my stomach. 'I love you and I will do anything not to lose you. That was why I hid the body. I just wanted to protect you.'

I put my hand on his hair and feel a rush of affection travel through me. I love this man. I love our daughter. I love the life we built together. Is there really a chance for us to make it back from the edge? 'I love you, Sebastian,' I say softly.

'I love you too, Fearne,' he says, but his words are slightly muffled through my jumper. 'And I promise that I will spend the next few decades trying to make up for everything.'

We stand in the doorway between the garage and the kitchen for another five minutes, Sebastian sobbing slightly, I think in relief. For the first time in a very long time, I feel the embers of hope flickering at the edges of my marriage. Perhaps we can get through this. Perhaps this was the impetus we needed to make the change.

But there is one tiny niggling question in the corner of my brain.

If Sebastian didn't leave that note, then who did?

Who did Jessica meet in the woods?

54

JESSICA

The warm glow I saw through the trees comes from a hundred battery-powered votive candles, scattered on the grass and across a circle of wooden stumps. In the centre is a fire pit, the flames rising high and kicking out a surprising amount of heat. To one side is a checked blanket and a wicker basket, a bottle of champagne sticking out of the top.

A low growl to my left causes my head to snap round. Storm and Shadow, the two huskies, are both wearing matching tuxedos, the bow ties around their necks at rather jaunty angles. I smile at them and the growling stops, replaced by the steady thump of wagging tails against the ground.

'You came.' Alvi sounds almost breathless as he spots me, a punnet of strawberries in his hand, the film lid the source of the previous rustling I heard.

'I...' I start to say but the words don't come. Instead I look around the rest of the clearing. It's beautiful. It's so... romantic.

My mind is reeling. This isn't what I was meant to see when I got here. I was meant to find a man intent on ruining me, a man who I would have to destroy to save myself and everything here in Ellsbury I've come to love. My body is flooded with adrenaline, prepared for the kill, my fingers already on the hilt of the knife.

But Alvi isn't here to threaten me. He doesn't want to hurt me. He's wearing an expression that is half smile and half trepidation; he's waiting for my reaction to the scene he has laid out in front of me. And all I can do is stand stock still like a fool.

He takes a few steps toward me. 'Are you OK?' he asks, his voice soft and tinged with concern. He stops just out of touching distance. 'You look shocked.' His face falls. 'It's too much, isn't it? Yes, it's definitely too much. I'm sorry. I should have thought. I—'

'It's perfect,' I say, interrupting him. 'I just... I was expecting something... I don't know... Sorry.' I pause and look at him, taking in every inch of him. He's wearing a pair of jeans with only a few small rips, a cosy-looking checked shirt in shades of green and grey over a plain white t-shirt. His dirty blond hair is swept back from his face, accentuating his cheekbones with their smattering of stubble. He looks good enough to eat.

He clears his throat as if he's about to launch into a big speech. 'Jessica Williams. I'm not the best at grand displays of affection. I'm not an expert in telling women how I feel about them. But getting to know you over the last month has been the highlight of my year. No, my decade.' He smiles, but there's a hint of bashfulness there. 'You are the most incredible woman I've ever met. And so I wanted you to know that.'

He looks down at the floor. I feel like he's prepared for this and so I let him finish without interruption. 'Jessica, I'm not the best man in the world. I have my flaws, my... foibles? Is that the word? I... it sounds weird.' He looks up hopefully.

'Yes, foibles is a word.' It's a good word, I too have my foibles, if you can call a propensity toward murder that.

'Great.' He sighs in relief and his body language relaxes a

little. 'So, yes. I have my flaws and foibles and I know I'm not the rich handsome prince that most women dream of. But I have all my own teeth and a pack of dogs. Oh, and a miniature pony I rescued this morning.' He grins. 'And I can make a mean *glögi*. The secret is homemade candied orange peel.' The grin morphs into a chuckle and I can't help but join in.

Can I really build a future here in Ellsbury? Build a future with this gorgeous man and his animals? One where Lena can also find a home? I want to. Oh, how I want to. But I never thought it was even a possibility.

'Hey.' He closes the gap between us. Up close, he smells of pine and spice and I allow myself to breathe him in. 'I know this is all a lot to take in. And perhaps I should have kept my declaration a little simpler.' He grimaces as he glances around the clearing and all the effort he's put into this grand gesture. 'But I needed you to know that I see you, Jessica. I see who you are, deep down inside. And I want to be part of your life.'

I look into his chocolate-brown eyes. I know he doesn't really see me, not the real me, not the me with a knife in her bag. But could I become the woman he sees? Could I stay here in Ellsbury and make a fresh start? I said before that I couldn't do that, that I wouldn't do that. But I'm tired. Tired of running and tired of looking over my shoulder all the time, waiting for fate to catch up with me. What if I could be happy here?

It has to be worth a try.

I don't say anything, but I reach out and grab the front of his flannel shirt, pulling him toward me. And then I kiss him.

He kisses me back, snaking his hand around me to hold me close. Then he pulls back and looks at me. 'Is that a yes?' he asks with a glint in his eye.

'Yes,' I say and then he's kissing me again.

* * *

Carl, AKA Santa, has another gig for the final few days before Christmas and so the grotto closes a day before the rest of the market. I think perhaps he really is Santa and needs to head back to the North Pole in time to prepare for the Christmas Eve present drop. I tell him to say hi to Hanna. He merely offers me a wink in return.

But the early closure gives me an opportunity. One that unfortunately necessitates a 4 a.m. wake-up call.

'What are you doing?' Lena asks, padding into the kitchen wiping sleep from her eyes.

'Sorry,' I reply. 'I was trying to be as quiet as possible.'

'You failed.' She helps herself to a glass of water. 'But now I'm awake you can tell me where you're going.'

'Just out for the day. I'll be back this evening for the party,' I promise her.

'But where are you going?' She sounds petulant and I'm once again reminded of just how young she really is. I definitely need to think about the long term and what she does next. I want her to go to college and get some qualifications and have... well... I just want her to have a normal life. A good life.

'Just a quick visit to see an old friend, that's all.' I hate lying to her, but the fewer people who know what I'm up to the better. It's a risk. But one I think is necessary.

I travel light, just a backpack, which can go under the seat in front of me. I want to be as quick as possible, in and out with barely a trace.

55

FEARNE

This year the market closes on 21 December and the final evening of trading is the best of the year. Crowds throng the footpaths and there are queues at every stall. Even the Scissor Sisters are struggling to keep up with demand. I walk through the people browsing the stalls. Some give off an air of festive joy as they revel in the atmosphere, clutching little cups of mulled wine and nibbling on hog roast baps from Porkies. Others are rushing around the stalls with poorly concealed panic, evidently trying to buy last-minute gifts before the market finishes.

'Does he even like whisky?' I hear one rather harried-looking woman asking the man next to her.

He shrugs. 'Doesn't everyone like whisky?'

She shoots him a filthy look. 'Well, I'm blaming you if it's wrong. He is *your* father after all.'

I smile at the poor woman in solidarity that I too have nightmare in-laws. She doesn't smile back. She probably thinks I'm a lunatic rather than an ally.

'I need more gonks!' yells a very excited-looking James as he runs past me. 'Luckily I have more stock in my car.'

The biggest crowd on the market though is clustered around Alvi's Last Chance stall and, as I get closer, I can understand why. A few days ago, he got a call from a woman up in Hornsley, a village about three miles away. She had opened her front door that morning to see a miniature horse grazing on her lawn, a ribbon tied around his neck and a note saying *A Christmas Gift for you*. She had no idea who it was from, or why the hell anyone would give her a horse seeing as she hates the things.

I have no idea where Alvi has sourced it from, especially at such short notice, but the tiny horse is dressed in a nutcracker outfit and there is a growing queue of little girls waiting to have their photo taken with him. There is even a box of tutus and other dressing-up options for the kids to choose from.

By 9 p.m., the crowds have thinned, replaced with just a handful of overly merry – i.e. pissed – people still milling around. The shutters come down on the stalls for the final time and the vendors emerge, everyone heading in the direction of The Apres-Ski.

Everyone is knackered, but with an undercurrent of happiness, a sense of a job well done. Tomorrow will be all hands on deck to do a full strip-down of the site, removing every scrap of evidence that we've ever been here in time for midnight mass and all the other services in the cathedral.

But, tonight, we will party and if this year is anything like 2024 it will be a very late night. Last year we literally drank the bar dry; Remi was ecstatic as it meant less product for him to take away the following day.

Immy is here, ostensibly to support the family, but in reality she is hoping someone might buy her a hot spiced cider. Remi is under pain of death – not to mention the risk to his licence – if he lets her drink. I don't mind her having the odd glass of wine at home, or even a few beers with her mates, but not on market grounds.

Lena has taken her under her wing and I'm standing on the edge of the party watching the two of them as they sit with their heads almost touching, gossiping and laughing together.

'Is she staying with Jessica permanently?' Sebastian asks, coming up behind me.

'Who? Lena?'

'Yeah.'

'I think so,' I reply. 'I just don't know how they'll make it work long term though, the cottage only has one bedroom and Hanna only rented it to her for the few months she was going to be here in Ellsbury. I mean, that might change now Jessica's with Alvi... but it's kind of a lot for a new relationship.'

'Yeah.' He's silent for a few moments as we watch the girls. 'They get on really well, don't they?'

'Immy thinks she's brilliant.'

'Well, something for you to think about, but we do have loads of space.'

I turn to look him in the eye. 'Are you saying we could take her in?'

He shrugs. As if it was nothing at all. 'We have a spare room. She could go to college.'

I smile. 'You're a big softy, you know that?'

'I... I...' He drops his gaze and looks at the toe of his shoe. 'I'm trying.' He sounds serious, solemn even. 'To be a better husband. A better father.'

I go to find Jessica. 'Hey. I know she's been staying with you. But. Umm... it's just that her and Immy get on so well...'

She cocks her head and looks me straight in the eye. 'Spit it out, woman. I don't think we need to be shy around each other any more.'

I laugh. 'You're right. Well, Sebastian and I were wondering if Lena would like to come and live with us. We have a spare room and she'd be more than welcome. And Immy would adore having a big sister.'

'Wow.' She smiles. 'I... that would be amazing. She'd love that.'

'Really? I don't want you to think I'm trying to steal her away or anything.'

'Not at all. And it's perfect timing. Someone's put an offer in on the cottage so I'm going to need to find somewhere else to rent.'

'Have you looked for places yet?'

'Not yet. I was panicking because finding somewhere in my price range and with a landlord who doesn't ask too many questions about the teenager who is kind of in my care was going to be tricky.'

'But you're sure you'd be OK with her living with us?'

'I couldn't think of anywhere better for her.'

'She could go back to college and I'm sure Immy's dance school would find her a spot.'

'It sounds perfect,' she says, and then her face breaks into a smile. 'Thank you.'

* * *

It's the day before Christmas Eve and I'm finally starting to relax into the festive spirit. Today's job is to start preparing some of the food and wrap the enormous pile of presents I've been hiding in the cupboard under the stairs. The only thing we keep in there is the vacuum cleaner, and I'm the only one who uses it so the gifts have remained undiscovered for weeks.

A car pulls onto the driveway just as I'm putting the Christmas ham in the oven to start working its magic.

DC Jenkins steps out of the car.

Fuck.

DS Krishnan also gets out.

Double fuck.

'Mrs Dixon,' DC Jenkins starts as I open the front door. 'May we come in?'

I nod dumbly. I feel like I'm moving through treacle. This is it, isn't it? The moment when I thought everything was going to turn out OK but really it was all fake and everything is actually about to crash down around me.

'We just wanted to come and see you. About Erin Winters. I know you were particularly worried.'

'Yes.' I try to swallow.

'On Friday her debit card was used in Aberdeen. The CCTV isn't great, but it showed a woman in a bright-red coat. And there has been some activity on her Instagram account.'

'So…'

'So we believe she's merely gone away. A few friends have corroborated receiving messages from her.'

'Well, that's a relief,' I tell them. 'I didn't know she had a link with Aberdeen.'

DS Krishnan shrugs. 'Apparently so.' She sighs loudly. 'Sorry,' she says quickly, regaining her professional composure. 'It's just frustrating and a total waste of police resources to have to find people who aren't lost.'

After I close the door behind them, I head straight to the Christmas tree in the living room. Yesterday, Jessica gave me an early gift.

'Just a little something to hang on the tree now you're finally getting into the festive swing of things,' she'd said, as she handed me a small red box tied with tartan ribbon. Inside was a wooden dog, a Scottish Terrier. I thought it was because she has dogs on the brain since that evening with Alvi. Maybe it had a little more meaning, like she'd been on a little day trip and bought me back a souvenir?

I reach out and touch the ornament. It's a sign that it's over.

The police won't continue to look for Erin.

Her body will never be found.

It's done.

I think it's time for a drink.

56

IN WHICH A NAME IS REVEALED…

I know that Jessica Williams isn't her real name. But I don't know who she was, once upon a time.

Does it matter who she was, when I know what she became? I think it does. I think it's one thing to see the reality of the person standing in front of you and another to know where they came from. What made them the way they are.

So far the only pattern I can really find is that there is no pattern: she has killed by many different methods over the years. Oh, and the vast majority of her victims are men. Bad men on the whole, men who it would be easy to say deserved the fates they met.

I need to go back in time to find her. But how far?

In 2014, there was a spate of stabbings in the Cornish city of Truro. Was that her?

What about the two convicted rapists found poisoned on a beach in South Shields in 2012?

Or the man found swinging from the rafters of his garage following an accusation of child abuse? The police determined there was no way he could have hanged himself, but there wasn't a huge amount of resources put into finding his killer. That was in 2011.

In 2010, Kirk Clarkson was found in his home. He'd been gagged and bound to a chair and his death had apparently been slow, his torture deliberate. A young woman was interviewed in connection with his murder, but no charges were ever brought. Her name was Eloise Gunner. There's a grainy picture of her.

It looks like Jessica. I'm close now, I can feel it. So close to the truth.

As if by reflex, I reach out to stroke the head of the dog snuggled in next to me.

57

JESSICA

My normal Christmas Day routine has remained unchanged for over a decade. I sleep in late, not bothering to set an alarm and allowing myself to snooze for longer than is generally considered decent. Then I get up and make myself a huge flavoured latte with whipped cream and cinnamon sugar sprinkles. If the weather is nice, I take a walk, peeking through windows at the families inside in their matching pyjamas. In the afternoon I find a soup kitchen that needs an additional pair of hands and help out doing whatever I can. Then I normally head to a local pub in the evening, under the excuse of escaping the rest of the family and find myself drawn into a million other people's lives who are all doing that same thing I've lied about. Comfortably pissed, I then take myself home and climb back into bed to get a good night's sleep before Boxing Day.

But this year is not a normal Christmas.

Lena wakes me up before it's light with a cry of '*It's Christmas!*' right in my ear. She's wearing new bright-red pyjamas and thrusts a package toward me. 'You have to put these on. Now.'

They match hers and are covered in little sausage dogs

wearing Santa hats and little jumpers. I put them on and do a little twirl for her.

We look ridiculous.

It's perfect.

I light the fire while Lena fetches the bottle of buck's fizz from the fridge.

'Is this alcohol?' she asks, wrinkling her nose as she sniffs it.

'Barely,' I reply. It's from Aldi and has half the alcohol of a light beer. 'You'd have to drink a lot of it to get drunk.' Should I give alcohol to my seventeen-year-old... what is she? She means far too much to call her my lodger. Friend feels weak. Ward feels too much like I'm a character in one of Fearne's books – the non-steamy ones obviously. And, besides, next week she'll be moving in with the Dixons and she'll no longer be mine to feel like I'm being a terrible parent to. So, I guess I should be the cool aunt. Does that work? The cool aunt who lets her drink buck's fizz and who she can tell about boys and makes sure she knows how to defend herself.

'Earth to Jessica,' Lena says, waggling the glass she's holding out to me.

'Sorry. I was just—'

'Yeah, whatever. Probably thinking about Alvi.' She flaps her hand dismissively, but there's a small grin on her face. She approves of him. I can tell. 'Anyway. Less mooning over some guy and more presents.'

She squeals with delight when she unwraps the PALETTES system I bought her from that Serendipity makeup place Immy and she had fawned over.

'Is it the right one?' I ask with a hint of trepidation.

'You're kidding?' she says, looking up at me.

I've got it wrong.

'It's perfect,' she says and I breathe a sigh of relief.

She's bought me a small paring knife from a fancy Japanese brand who inlay the handles with resin so it glitters in the firelight. It feels almost heavy in my hand, the weight perfectly balanced.

'Apparently it's very good for slicing tomatoes.' She winks as she says it, drawing out the word 'tomatoes' so I know that isn't what she means at all.

'It's gorgeous,' I tell her, admiring it more closely. Should I tell her that I won't be using it for... well, you know what. That I'm not going to be doing that any more. I'm turning over a new leaf. I need to be able to stay in Ellsbury.

But I'm saved from saying anything more by the ringing of the doorbell.

'That'll be Loverboy,' Lena says in a grandmotherly voice. I laugh. Sometimes she says things that are so out of character for her age. She's weird and a little kooky and I love it.

When I asked Lena if she minded me inviting Alvi to spend Christmas with us she merely raised an eyebrow. 'A misfits Christmas? That sounds perfect. But he'd better bring some of the dogs.'

I open the front door of the cottage to see that he has very much upheld his side of that bargain. The huskies, Storm and Shadow, are dressed in the same tuxedos they wore that night in the woods. Figgy the Iggy is tucked behind Shadow in a full onesie to keep her warm, her sad eyes peeking out at me. He's also brought the labrador and the black and white collie I've met a few times before.

'It's going to be a tight squeeze,' he tells me as he lifts the collection of leads in his hand.

'Lena will be thrilled,' I reassure him and motion for them all to come inside.

Lena is indeed thrilled and practically throws herself onto the floor to give all the fur babies cuddles.

Alvi squeezes past the pile of wagging tails and Christmas-pyjama-clad limbs and takes me in his arms. 'You look adorable,' he whispers in my ear before kissing me lightly on the lips. 'Happy Christmas, Jessica.'

I pull him into the kitchen, away from prying teenage eyes, to give him a proper Christmas kiss, breathing in the scent of him and the taste of peppermint on his lips.

We promised each other we wouldn't buy gifts but he hands me a small box wrapped in green and red paper.

'I thought...' I start, taking it from him.

'It's only something silly,' he assures me, the skin around his eyes crinkling as he smiles.

I unwrap it to reveal a special roller to remove dog hair from clothes.

'I figured you'd need one if we're going to be spending more time together.'

We spend the day watching Christmas movies and drinking buck's fizz and grazing from the charcuterie board I splurged on from Marks and Spencer. I also bought a turkey crown and pre-prepared veggies and trimmings, so Christmas dinner is an absolute breeze. We eat just after darkness has fallen, the room illuminated by a glut of candles placed on almost every available surface.

It's a very different Christmas Day to the ones that have gone before it.

But it's utterly perfect in every single way.

* * *

At around 8 p.m., I head into the kitchen to make some dessert; we've opted for a rather non-traditional sticky toffee pudding – although it is in the shape of a Christmas tree so it isn't too much of a concession – with brandy butter on the side and a vanilla sauce imbued with Baileys to pour over the top.

I sense him behind me and lean in as he wraps his arms around my waist.

'I had something to ask you, Jessica.'

I love the way my name sounds on his lips. Even if it isn't my real name. That is something he can never know, however much I want to tell him everything.

'I know the cottage has been sold.' There's a sadness in his tone. He has so many memories tied up in this place it's going to be hard for him to let it go. 'But I was thinking... umm... how about you come and stay with me?'

I turn to face him. 'Are you asking me to move in with you?'

'Uh... yes.' It sounds like a question, like if I turn him down he can always say that wasn't what he was asking.

'That sounds utterly perfect.'

His face breaks into a smile. 'You're sure?'

'Positive.'

58

FEARNE

Normally I'm the first one up on Christmas morning. Immy has never been an early riser, even when she was little we had to crowbar her out of bed to open her presents. And don't get me started on Mr Grumpy Pants, aka Sebastian, who would bitch and moan if I tried to get him up before nine.

But this year I wake up at eight to the aroma of coffee and pastries and turn to find myself nose to nose with a wooden tray stacked with goodies.

'I made those croissants you like,' Sebastian says, standing in the doorway wearing a Santa hat and a jumper with prancing reindeer emblazoned across it. 'Immy's just having a shower and then let's open presents. See you downstairs in about half an hour.' He scuttles away and I stare at the space where he was. What the hell has happened to my husband?

The croissants are fresh from the oven and still warm. I spread a thick layer of butter across them and watch as it melts into the pastry. Divine. The best start to Christmas morning.

I can hear clattering in the kitchen as I get dressed, pulling out my own festive jumper and a pair of buttery soft jeans that have a bit of stretch in them. I read something last year about how the average person consumes over six thousand calories on Christmas Day. I'm treating that as a challenge that I fully intend to beat. It's almost half past eight, which means I need to put the turkey in the oven in about half an hour. So much for Sebastian's 'let's open presents'. Every year, he and Immy have a lovely time while I'm forced to keep popping in and out of the kitchen to make sure the dinner stays on track. All the while topping up drinks and snacks for everyone else. Oh well, at least he made breakfast. I guess I should be grateful for that.

But, when I get downstairs, I find a glass of sherry waiting by my spot on the sofa, along with a box of my favourite Guylian seashell chocolates, already opened and tilted at the perfect angle for me to reach them. All twenty are intact, he didn't even sneak one 'to test it' like he usually does.

I peek into the kitchen. The turkey is out of the fridge and in its roasting tin. A copy of *Delia's Happy Christmas* lies open on the countertop with Sebastian poring over its pages.

'What are you doing?' I ask.

'Cooking,' he replies before turning his attention back to Delia.

'But...' I trail off. I was going to say that he doesn't cook. That he has no idea what he's doing. But neither did I. That first Christmas after I'd moved in with him and Immy I had to wing it, armed only with a cookbook and a panicked call to my mum who was still mad as hell about me moving in with Sebastian and used the day as an opportunity to unleash even more passive-aggressive bullshit than usual.

'You go and sit down. Chill out. We've got this.' He turns and gives me what I assume he thinks is a reassuring smile. There's something almost of the grimace to it.

'We?'

'Happy Christmas, Mum!' Immy yells as she comes thundering down the stairs, her wet blonde hair in two plaits. 'Daddy and I are doing everything today so go and sit the hell down.'

'Language,' I say on autopilot.

'It's Christmas,' she replies sweetly and blows me a kiss. Well, I suppose if there's any day you can relax the rules, it's today.

'Was this your idea?' I ask her.

'No.' She shakes her head. 'This was all Dad. He promised me we can go to Mykonos on holiday in the summer if I help.'

'Oh.' I bite down the urge to say that perhaps we should discuss going on fancy holidays as a family. But, let's be honest, Mykonos does look rather lovely.

Fifteen minutes later, I've eaten five of the chocolate seashells, drunk the sherry and downloaded a new delightfully Christmassy steamy romcom – imaginatively titled *Santa's Coming* – onto my Kindle. Immy has put on a Lindsey Stirling album and so my feet – raised up on the recliner – occasionally jig to the upbeat renditions of Christmas carols played on a violin. Now *this* is how you do Christmas. Even if I do feel a little guilty that the rest of the family is slaving away in the kitchen, which is slightly mad given this is what they did for years and I bet they never gave me a second thought.

Immy appears at the door with the bottle of sherry. 'Top-up?' she asks, even though it feels like a slightly defunct question. 'Umm, Dad said we weren't allowed to disturb you to ask specific questions...' she trails off.

'What do you need?' I prepare myself internally to get up and go to help them.

'Just to ask how many potatoes we should do?'

Has anyone ever perfected the exact number of roasties to do for Christmas dinner? I doubt it. Plus, have you ever had leftover ones in your turkey sandwich on Boxing Day? Delicious. 'Just do what you think, then add another ten,' I tell her.

'That feels like a lot of potatoes.'

'It's Christmas.'

She scurries off and I glance at the time. I can probably have another twenty minutes of *Santa's Coming* before they peel all of those and so I settle back against the cushions. I think I could get used to this. Perhaps all women should tell their husbands they would have let them get murdered, in order to buck up their ideas? I guess it helps if you've already killed someone, just to make them take the threat a bit more seriously. Sorry, I'm being flippant. I think it might be the sherry talking.

Eventually all the prep work is done for the meal and Sebastian and Immy come into the living room to open the presents. They are armed with plates of sausage rolls, caramelised onion chutney baked into them, and splodges of tomato ketchup for dipping.

'Oh, and the batter is in the fridge,' Sebastian tells me.

'Batter?' I ask.

'For the Yorkshire puddings.'

'But we're not having beef.'

'I know. But they're your favourite so let's live a little.'

The 'great opening of gifts' has become less and less exciting over the years as Immy has grown up. Mainly because her childish delight at opening surprise gifts selected after hours of me poring over the catalogues and magazines has been replaced by wish lists of all the exact things she wants. And when I say exact... her list for this year was extraordinarily specific.

Pair of Lululemon leggings: high-rise, 28-inch length, graphite grey.

Hoodie from Aelfric Eden: star-graphic, khaki, size small.

New PALETTES kit from Serendipity and a gift voucher to fill it with things only she can pick out.

Pair of Nike AirJordan1 Low trainers: aluminium/white, size five.

Doing her Christmas shopping this year felt more like being a PA to a slightly bratty young executive than buying gifts for my daughter.

But now, watching her squeal with delight and immediately take photos to send to Riya, I realise it was all worth it. Teenage girls can be difficult to keep happy, but I think Sebastian and I are doing all right with Immy. I hope we can do the same for Lena when she moves in early next week.

My gifts from Sebastian are basically the same thing he's given me every year for at least a decade. And, don't get me wrong, that's not a bad thing. We both agree that Christmas gifts should be things you wouldn't otherwise buy for yourself, so I tend to get posh or fancy versions of 'everyday' things. So there's a pair of gorgeously soft bamboo pyjamas. Some extra fluffy bed socks made with real cashmere. A new case for my Kindle so it'll feel like I've had a major upgrade. A bottle of the most incredible gin from this tiny little distillery on the edge of Dartmoor. A giftset of my favourite perfume.

On the flip side, Sebastian has similar gifts from me. A new hat and scarf set made from alpaca wool for amazing warmth. A coffee machine for the office so he doesn't have to keep schlepping up and down the stairs every time he wants a drink – although I may have had an ulterior motive as it means he won't pester me when I'm writing either. A subscription to 'Dull Man's Monthly' – actually it's called *How it Works*, but I think my title is more accurate.

But I did buy a few extras this year. Frivolous things for both Immy and Sebastian. Things they didn't ask for. It's a risk.

Immy's eyes light up when she unwraps her gift and opens the box inside. I've made her a hamper of new dance things: the boatneck leotard she's been coveting, new warmups, a pair of the new jazz sneakers she's watched a million TikToks about. And nestled in the centre is a voucher for a summer intensive course in London, the one she's been dreaming of doing but that costs hundreds of pounds. 'This is amazing, Mum,' she says, the awe in her voice unmissable. She leaps up and gives me a hug. 'Or should I say thanks to Cherry Dubois?' she whispers in my ear so only I can hear and then goes to hug her father, who is looking a little puzzled about the contents of the hamper.

Sebastian's extra gift is surprisingly large and extremely heavy.

'What the...' he half says as I motion toward where I tucked it behind a chair.

He frowns as he crouches in front of it and carefully begins to unwrap it, as if it might be a bomb that's about to explode in his face.

'Oh. Oh. Oh,' he exclaims a few times as he reveals elements of the box. Immy rolls her eyes at me at the noises he makes and I stifle a giggle. 'But this... oh...' He stops and stares at it for a few moments and then turns to face me, his mouth a perfect O.

'It's a Lego *Titanic*,' I tell him.

'It's...' He turns back to look at it. 'I... I have wanted this since I first saw it.' He turns back round to me. 'How did you know?'

I've seen his lingering look at the set in the window of the toy store just down the road from the market. The collection of *Titanic* books on a shelf in his office. The couple of times he's mentioned that he used to love building Lego when he was a kid, his tone always so lamenting of being a grown-up, like you can't still enjoy the things you used to just because you've reached a certain age.

'I love it,' he tells me, with absolute seriousness. 'Oh, and this is a little something extra for you.' He hands me an envelope and a slight blush spreads across his cheeks.

Inside are tickets for a few nights away next week. He has booked a treehouse in the grounds of a mega-fancy hotel and it looks incredible.

'Just you and me and full access to the spa, plus unlimited room service,' he says.

'It sounds like heaven.'

* * *

The treehouse *is* heaven. It's huge, with a separate living room and these incredible views out into the forest. It feels like we're in the middle of nowhere, tucked away under a canopy of trees and stars.

I'm on FaceTime, showing the living area off to Immy while Sebastian has a shower.

'It looks amazing, Mum,' Immy says as I show her the fully stocked fridge and snack tray, the terrace with its two-person hammock and hot tub, the sofa with cushions as soft as clouds.

'How's Lena settling in?' I ask.

'Good. We've been into town to get some things for her room.'

'And you're sure you're OK with her moving in?' I ask for what feels like the millionth time.

'Of course, Mum. She's great. And it's going to be fab to have a big sister.' She smiles and I feel myself relax a little more. Maybe this will work out after all. 'Now, get off the phone and enjoy the trip.'

'OK, OK.' I laugh. 'Love you millions.'

'Love you too.'

I pour two huge glasses of Pinot Noir from one of the fancy bottles and then settle down on the plush sofa, drawing a super-soft blanket over my legs. There's an iPad to control everything in the room, so I use it to dim the lights, allowing me to better appreciate the stars in the night sky outside the huge windows. The wine is delicious, a burst of cherry flavours on my tongue.

'Good evening, my lady,' a deep voice says from behind me.

I turn and almost drop my wine when I see the vision before me.

'Theron?' I whisper.

'At your service, my lady.'

Sebastian is wearing black trousers and a white fitted old-fashioned laced-up undershirt. Over that he's added deep-brown leather armour, adorned with Nordic-inspired wolf art, a black cloak pinned to the shoulders. He looks exactly like Theron, the seriously sexy human form of the werewolf protagonist in the book I was nominated the Steamies award for.

'I did a ton of research and I hope I got it right,' Sebastian says and wiggles a little uncomfortably.

I feel a flash of irritation that he's ruining the moment by overthinking things. But that is the man I married, someone who worries about the small things. And it does mean he has nailed every detail, even down to the sword he's holding in one hand, his grip tight on the hilt as if he would be ready at any moment to take on my adversaries.

'Oh, and obviously I'll wear something a little more... well, like a suit or something. When we go to the Dorchester.' He smiles.

'You mean...' I trail off. Surely he *doesn't* mean the Steamies.

'You think I'm going to let my brilliant wife miss out on accepting her award in person?' He sounds aghast at the very thought.

'I haven't got a hope of actually win—'

'You have every hope,' he interrupts. 'And I'm so proud of you.' Then he shakes himself and paints a more serious expression on his face. 'But first,' he reaches out his hand, 'if my lady would join me...' His voice is lower than normal, the words coated in honey.

My stomach fizzes. 'Theron,' I say and stand up from the sofa, placing my wine on the coffee table. I take a few steps so I'm standing directly in front of my husband.

'Your wish is my command, my lady.'

'And what do you think I wish?' I ask.

'I think you wish me to take you into the bedroom and ravish you.'

'Ravish me?'

He closes the inches between us, his hand snaking into my hair at the base of my neck. 'I will do anything for you, Fearne.' He's earnest, forceful. 'I would go to the ends of the earth and back again if you asked me to. Fight the whole world for you. I live and die in the service of you.'

'Take me to bed,' I whisper. But it's more of a plea. I haven't been this turned on for a very long time.

59

IN WHICH THERE WAS A CHRISTMAS MASSACRE...

A more detailed search for Eloise Gunner reveals a story from the *Wiltshire Herald* from late December 2007.

A Christmas Massacre

It's the kind of thing that nightmares are made of. A masked man at your back door. A masked man with a knife. Your wife and children are home.

But for George Gunner, businessman, member of the town council and vociferous supporter of local causes, this wasn't just a nightmare. This was reality. And it happened on Christmas Day.

Police were called to the area after neighbours spotted sixteen-year-old Eloise Gunner wandering down the street drenched in blood. She was in a trance, unable to utter a single word of what had happened to her and her family.

At the family home, police were met with the kind of scene that will be ingrained in their memories forever.

'There was blood everywhere,' an officer told the *Herald*.

'All over the floor, on the walls, spattered across the ceiling. And the smell...'

With Eloise still unable to speak, CCTV footage was gathered to understand what had happened. A masked man had let himself into the garden and broken down the back door, forcing his way into the house. Ten minutes later, he ran back out of the property and vanished into the wooded area at the rear of the property.

The man has yet to be formally identified. However, a source close to the paper has revealed a local man, Kirk Clarkson, has been taken into police custody for questioning.

Kirk Clarkson was the man found murdered in 2010. Was he the first person she killed, in revenge for what she thought he did to her family? Did he really kill them? The police didn't think so, they released him after less than twenty-four hours and no further charges were brought against him.

Is she a vigilante or a killer?

Does it really matter?

Does it change anything?

60

JESSICA

It's 6 January and I'm standing in the middle of the cottage's living room. All the Christmas paraphernalia has been packed away into boxes ready for next year. Where will I be then? If everything works out, I'll be with Alvi at the farm, decorating the kennels for all the dogs and probably needing a *lot* more in the way of tinsel and fairy lights.

I feel like I'm standing on the edge of a precipice, but my fear of falling is matched with anticipation. Perhaps I won't plunge to my death, but instead I will soar into the sky. I never thought happiness, true happiness, was part of my future. I never thought that happy-ever-after was something I could even contemplate.

I was sixteen years old when a masked man broke into my house and killed my entire family on Christmas Day. I couldn't protect them, I couldn't save them. I couldn't even die with them.

But I could avenge them. Eventually anyway. The police had decided there was insufficient evidence to arrest Kirk Clarkson and so I set out to do my own research, to build my own case against him. It took me three years to finally be sure of his guilt and to muster the courage to do what needed to be done. I surprised myself though; I had been driven by a deep rage and a desire for retribution, but with Kirk in front of me and the knife in my hand all I felt was peace. There was a beautiful inevitability to what I was doing, a sense of the scales being balanced.

And, in the process of researching Kirk, I found so many other people who had committed heinous crimes, who deserved to be punished and just... well... weren't. They were walking free, skipping off into the sunset to do those terrible things again. Where's the justice in that? With every kill I felt more alive, my life driven by purpose and meaning.

I don't want to stop, the voice whispers in my brain as I look around the cottage for a final time. But sometimes we have to make compromises, we have to accept that change is necessary for survival. I want to build a future for myself. A future full of love and laughter and dog hair. Alvi cannot know who I was and what I became; you can't have a boyfriend and continue to kill people on the side, that's just not reasonable. Unless you fall in love with another killer, but what are the chances of that?

'You ready?' Alvi asks me from the doorway.

I nod and then turn toward him with a smile on my face. I always knew I'd be leaving here in January, I just thought I'd be moving on to pastures new and not moving in with a totally hot man and his pack of misfits.

A new Jessica Williams awaits.

I'm excited to meet her.

* * *

We arrive at the farm and Alvi leads me inside the house and into the kitchen. It's a large room, with wooden cabinets and a huge Aga taking up most of one side. A massive table with bench seats dominates the other half of the space. It's old fashioned, but in a way that looks well utilised rather than merely unloved. It's exactly the kind of decor you would expect from a man like Alvi.

'I'll make tea,' he says and heads toward the kettle. He seems nervous, like he's on edge.

'Is everything OK?' I ask gently.

'Fine,' he says quickly.

But I can tell that everything isn't fine as he stands in silence and waits for the water to boil. I watch as he takes two mugs out of the cupboard, throws the teabags in and then adds the hot water. His shoulders are stiff, his back ramrod straight. I can feel the tension coming off him in waves.

'Please tell me what's wrong.'

'Nothing.'

He plucks a spoon from the drawer in front of him and uses it to squeeze the teabags. I take a few steps to the fridge and get the milk. He takes it from me but doesn't meet my eyes.

A ball of fear forms in my stomach. Is he having second thoughts about me moving in? Is this all too much, too soon, and he's realised how reckless it is to ask someone to move in only a couple of weeks into the relationship?

'I... err... I...' he stutters. 'I'm going to the kennels.' He picks up one of the mugs of tea and heads toward the back door. 'I need you to read the folder on the table.'

That sounded ominous.

I stare at his back as he leaves before crossing over to the table. I perch on the bench and open the folder. It's full of printed pages; of newspaper articles, Google search results, adverts for podcasts and YouTube accounts.

A Christmas Slay Ride.
May All Your Christmases be Red… Blood Red.
Rosie Investigates.
Body Found in Morley.
Second Body Found in Morley.
Third Stabbing Victim Found in Truro.
Two Found Poisoned in South Shields.

It isn't just a folder.

It's a dossier.

He knows. He really knows. There is no way out of this, no telling him he's wrong and barking up the wrong tree.

Is our whole relationship a lie? A mechanism for him to get close to me, to get me to drop my guard as he investigates me?

What will he do now? I know what I would do to someone I thought was a serial killer.

He wants me to meet him in the kennels.

How can I have been so stupid to think he wants me, to think he wants to build a life with me? He doesn't 'see me' or whatever other bullshit he said that night that made me let my guard down and let him into my heart.

Stupid stupid stupid.

No one can be trusted.

Well, I guess happy-ever-after is only something we find in fairytales. In real life people turn out to be someone else entirely.

But, hang on, there's more.

Man Dies in Bristol House Fire: Arson Suspected.
Second Body Pulled from Tilgate Lake Sparks Murder Investigation.
Peterborough Couple Killed by Home Invader.

I shuffle through them, my confusion growing the more I read. I didn't make these kills. They aren't mine. The rest of the dossier was so well researched, so meticulously cross referenced to me. But these? I wasn't even in the country in late February 2023; I was in Vegas taking part in The Downtown Poker Tournament and I came fifth so there's plenty of evidence online.

Who are all these victims? And why does Alvi think I killed these people too?

I pull out my phone and tap the first name into Google, scrolling down past the articles about his murder to the less sensationalist search results. In 2022 Markus Pattinson was convicted of animal cruelty for... well, I'm not going to repeat what I just read. I feel my anger rising at the mere thought that scum like this walk the earth. Or walked I suppose.

Aaron Kelsall ran an illegal dog-fighting ring.

Searching for Ethan and Sienna Doolin brings up a Companies House listing for Pedigree Puppies Online Ltd. I can only imagine they run – ran – a puppy farm.

I sit on the bench and look at the pages spread out across the table. All of these victims were guilty of animal abuse. So maybe they weren't victims at all. Or at least not *innocent* victims anyway.

Is it Alvi?

Is he the one hunting down the dregs of our society and righting the wrongs committed against these innocent animals?

When he says he 'sees me', does he mean he *really* 'sees me'? Does he look at the monster inside me and see himself reflected back?

What waits for me in the kennels?

My own demise?

Or a perfect future?

61

ALVI

She's been over an hour and I can't bear it any longer.

What if I'm wrong? What if she is in fact just a wonderfully kind woman who loves Christmas?

But she is definitely the teenager who survived the so-called Christmas Massacre. Eloise Gunner is one hundred percent Jessica Williams and you don't go through something like that and not come out the other side a different person.

Shall I tell you where this all started? With me, I mean. Apparently, I've always had what my parents called 'a strong sense of right and wrong' and even as a little kid I'd get very upset if people weren't punished for their wrongdoings. I think I must have been a bit of a nightmare if I'm honest.

But then when I was eighteen – I'd just moved to the UK for university and was staying here on the farm – a man from a rival stud broke into the stables and poisoned the horses' water troughs. Three of them died. The man was convicted of some bullshit crime like breaking and entering and given a six-month custodial sentence, but it was commuted for time served before the trial. An absolute farce. He killed three innocent horses and walked away. So I made him pay for what he did.

My aunt and uncle moved away after the break-in; I think it was too painful to look out over the stables. They let the farm for a few years, before I asked if I could take over the lease for the Last Chance Rescue Centre. I wanted to make it all right again, another way to rebalance the scales.

But there was an itch I couldn't scratch and a burning desire to help the animals, to make sure the crimes against them didn't go unpunished. Do you know how lax our judicial system is on animal offences? It's shocking, it really is. But I'm doing what I can to make sure people get what they really deserve and I've fallen into something of a groove, travelling a few times a year to make sure that the worst offenders are dealt with.

And then Jessica turned up in Ellsbury and Hanna offered her Mum's cottage. I wanted to make sure my sister wasn't getting conned; she does have a tendency to take in waifs and strays. I guess that runs in the family.

But when I dug a little into who this Jessica Williams was, I found... well, I found that everywhere she had been also had a string of unsolved murders. As you'll imagine, I like to keep track of unsolved cases, true crime documentaries, that kind of thing. It's really a good idea to know which murders are getting attention and then putting that learning into practice to avoid the same pitfalls with my own activities. And then I discovered she hadn't always been Jessica Williams and everything kind of fell into place.

I glance at my watch. One hour and ten minutes now.

'What if she doesn't come?' I ask out loud.

There's a muffled noise from the man in front of me, but I can't make out the words through his gag.

'You think she'll come?' I ask him, unable to take the hope from my voice.

His eyes widen in fear.

The door creaks open and I snap my head toward the sound. She's here.

'Alvi?' She pokes her head into the kennels.

'I'm in here,' I reply, rather unnecessarily as she can now see me. But nerves always make me act like a gibbering idiot and I am utterly terrified. What if she rejects me? Or worse. She could have called the police. There could be an entire swat team behind her, waiting to storm the area.

'Is it true?' she asks.

I take a breath. 'Yes.'

She takes a step inside the kennels. 'And who is he?' she asks, motioning to the man sitting on a chair in the middle of the space, his ankles bound and his wrists zip-tied together.

'This is George.'

'Hi George,' Jessica says in a high-pitched, girlie voice. 'And what did George do to warrant being in this position?'

'George broke in a few nights ago. He was looking for bait dogs.'

I watch the anger skitter across her face.

'Bastard.' She spits the word. I think it's the only time I've ever heard her swear. 'And what happens to George now?' she asks, her eyes lifting from the man to meet mine.

'Well, that depends on you, my love.'

'Love?' she asks.

I nod.

'Even after everything you know about me?'

I nod again.

'I love you too, Alvi Jakkinen.'

'Even after everything you know about me?' It's my turn to ask this time.

'Of course.'

I close the gap between us and take her in my arms. My mouth meets hers, the kiss soft and tender. I feel her relax and we melt into the kiss, my hands in her hair. But then I pull away a little so I can look into her eyes.

'You are the most incredible woman I have ever met,' I tell her. 'And later on, I want to take you upstairs and make delicious slow love to you.' She bites her bottom lip and I want to take her upstairs now.

'But first...' I trail off and motion to George. 'What do you think we should do with him?'

Jessica grins and steps away from me, pulling a paring knife from the back pocket of her jeans. 'Well, you know what they say. The couple who slay together, stay together.'

* * *

MORE FROM SARAH BONNER

In case you missed it, *How to Slay on Holiday*, Sarah Bonner's previous title, is available to order now here:

https://mybook.to/HolidaySlayBackAd

ACKNOWLEDGEMENTS

Firstly, a huge thank you to my wonderful agent Hannah Sheppard. I am so lucky to have such an incredible champion for my career.

To the fabulous Francesca Best for deploying all your editorial expertise to whip the novel into shape and for your unfaltering enthusiasm for my books. To Amanda Ridout, Nia Beynon, Wendy Neale, Niamh Wallace, Marcela Torres, Isabelle Flynn, Leila Mauger, Grace Cooper, Hayley Russell, Ben Wilson, Paul Martin, Justinia Baird-Murray, Arbaiah Aird and everyone else at Boldwood for all your hard work in getting my books into the hands of readers.

To my family and friends for everything you do, especially to Mum for being my first reader. A huge thank you to my amazing husband who rescued this book from the wilderness by both suggesting I set it around a Christmas market and then creating a winter wonderland for me to write in through the spring (complete with tree and twinkling lights and festive-themed Lego!). I couldn't do this without you (and Lily, of course). A special mention to the Sbooky Bitches; there is no better writers' WhatsApp group!

And finally a massive thank you to all the other authors, reviewers, bloggers, and readers. Bookish people really are the best people!

ABOUT THE AUTHOR

Sarah Bonner is the author of bestselling psychological thrillers, including *Her Perfect Twin*. She lives in West Sussex with her husband and very spoiled rescue dog.

Sign up to Sarah Bonner's newsletter for news, competitions and updates on future books.

Follow Sarah on social media here:

- X x.com/sarahbonner101
- facebook.com/sarah.bonner.35574
- instagram.com/sarahbonner101
- tiktok.com/@sarahbonner101

ALSO BY SARAH BONNER

How to Slay at Work

How to Slay on Holiday

How to Slay at Christmas

THE *Murder* LIST

THE MURDER LIST IS A NEWSLETTER DEDICATED TO SPINE-CHILLING FICTION AND GRIPPING PAGE-TURNERS!

SIGN UP TO MAKE SURE YOU'RE ON OUR HIT LIST FOR EXCLUSIVE DEALS, AUTHOR CONTENT, AND COMPETITIONS.

SIGN UP TO OUR NEWSLETTER

BIT.LY/THEMURDERLISTNEWS

Boldwood

Boldwood Books is an award-winning fiction publishing company seeking out the best stories from around the world.

Find out more at www.boldwoodbooks.com

Join our reader community for brilliant books, competitions and offers!

Follow us
@BoldwoodBooks
@TheBoldBookClub

Sign up to our weekly deals newsletter

https://bit.ly/BoldwoodBNewsletter

Printed in Dunstable, United Kingdom